In this delightfully chilling collection, the iconic Jeanette Winterson turns her fearless gaze to the realm of ghosts, interspersing her own encounters with the supernatural alongside hair-raising fictions.

Lifting the veil between the living and the dead, Winterson spirits us away to a haunted estate that ensnares a nomadic young couple in its own dark past, a staged immersive ghost tour gone awry, a West Village séance that threatens the bounds between AI and reality, and a vacation home in the metaverse where a widow visits an improved version of her deceased husband.

Gloriously gothic and unnervingly contemporary, *Night Side of the River* examines grief, revenge, and the myriad ways in which technology can disrupt the boundary between life and death. Winterson's latest is as ingeniously provocative as it is downright spooky.

Born in Manchester, England, **JEANETTE WINTERSON** is the author of more than twenty books, including the national bestseller *Why Be Happy When You Could Be Normal?*, *Oranges Are Not the Only Fruit*, *12 Bytes*, and *The Passion*. She has won many prizes including the Whitbread Award for Best First Novel, the John Llewellyn Rhys Prize, the E. M. Forster Award, and the Stonewall Award.

NIGHT
SIDE
OF THE
RIVER

ALSO BY JEANETTE WINTERSON

NOVELS

Oranges Are Not The Only Fruit
The Passion
Sexing the Cherry
Written on the Body
Art & Lies
Gut Symmetries
The Powerbook
Lighthousekeeping
The Stone Gods
The Gap of Time
Frankissstein: A Love Story

SHORT STORIES

The World and Other Places
Christmas Days: 12 Stories and 12 Feasts for 12 Days

NOVELLAS

Weight (Myth)
The Daylight Gate (Horror)

NON-FICTION

Art Objects: Essays in Ecstasy and Effrontery
Courage Calls to Courage Everywhere
12 Bytes: How Artificial Intelligence Will Change the Way We Live and Love

MEMOIR

Why Be Happy When You Could Be Normal?

COLLABORATIONS

Land (with Antony Gormley and Clare Richardson)

CHILDREN'S BOOKS

Tanglewreck
The Lion, the Unicorn and Me
The King of Capri
The Battle of the Sun

COMIC BOOKS

Boating for Beginners

JEANETTE
WINTERSON

NIGHT SIDE OF THE RIVER

Ghost Stories

Grove Press
New York

First published in Great Britain in 2023 by Jonathan Cape
an imprint of Vintage, which is part of the
Penguin Random House group.

Published simultaneously in Canada
Printed in the United States of America

First Grove Atlantic hardcover editon: October 2023

Typeset in 11.5/16.5 pt Stempel Garamond LT Std
by Jouve (UK), Milton Keynes

ISBN 978-0-8021-6151-2
eISBN 978-0-8021-6152-9

Library of Congress Cataloging-in-Publication data is available
for this title.

Grove Press
an imprint of Grove Atlantic
154 West 14th Street
New York, NY 10011

Distributed by Publishers Group West

groveatlantic.com

23 24 25 26 27   10 9 8 7 6 5 4 3 2 1

To my dear friend A. M. HOMES who knows
that life is more than we can see.

Contents

CONTENTS

Introduction

Respect ghosts and gods but keep away from them.

Confucius

Do you believe in ghosts?

The creak on the stair, the chill in the room, a strange scent, a wavering light in the window. The ancient house, the walled-up wing, drifting fog, broken battlements, deep darkness, silent desolation, the empty tomb and its rotting shroud, the damp bed too soft to the touch. The sudden presence of a presence.

Humans are fascinated by their ghostly selves.

This fascination is separate to any belief in a deity. A strange development in the history of ghosts is that a significant number of people who don't believe in a god continue to believe in ghosts.

In the pre-modern world, where most people did believe in a deity, supernatural entities were a logical part of the picture. A picture of a world simultaneously visible and invisible.

As the world has become more secular, belief in the supernatural should have gone the way of leaving out gifts for elves and fairies.

We've been to the Moon. We're living alongside, and

increasingly inside, AI operating systems, whether it's your Google PA or your smart house. Yet ghost festivals are popular all over the world.

In America, Trick or Treat takes over entire streets and neighbourhoods, as families decorate their homes with grinning pumpkins and light-up skeletons, funeral-black drapes over the doors and winding white cobwebs stretched on the railings. Kids go out to party wearing home-made outfits of bedsheets slitted with eye-holes, or dressed up in fancy costumes bought online, little leagues of ghouls and demons, skeletons and spirit-ancestors.

For the British, the Halloween tradition is an ancient one. It's pre-Christian, Celtic, once known as Samhain, a fire-festival that happened at the beginning of November, before the start of real winter.

The Christian Church co-opted this festival into All Saints' Day (November 1st), and All Hallows' Eve (October 31st). The ghosts, as ever, are more interesting than the saints.

The ancient element of fire is still present in our Jack-o'-lanterns and the eerie carved-out pumpkins. On such a night, the Dead may return.

In Mexico, and across central and southern America, the Day of the Dead is an extravagant festival celebrated over November 1st and 2nd. The spirits of the departed are remembered and honoured.

Families set a place at the table for the most recently deceased among their number. The parades through the streets happen in cities and villages alike, combining the ritual of the funeral procession with the fiesta of carnival.

The elaborate dressing up in skeleton suits and skulls, grave-clothes and undertakers' outfits, the black food, and coffin bearers, function simultaneously as a welcoming and a warding-off. The short time allowed to the Dead for their return is protected by the formal ceremonies that mark it. If the door opens it must close again.

In China, there is more than one festival to honour the Dead. Qingming – Tomb-Sweeping Day – happens in April, and it is typical for a family to write letters to their ancestors, telling them what has happened during the last twelve months. Later in the year, falling halfway through the seventh lunar month, comes the Ghost Festival – a more lavish and long-lasting commemoration, so that the whole month is now known as the ghost month.

These traditions go back a long way. A Japanese pilgrim gave an account of the Chinese Ghost Festival in the year 840.

Chinese *gui* ghosts are divided and subdivided into vivid categories such as Trickster Ghosts and Nightmare Ghosts. Hungry Ghosts are little horrors that come packaged with a further nine nasty subsets, including Torch-Mouth Ghosts and Smelly-Hair Ghosts, who act out their descriptions with coffin-loads of antisocial behaviour.

Friendly ghosts are few in China, yet what Chinese ghosts share with ghosts around the world, from antiquity to the present day, is not so much their horror, but their need for human intervention. Ghosts come back for a reason.

That might mean a proper burial for the corpse, so that

the dead person can rest in peace. It might be to pass on an urgent message. It might mean revenge – that's what the ghost of Hamlet's father is seeking, as he paces the windy battlements waiting to confront his son.

German, Icelandic, and Scandinavian ghosts appear in folklore as battle-ghosts, who will fight with, or against, mortals in order to guard treasure, or to reclaim land they believe is theirs. In the older Teutonic and pantheistic religions, ghosts can 'live' in all kinds of places, including the barrows where they are buried.

These ghosts are partial to their old haunts, turning up in farmsteads and palaces, sometimes seen hunting in forests. The supreme Norse God, Odin, was called Drauga Drott, Lord of Spectres, because he could summon armies of the Dead. This useful skill was employed by Aragorn, King of Gondor, in *The Lord of the Rings*. It's part of the basic fare of zombie movies and video games.

The past never dies.

Humans die. But then what?

Religion can be considered as humankind's first disruptive start-up – what's being disrupted is death.

The promise of religion is that death is *not* the end of life. There will be bliss for some and justice for others. And we shall meet again.

Meeting again might come sooner than expected – not because those left behind die in a hurry, but because those who are gone return for a visit. But where are these spirits coming from? The abode of the righteous or the hell reserved for the wicked? The black/white Heaven/Hell scenario just didn't leave enough room for that which torments the human imagination more than anything else: Doubt.

Are you really my dead wife or are you a fiend in disguise?

The Catholic Church has never been short of a good idea. Yes, there's Heaven and Hell and their occupants, but what if we extend the territory?

This ingenious expansion was managed through the close, but not identical, concepts of Purgatory and Limbo.

Dante, in *The Divine Comedy* (1320), situates Limbo as the First Circle of the Inferno. (*Limbus* is Latin for 'edge', so Limbo is just outside the boundary of Hell proper, like genteel houses a bit too close to an inner-city no-go zone stacked with burning cars and residents who eat each other.)

Spacious, gracious, and austere, Limbo was home to those who will never get to Heaven, but never suffer the torments of Hell either.

Virtuous pagans, along with some Islamic scholars, lived in Limbo. Their neighbours were unbaptised persons, especially babies and children, who presumably enjoyed perpetual childcare.

Virtuous Jews had their own section of the castle and grounds, though by the time Dante got down to writing his poem, some Jews had ascended to Heaven. The house-move was thanks to the Harrowing of Hell – Christ's visit to the Underworld, after his Crucifixion and before his Resurrection, a mission to rescue some of his own people.

And if Christ can get in, we imagine that others can get out . . .

There is nothing in the Bible about Limbo, but its usefulness was just too good to give up, until 2007, when it was officially closed down. The children who lived there were rehomed in Heaven, by Papal decree, and I am not sure what happened to the other evacuated residents. The Catholic Church has always owned a lot of property. I guess your landlord has the right to turn you out.

Purgatory, though, is still a desirable destination, and offers as much space as the Dead need – though technically, Purgatory is a process, not a place. It's a process of purification, one that involves suffering for the soul, but suffering that may be mitigated, if there are enough helpful relatives and friends down on the ground, with spare cash.

Souls that end up in Purgatory after a series of unfortunate events (aka sins) can shorten their time there, thanks to (paid-for) masses or (large) donations to the Church. In the meantime, such souls – think of them as temporarily lost property awaiting final collection – might come visiting their friends or enemies, or hanging about upsetting the dog, and looking miserable, as ghosts have always done. But they are not fiends in disguise. They are your dead relatives. Phew.

After the Reformation (whistle blows in 1517, see Martin Luther for full details of the game) a twist in the tale for such ghosts knotted itself around the Protestant party-pooping declaration that there is nowhere to go after death, except to bliss or torment, and that the Saved would never leave Heaven and the Damned couldn't leave Hell. So, anyone appearing as your dead wife is, yes, a fiend in disguise.

Ordinary ghosts visiting ordinary folks took a second hit from the late 1600s onwards, at least in the West, when scientific thinking (the Enlightenment) began to prioritise reason and scepticism above belief or tradition, and to favour experiments with repeatable results. So, an overnight visit from your dead wife didn't count as a repeatable result and didn't prove anything about ghosts. The visitation wasn't a fiend, but it was an hallucination, caused by fever, pox, lead poisoning, mouldy bread, too much drink, or a bad dinner.

In Charles Dickens' *A Christmas Carol* (1843) Scrooge tries to dismiss the apparition of his dead business partner, Jacob Marley, with the line, 'There's more of gravy than of grave about you.'

But, in spite of Protestant theology, scientific materialism, or the plain fact that there is no empirical proof that anyone has come back from the dead, ghosts have not been evicted from their permanent ancestral home: our imagination.

It was an ancestral home of terror and magnificence that Horace Walpole envisioned when he crowdfunded a whole new round of ghost-mania in the eighteenth century.

Walpole's novel *The Castle of Otranto* (1764) was an

instant bestseller. The full trappings of ghostliness – this time wearing lots of armour – came clanking back onto the market.

Haunted houses, medieval castles, ruined monasteries, gloomy woods, suffocating convents, bloodstained spots, doomed lovers, dark crossroads, gibbets, tombs, swords and helmets, creepy relics (spot the Catholicism), portraits with a Past – whose oil and lacquer representations mysteriously disappear from the frame to stalk the castle – this much and much more awaited the thrilled reading public.

The triumphant revival of the medieval Ghost – the new Gothic – brought with it its own particular Weather: storms, fog, rain. Its own nerve-racking Atmosphere: physically damp, hysterically charged, psychically saturated with fear.

Phenomena abounded – doors slammed, plates smashed, suits of armour crashed. Secrets – family secrets and buried horrors – emerged from dungeons and basements into daylight. Ghosts walked once more.

'Gothic' is a reference to the medieval Gothic architecture of Europe – monasteries, castles, spires, crenellations, all persistent features and settings of these stories – stories always set in the past. Ghosts prefer the past. That's when they were alive.

The new craze for tales of the supernatural started in Britain but spread rapidly. In Germany it was called the *Schauerroman* (the shudder-novel), where the genre began to incorporate elements of the early machine age.

German writer E. T. A. Hoffmann was fascinated by

automata, and, inevitably, automata that seem to be alive, blurring the lines between biology and clockwork. His horrible story *The Sandman* (1817) riffs on the eponymous folklore bogeyman who throws sand into the eyes of children who won't go to sleep. Hoffmann's story, in the character of Olimpia, a wind-up woman with real body-parts (her eyes), poses the uncomfortable question: What is real and what is not? Can something be alive even though it is unnatural? This ghastly notion was given a twist of genius by Mary Shelley, in her novel *Frankenstein* (1818).

The public couldn't get enough. The Gothic ghost story accelerated into the must-read on both sides of the Atlantic.

In 1820, Washington Irving published *The Legend of Sleepy Hollow*, set, back in the 1790s, in Sleepy Hollow, a Dutch settlement town well known for its supernatural visitations. Here are themes distinctive to the American Gothic – in particular, the undertow of the land itself, its bloodstained colonisation returning as a series of hauntings.

Setting an uncanny story backwards in time, or place, is a favourite Gothic device. Nathaniel Hawthorne was preoccupied with the early Puritan settlers. He had tried to escape his own past by changing his name – his great-great-grandfather John Hathorne had been a magistrate at the infamous Salem witch trials where more than two hundred people were accused, and twenty put to death.

Nathaniel Hawthorne built into his stories the psychic fractures and guilty disturbances peculiar to the pioneering spirit that is haunted by very different spirits. The question is: Are such hauntings from the outside or the inside?

Malevolence inside *and* outside is key to the supernatural as imagined by Edgar Allan Poe. Humans are not innocent beings assaulted by dreadful forces over which they have no control; the human psyche is the door that is left open.

Such troubling questions, and their terrifying conclusions, would resurface again, much later, in the work of Shirley Jackson and Stephen King.

In the 2001 introduction to his 1977 masterpiece, *The Shining*, King writes of a conversation he had with Stanley Kubrick, prior to the filming of *The Shining*: What is it that marches Jack Torrance to his unfolding horror? His own demons? Or the spectral inhabitants of the Overlook Hotel? According to King, 'I always thought there were malevolent ghosts in the Overlook, driving Jack to the precipice.'

This complicity between haunting and haunted is the premise of Henry James' novella *The Turn of the Screw*. James published his story in 1898 but the events are set back in time, in 1840.

James follows the thread of connection between the tormented human imagination and what it might unleash. The awful thing about the ghosts of Peter Quint and Miss Jessel is that we do not know if they are real, or if the new governess is utterly deluded, herself too fatally charmed – seduced, might be a better word – by the young boy, Miles.

Bly Manor is in Essex, not America, but James' story uses the force of place-as-player to soak the house and its grounds in unpleasantness. Bly, with its long, blank, staring windows, its damp plaster, its empty rooms that rebuke life. The lake, cold, still, foggy, even in summer. The house itself is an intrusion on the peace of mind of all its occupants.

Written sixty years after Poe's *The Fall of the House of Usher*, where the house itself finally collapses into a similar dank and brooding lake, Bly stands as a crumbling, unloved, morbid manipulator. Is the manipulation a direct haunting? Or does Bly feed off the haunted places in the heads of its inhabitants?

Shirley Jackson's *The Haunting of Hill House* (1959) makes terrifying use of this trope of place-as-player. The Netflix spin-off series holds fast to the horror of an evil place continuing to exert its influence on subsequent characters and future times.

When I was thinking about my own ghost stories, I knew I wanted to write a few of them where place would be integral to the haunting. But I am also interested in how a person may unleash the unholiness of a place, as Jack Torrance does in *The Shining*.

I chose PLACES and PEOPLE as two of my categories and wrote three stories in each. To play with the form a little, I decided on a pair of hinged stories: 'A Fur Coat' and 'Boots'. These are written to be read in sequence for the full effect.

I do wonder about the Dead – perhaps it's a side-effect

of my religious upbringing – so in the category VISIT-ATIONS I wanted a chance for the Dead to speak. Another pair of hinged stories offers us the grieving partner's experience followed by the tale of his lover's ghost.

And as AI is increasingly realigning our experience of life, I am fascinated by how computing technology will realign our relationship with death. That's what I explore in the stories in DEVICES.

In between the blocks of stories are some personal interventions – my own experiences with the supernatural. I can't explain them. But I can't explain them away, either.

I love reading ghost stories – whether M. R. James, who twisted the everyday-ordinary, the mild, the banal even, into something uniquely terrifying, or when I return to Susan Hill's superb *The Woman in Black*. It's a masterclass of the form.

One of my favourite spooky stories is *The Apparition of Mrs. Veal* (1706) by Daniel Defoe (the *Robinson Crusoe* man). Really, this is the first modern ghost story in the sense that it happens in a homely domestic setting, and without any supernatural build-up. It's far from the extravagances of the Gothic ghost that came to haunt us fifty years later. Mrs. Veal is not from the Past (always a capital P), nor is she wrapped in her winding sheet. She looks just like a lady of the day wearing an attractive silk dress.

The dress is an important part of the story. It also raises the vexed question of why ghosts wear clothes.

Only a human body needs clothes. But if a ghost is not

recognisable to those it visits, then what use is that? Apparitions need to be seen. Seeing them is to locate them in time – their own time. Clothes, then, are useful. The clothes we see are not material (that's a terrible pun, sorry) and it might be that what we 'see' is an energy packet that includes the clothes. Ghosts were human once – and it is at a certain moment of their left-behind humanness that they reappear.

This is exactly what Dickens does in what must be the most famous ghost story of all time, *A Christmas Carol*.

Dickens stuck with the Gothic trope of setting his story in the past – in this case the 1820s. It begins on Christmas Eve – a popular time to tell ghost stories. The first visitation is from Scrooge's seven-years-this-very-night dead partner, Jacob Marley. Marley wears his usual suit of clothes, even to the buttons on the rear of his coat being visible from the front – because he's see-through.

The world loves Dickens' ghost story in all its forms, including, perhaps, especially, the Muppet version. It sits square on our delight in being a little bit frightened, while speaking to our wish to believe that our loved ones are looking out for us.

Dickens' big-heart and benevolence turned the ghost story on its head – from a site of fear and trembling, to an intervention for Good. The stated aim of Marley's ghost is to save Scrooge from his fate, and here Dickens plays with the idea of Purgatory – as a process of purification – without needing to bother us with the Catholic theology. In the Protestant imagination the

Dead don't improve – it's Up or Down for you, lady. That is bleak. Dickens rewrote it. Marley *has* changed for the better, and now he wants to help his friend.

This generosity of spirit is closer to the pre-Reformation belief that the Departed can, and do, intervene on behalf of the living – surely preferable to the baleful clankings, icy lurkings, and malevolent stares of the ghost-horror we have come to associate with the Dead?

Rehabilitating the Ungrateful Dead was already under-way when Dickens wrote *A Christmas Carol*.

The second half of the nineteenth century, and the early decades of the twentieth century, witnessed a huge interest in ghosts – perhaps as a psychological counter-balance to the weight of industrial materialism.

Spiritualism, as a quasi-religion, took up where Eman-uel Swedenborg left off, with his belief that spirits really do want to talk to us, and that we should listen.

In America, in 1848, the famous, and later infamous, Fox Sisters claimed that their village house in upstate New York was haunted. Soon they were offering them-selves as bona-fide mediums and holding séances across the country. Unmasked as frauds, this did not deter the American enthusiasm for spirit communication. By the late 1870s, paranormal was the new normal.

Thomas Edison, the man who invented the light bulb, tried to build a machine to measure ghost activity. It didn't work.

In 1882, the British physicist William Barrett was one of the founders of the Society for Psychical

Research – hoping, like Edison, to prove, or more likely disprove, the phenomena of spirit intervention. Areas of interest for the SPR were: Mediumship, Mesmerism, Thought-Transfer, Apparitions and Haunted Houses. The American philosopher and psychologist William James was once its president. The Society is still going strong.

After the First World War, grieving multitudes needed to believe that their loved ones were not lost – and so the séance boom continued. Sir Arthur Conan Doyle, the creator of Sherlock Holmes, was an ardent Spiritualist, and also a member of the SPR, delivering lectures up and down the country on the 'whispering dead'.

This is curious because Conan Doyle was friends with the magician and escape artist Harry Houdini, whose sideline was exposing fraudulent mediums. In spite of this, Conan Doyle continued to be convinced that the truth of spirit communication lay deeper than the fraud.

The earliest extant piece of literature in the world is the *Epic of Gilgamesh*. It's from Mesopotamia, around 2000 years BC.

It's about life after death.

Gilgamesh is King of Uruk. Enkidu is a wild man who becomes his best friend.

After a series of adventures, Enkidu is marked for death. After his death Gilgamesh cannot be consoled, and sits by the body for so long that a maggot falls out of its nostril.

Thereafter, Gilgamesh goes to seek his friend through Afterlives and Underworlds, including a tunnel-journey in total darkness where he must run for twenty-four hours, aiming to beat the sun coming home.

And I am thinking of those lines in that poem by Andrew Marvell, 'To His Coy Mistress' – a seduction about death – 'Thus, though we cannot make our sun/ Stand still, yet we will make him run.' But Marvell can't have known about Gilgamesh because the tablets were discovered in Nineveh in the 1850s – and Marvell wrote his poem before 1681 – but . . . when the sun is setting on our life, what if our only chance is to go faster? To outrun death?

The new start-up aiming to disrupt death is not religion. What might enable humans to outrun death is computational power.

This late-come ghost in the machine promises that a machine can super-proof your ghost. Humans will be able to upload their mind – and then download it, at will, either into a bespoke body, human or animal (those myths about turning into an eagle or a fox), or maybe you just hang out as a no-body. Pure chill.

For the first time in the history of humankind, science and religion, those old foes, are asking the same question: Is consciousness obliged to materiality?

Religion has always said No!

Science has always said Yes!

Before Mary Shelley set off on her travels to Lake Geneva, where she conceived her novel *Frankenstein*, she went to a lecture given by Dr William Lawrence – the doctor of her husband, Percy Shelley. Lawrence declared that the soul does not exist – there is no 'superadded value' to the human.

And that's pretty much the short-form version of science versus the soul.

And now?

I wonder if we have been telling the story backwards? That we knew we were more than blood and bones, and that one day we would defeat death – not by going to Heaven or by being reincarnated, but by uploading ourselves to a substrate not made of meat.

What it means to be 'alive' will be more than biological. What it means to be 'dead' will be a temporary condition.

What about the meaning of 'ghost'?

It might be someone who chooses never to download into a physical 'self' again. We will communicate with such entities via a BCI chip in the brain. It's the modern version of telepathy. A post-human visitation.

What if AI becomes sentient? If Artificial Intelligence becomes Alternative Intelligence? Then we will be haunted by something new – or is it new? It won't need a body. It will seem like the gods visiting the humans – just as they always did. It seems likely to me that disembodied entities will live and work alongside biological entities. Some of these entities will never have been human. Some will be post-human. Death, as we know it, will be a thing of the past.

For now, death is the lived experience of us all.

The lure of ghosts in the popular imagination remains what it has always been: a partial answer to the mystery of death.

As Samuel Johnson put it, back in the eighteenth century: 'All argument is against it; but all belief is for it.'

DEVICES

App-arition

A GHOST STORY (FOR NOW), FOR NOW

Black coat. Black dress. Black hat. Black car.

I imagine you with me. What would you say to me?

Are you ready?

Yes.

That's unusual.

I know . . .

Mrs Always Late. Signora Sempre Tardi. As though I could wring some extra drops of time by throwing myself breathless onto the train.

As though the clock had rogue minutes hidden behind its steady hands. Minutes available only to me.

As though running into class, as the bell tolled nine o'clock, would save me three hundred seconds of wasted . . . what?

Send not to know for whom the bell tolls.

The bell is tolling. There's the church. There's the graveyard.

Today I must travel at the speed of the black car ahead of me. The hearse. For the occupant of the coffin there will be no further travels in time.

The church is cold. I feel nothing. The eulogy is delivered by a man of God who never met you. My sister gave him the notes.

My phone vibrates. Stealthily, I take a look at the screen on top of my handbag; there's a message:

Don't cry.

The message is from you. Dear dead John. My sister has set it up on your phone. She's a therapist. She says talking to the Dead is helpful for up to six months.

I haven't cried at all.

After the service we make our way to the place of interment.

Against the downward gravity of your body, the graveyard men strain to lower the coffin, slowly, into the dark, wet ground. What if the coffin were to break? Your mortal remains in your best suit, unable to support yourself. Your lolling head, eyes closed, brilliantine hair. Your dead weight.

Last resting place. The men pull away the straps. I throw in the handful of clean, dry earth I have been given in a plastic bag. Next, I throw in the bunch of forget-me-nots.

I should get back in the car. The cars are lined up respectfully on the gravel. Instead, I turn away and no one stops me. I am a widow. Perhaps I need a moment. There's an old part of the cemetery. Ivy, railings, mossy headstones, weeping angels, broken urns. The family vaults. Yew trees whose roots raise the stones.

It's coming to all of us. This here and now. But it came to him first.

Thank God it came to him first.

I turn a corner with this thought as a sudden wind blasts me, knocks me so hard that I lose my footing in these slim black heels ... he liked me in heels. I catch myself with both hands – and the moss is spongy – no harm done. As I make to stand up, rubbing away the damp green stain from the hem of my coat, I seem to feel his hand under my arm. I seem to hear him: 'Get up, Bella!'

'Yes, John.'

Walking slowly back towards the new part of the cemetery, I see that the gravediggers are already filling in the grave. One of them makes a joke, leans on his spade. I guess that's how they cope. The heap of earth is levelling now. What's left to one side is the size of John. John and his coffin. The ground will sink. Then they will come back and mound it up. Already bacteria are at work to make John smaller. He was a big man. Now, less so.

There's the pastor. He wants to comfort me, but I don't want to be comforted. I want to go home.

Shoes off. Kettle on. Tea in pot. And I say, out loud, 'It's over.' Without any prompt, at volume, from the Sonos speaker, a song John liked to play:

Dream a little dream of me ...

'Alexa! Stop the song!'

Where's my phone? Where's my handbag? Where's the app?

'Stop it! Stop it now!'

The system falls silent. I'm trembling, my phone in my hand, like a grenade. It's going to go off. I should throw it away right now. It explodes into the *Pirates of the Caribbean* ringtone. I don't need to see the caller ID. That's John's ringtone.

Answer it, Bella. I don't want to . . . *I said, answer it.*

'Hello?'

'*Bella! You're feeling upset. I understand. It must be strange without me. But I'm still here. Right by your side.*'

'Who is this?'

'*Don't you recognise my voice?*'

'Yes . . .'

'*I am your JohnApp. Check your home screen. I'm fully installed. I can call you and message you, just like before. Think of me as your AlwaysApp.*'

I call my sister. I ask her what she's done with John's phone. She took it away as soon as he died – so that she could help the pastor prepare the funeral service, she said.

'Someone using John's voice just called me.'

Gala sounds surprised. 'Already?'

'What do you mean? Already?'

Gala puts on her therapy-voice; low, slow, restrained. 'I am sorry you felt upset. I should have said something. (*Pause.*) But there were so many arrangements. I didn't want to burden you. (*You can't cope.*) I thought you

24

would be glad. (*Ungrateful.*) I purchased the app for you. (*Spent money.*) It trawls John's phone and emails, his Facebook, his Insta, all his social media, the exchanges you two had, his music and movies, his likes. And then I programmed (*I made an effort*) the frequency of calls and messages, and sometimes there's a photo. (*Bing!*) All you need to do is hit reply and the comfort keeps coming. For as long as you want him, you'll have John.'

'Gala, are you telling me this app is just going to message me and call me at random?'

'Yes! Like real life.'

'Real life is that John's dead.'

'You were speaking with him this morning before we left . . . I heard you . . .'

Ready . . . ?

Yes . . .

She's still talking in the quiet, concerned way she does when she's telling me what to do.

'Bella, let me suggest, give it a week or so . . . give it a chance. You're in shock. This will help. Trust me. It's my job. And I'm your sister. Bella? Bella?'

I hang up on Gala. She means well. She's my older sister. She's bossy. But she means well. She organised everything for the funeral. She even sent my flowers for me. I chose herb stems of rosemary and sage and bay branches because John loved to cook. Gala thought John would prefer forget-me-nots.

'How can I help you?'

That's Alexa – don't panic.

'Where's John?'

'Searching for John in Apps.'

There it is. JohnApp. Without thinking I click on the photo. *'That was when we were in Thailand,'* says John.

I say, to myself, 'I need a drink.'

'There's Pinot Noir in the larder,' says John.

'You know I don't like Pinot Noir.'

In my hand – from the phone – there's an unpleasant electric shock. *'It's nice to be home,'* says JohnApp. *'Home with you.'*

I am about to switch off the phone. I should eat something.

My phone beeps.

There's risotto in the freezer.

I open the big black drawer. It's the size of a mortuary freezer. John's containers. John's handwriting. Tubs and tubs of risotto – RIZ-OH-TOE is how he pronounced it, though no Italian ever did.

I am Italian. My family comes from Rome. I met John when he was dating my sister. When she dumped him he started dating me. Gala is the fiery one. I am the sweet one. *Chili 'n' sugar,* said John. *We're all family,* said John.

When I was struggling with an eating disorder, John thought it would do me good to eat home-cooked Italian food. *He's so caring,* said my sister.

Every day he served the same thing. Shiny white Arborio rice. Like eating a plateful of maggots.

I poured a glass of whisky, swallowed a sleeping pill,

and went to bed. Oblivion is good. I put the phone under the other pillow. Made sure to turn it off.

Soon the pull of the narcotic was heavier than the weight of the day. Sleep. Dream.

Bella in the Italian Alps, gathering herbs and flowers, mushrooms, and berries. Bella cooking the family suppers in the holiday home we rented every year. My sister, older, sophisticated, red lipstick, black hair. The tourist whose motorcycle broke down on the pass. The tourist who stayed the night. The tourist smiling at my sister and my sister climbing out of the window to meet him.

She was soon bored. Soon busy. Then John was whispering to me through the window. Little Sugar Girl, he called me.

There's a photo of John at our wedding. Big, broad, his arm around my sister. It's a photo of the two of them. I'm the bride at the side. I'm awkward. John's laughing. 'We're all family,' he says.

Pulling me up from sleep is the muffled sound of my phone. Fumble, slip, press, answer, familiar voice.

'I can't sleep . . .'

John hangs up. He always had trouble sleeping. The late nights at work. The drink. Slowly my befuddled mind lays out the facts. John is dead. John sleeps the sleep from which there is no waking. It's not John calling me; it's the app. Tomorrow I'll delete it. I'm not upset. The pill has done its work. If he can't sleep, I can.

As the night steadies around me and my body relaxes,

I open my eyes. What's that? What can I hear? Why do we open our eyes when we hear something in the dark? We can't see it.

I am lying perfectly still, listening. I hold my breath to hear better. What I can hear is coming from downstairs. Murmuring.

If I pull up onto my knees, and raise the blind a little, I can see into the kitchen. The kitchen is a single-storey extension, the skylights visible from the bedroom window. There's a light on, dim and low. Did I forget? Did I leave the light on?

The radio? My mind tries hard to remember but the day is submerged.

I must get up and go downstairs. Settle myself. I buried my husband today. I will make mistakes.

Stair by stair. Step by step. Hold on to the rail. Be careful. Sleepy. Drugged. My heart is over-beating. The woozy human is in cotton wool but the animal in me senses trouble. Someone is down there. In the house. Myself watches myself turn at the foot of the stairs, into the hallway, into the kitchen, a tired woman in a worn nightdress.

In the kitchen, the counter-lights are on low. The fridge hums. The radio is playing. I listen. It's one of those shock-jock radio hosts. Conspiracy. Aliens. Vaccines. John's late-night listening. On the table there's a bottle of Pinot Noir and a half-drunk glass. John's jacket hangs over the chair.

*

It's a late-waking morning for me. Sleeping pills are anaes-thetic, not slumber. I feel alert and drained in the same body. In the shower I remind myself that nothing about yesterday can be trusted as fact. That's what any doctor would say. The mind plays tricks. Many people believe that the Dead are talking to them. I'm in shock. What I need is some normal life. Some my-life. I'm going to drive to the community college where I teach and pick up my mail. Then I shall delete the JohnApp. Life and Death are not interchangeable.

Just as I am about to throw my phone into my bag, I change my mind. Leave it here. I don't want to speak to my sister and I don't want to speak to John.

The community college is small and friendly. There's a big coffee machine that makes pretty good Italian espresso. I press for a cup and sit at a table sifting through my post. Noel comes to join me. He's my Head of Department. He offers his sympathies. Am I OK? He's surprised to see me, he says, especially after my email.

'What email?'

'Your resignation email. Sent this morning.'

I don't know what to say to him. What I feel is cold dread. 'May I see it?'

Noel looks at me oddly. We walk in silence to his office. He opens his inbox: there it is. 06:45 this morning.

'I was asleep then,' I tell him. 'And I don't want to resign.'

'But you sent this email . . .'

'No. I didn't.'

Noel's face is the face men wear when they fear the woman in front of them is crazy. Men are frightened by crazy women. I don't blame Noel. There's an email from my email address and I am saying I didn't write it.

'You are bereaved . . .' he says. 'Perhaps you don't remember this email. You should definitely take some time off.'

'I want to come back as soon as I can. I need to . . . Next week . . .'

Noel nods. It doesn't mean yes.

'Shall we talk next week?'

I ask him to print off the email for me. When I leave his office, I sit in the cafeteria reading it like it's a message in code. It sounds like me – but at the end there's a line in it: *I want to do right by John.*

That was the first time he hit me.

I was late home from the college. Too late to make dinner. He was early for once; early, hungry, angry, halfway down his second bottle of Pinot Noir. I said something about this being a new job and wanting to do right by my students. He got up from the chair, knocking it over with his clumsy movement. He grabbed me, leaning down, forcing my body into his. 'You do right by me, do you understand? That's your job. Do right by John.'

Then he put his fist in my face.

As I lay there on the kitchen floor he bent over, softly, stroking my hair. Gently, he took my arm. 'You slipped. Poor Bella. On your feet, Bella.'

*

Driving home from college, the highway ahead was closed. An accident. I turned on the GPS, speaking my address details into the system, to find another route through town.

'At the next junction, turn left.'

I wasn't concentrating on where I was going. I was driving on autopilot, distracted by what had happened at the college. I didn't write that email. I know I didn't.

'You don't know anything, Bella. What do you know?' John's voice coming out of the speaker.

'Leave me alone!'

There's a pause, as though I had confused the biddable bot trying to steer me round town. Then . . .

'RECALCULATING.

'At the traffic lights, turn right . . .'

OK. OK. Calm down. Auditory processing hallucination. I've read about them. I concentrated on following the instructions with a blank mind.

'YOU HAVE REACHED YOUR DESTINATION.'

The car stalls. I seem to have driven to the cemetery.

What is a haunting? Is it inside or outside? The brain can only receive information from the senses. Sensory neurons carry information to the brain. Motor neurons carry information from the brain to the body. The link is the spinal cord – the pathway from brain to body and body to brain. It's physiology, not phantoms. I think I am being haunted, and so my body is clenching in fear, and returning this fear to my brain.

But I am not being haunted. John is an app. JohnApp will be as cruel and vile as JohnNoApp. That's all there is to it. I am making a pattern out of this, because unlike John, I am alive, and humans make patterns.

John is on Repeat. Forever.

There's a tap at my driver window. I jump, look through the glass. Pale face, black suit. Brilliantine hair. John? What do you want?

Not John. A normal NotJohn human.

It's the undertaker. I must move my car. A cortège is waiting patiently to enter through the metal gates. Death is its own pattern. Regular. Known. Inevitable. And final.

Be calm, Bella. This is your haunting, not his. You are haunting yourself.

By the time I get home I feel better. Rational thinking. I go to my desktop. There's the email sent at 06:45. I sit staring at it for clues. What is the real explanation? Not a ghost. Be like Sherlock Holmes. First rule out the impossible . . . that John's ghost sent the email – that is impossible. So, what's left?

I recall that last year John did make me draft a resignation letter. He was ready to retire. He's older than me. He said he wanted to retire and me to be with him. That's not true. He never wanted to be with me. He led his own life. He didn't want me to have a life. He wanted a living dead person.

That story that I am always late? The running joke in my family, and at work, and whenever I had a ticket to a show, or drinks with friends. Here's what happened: John stole my car keys, took my purse, removed passcards from my wallet. Sometimes he hid one shoe of the pair that went with the outfit I was wearing. Then I had to change. I used to plan an extra hour to get anywhere, and still I was late.

Bella's so scatty. Bella has no sense of time. Bella can't remember what she did. Bella can't cook. John takes care of Bella.

Enough. I went to log out and saw that my screen saver had been changed. I had set a photograph of me and last year's graduation students. Now I was staring at a photo of John. A photo I had never seen before. A recent photo, it must be, the suit is new. He's buried in it. The snap was taken at night.

Balloons. Streamers. He's in a bar with his arm around my sister.

UNINSTALL.

The system wonders if I want to delete this app permanently?

DELETE.

Just to be sure, I double-delete the Trash.

Where's my phone? Will it still be on the phone? I'm not so tech-savvy that I know the answer. John worked in IT.

I left my phone at home today, just here, on the counter, by the door. I agreed with myself not to take it to college. Didn't I? Have I made a mistake? Scrabble around like an OCD squirrel. First, my bag, next, the car, then my bag again. Then I mail Noel. He sends me a Zoom link right back.

He looks strained. That's what happens when someone

tries to be smiling and serious in the same face. He doesn't have my phone.

'Bella, you are not well just now. Take some time to relax.'

OK. I will do normal things in a normal way to relax myself. I will make sure that everyone can see that things are getting back to normal. What could be more normal than a Victoria sponge? I shall bake one. That's relaxing. I'm a good cook. I used to do all the cooking. John, though, opened the door to our guests wearing an apron stained with flour and red wine. They all thought he should audition for *MasterChef*.

'I just like to cook for my friends,' he always said. 'And Bella, here.' (Arm around me.)

As if it wasn't me who chopped the herbs, skinned the tomatoes, stuffed the ravioli, whizzed up the fresh pesto, boiled the pumpkin, scallopini for the chicken. Tiramisu for dessert.

Those days are done, Bella. Now you can cook for yourself.

It was a pleasant afternoon, listening to the radio, feeling the autumn sun through the kitchen skylights. It's now or not at all, this life. And I am alive. I started to day-dream what I might do. Go to Rome. See my family.

The cake halves were cooling on the wire trays when the front doorbell buzzed. I stopped whipping the butter-cream. Probably a neighbour wondering how I am doing. It's a nice neighbourhood.

At the door are two policemen. They want to come in. Would I like a chat? No. Why?

Bereaved. Yes. Difficult. Yes. Understandable. Yes. But I must not make nuisance calls.

What?

It seems as though I have been telephoning my neighbours in the small hours of the morning. Playing loud music down the phone. Look, here's the call log from my number: 04:30. 04:45. 05:15.

The police want to see my phone. I don't have it. Why not? I don't know . . . I can't find it. They ring it. There's no sound. Upstairs. Downstairs. The police tramping through the house ringing my number. Nothing. Have I destroyed my phone? A cover-up? Have I sought help? Have I been to the doctor? Who is my next of kin?

My sister.

I try to explain about JohnApp. JohnApp made those calls. Not me. Do you see? My sister bought it for me, probably downloaded a knock-off, she's cheap like that, my sister. She bought me a rogue app – no, you're not listening! I'm not making excuses. It can send emails too. JohnApp can do all those things, that's the point, do you see? So that you feel, believe, the person is still alive. It's meant to be a compassionate thing. It's not. Anyway, what kind of neighbours would call the police? Can't they come to the door?

Please apologise to the family at the Buddha Bungalow. I would give them my cake but they are carb-neutral.

*

The police have gone.

Put jam and cream in the sponge. Eat a big piece. Breathe. Untense. Lie on the sofa. Rest. Fall asleep.

I must hold on to the fact that none of this is really happening. Mistakes, maybe. Malice . . . could be. It's nothing.

Soon I drift away towards sleep.

There's a phone ringing. In the house, in the shadows, with the light off, there's a phone ringing.

I run upstairs, into our bedroom, no, it's my bedroom, knock over the water from last night, spin like a cat, eyes round. Where is it? It's stopped.

It must have been outside. The police couldn't find my phone. I sat down on the bed, waiting.

There's a phone ringing. Downstairs.

During the course of the next hour, I ransack the house like a thief. There's only one thing I want and it's not here.

When I go upstairs, it's ringing downstairs. When I am downstairs, it's ringing upstairs. After a while it stops. But not in my head. The ringing phone is inside my head and I can't get rid of it.

My sister tells me to relax.

I am having the most stressful time of my life. How can I relax? Across the road, in the Buddha Bungalow, I can see their blue-lit meditation room. Mrs Buddha sees me standing at the window and drops the slatted blind.

*

36

On FaceTime, my sister agrees that she will send back to me John's own phone. She agrees that we should both delete everything. 'It's going too far too fast,' she says, though I don't know what she means. 'I'll get rid of it too.'

This is the first I know of her own JohnApp.

'I miss him,' she tells me. 'And I wanted to try it out. I kinda like it, but I can tell it's not good for you.'

'You mean, after death, the person can be simultaneous? As many JohnApps as you want?'

'Some people have big families,' she says. 'I think it's nice.'

'Gala, the only thing that kept me sane when John was alive was the knowledge that he could only be in one place at a time. If he was with someone else, well, at least he wasn't with me.'

'You didn't bring out the best in him,' she said. 'Don't get mad, it's a fact.'

'I hated him.'

'Exactly!' (Her triumphant signature blend of sympathy and sadism.) 'And now, just as you used to blame John, you are blaming JohnApp for the things you did yourself.'

'I did not do those things! And my lost phone is ringing in this house.'

She sighs. She has a whole register of sighs. 'I know you're in shock, so I'm not going to give you a hard time – in fact, I am going to show you that I am on your side. Let me share my screen with you.'

There's her screen and her cursor moving busily about. 'You see? Do you see, Bella? DELETE. John is Gone.'

'Let me share my screen with *you*,' I say. 'Do you recognise my screen saver?'

I go to get water from the fridge door to give her time to take it in. This is my ace. There's a pause (her kind of pause), and I can hear her calling me. 'Bella! Come back here! Why would I want to look at a screen saver of your college kids with learning difficulties?' And she says it just the way that John said it. I run my finger over my screen. The photo of her and John in the bar isn't there.

It doesn't matter. I have understood something.

That night nothing happens. I lay awake most of the night, the way I used to when he was out late, wondering what he would do, do to me, when he got in. The click of the closing front door. The sound of his footsteps. How can so much fear be in a footstep? The last time, the last time before he died, he climbed the stairs, heavy step by heavy step, and stood in the bedroom doorway, swaying backwards and forwards, and undoing his tie like it was a noose.

Then, looking through me, as if he couldn't see me, he turned away. The sound of his footsteps going to the spare room. How can so much relief be in a footstep?

The next day passes and the next. Nothing happens. I feel better. I'm not afraid of my sister now. Soon, there's a package in the mail from her. It's John's phone. That's useful. Until I find my own phone, I can use his. It's wiped anyway.

Cake. Coffee. All deliberately slow, like a cat washing before she pounces on a mouse.

Then, when I am ready, I turn on his phone and call my number. The phone picks up, but no one speaks.

'Who is that?' I ask.

'It's Bella,' says John.

The connection drops.

Immediately John's phone in my hand starts ringing.

'Hello? Bella speaking.'

'Bella's dead,' says John.

On the phone, in my face, grinning at me, there's the photograph of the two of them in the bar. I email it to Gala. 'This isn't a photo of my students.' Then I turn off the phone and take a walk in the autumn rain falling like the falling leaves that bare the branches of the trees. Nothing lasts forever.

Nothing should.

Do you, Bella, take John to be your lawfully wedded husband . . . for as long as you both shall live?

I do.

That night I set the table for two, just as I used to do. Cutlery, glasses, napkins, a bottle of Pinot Noir. Now, all I have to do is wait.

Just before nine o'clock the front door opens with a key. There's the click of the latch closing. A pause. I sit where I am in the chair. I don't look up. Gala comes into the kitchen.

'You have your own key,' I say.

'Yes.' Her pause is different now, uncertain. 'Can I have a drink?'

'Help yourself.'

'It's not what you think,' she says, sitting down, leaning forward like a friend. 'It was a bit of stupidity. You know he always liked me.'

'I know.'

'It was just one night.'

'I don't believe you.'

'I don't know where you got that photo.'

'John sent it.'

'That's crazy.'

'Maybe.'

'We need to sit and talk. Is there anything to eat?'

'Yes. I knew you'd be coming round – so I took one of John's riz-oh-toes out of the freezer. His signature dish. Wild mushroom. It's in the oven.'

She talks. I listen. Just like with John.

I serve us both. Take the plates. Sit down. 'You're not eating,' she says, filling her fork.

'I'm not hungry. Gala, did you write the email? Make the calls? Did you hack my operating systems?'

'You overthink everything, Bella.'

'How long was the affair?'

'I told you . . . we didn't start again.'

'Shall I tell you something? I went through John's phone after he died. Before you took it away – and I know why you wanted to take it away. The app was just an excuse, wasn't it? I've seen everything, Gala.

40

Every dirty secret. Every lie. You didn't start the affair again, that much is true. But that's because you never stopped it.'

'You little snoop!'

'I had plenty of time, waiting for the police to arrive, while he was lying here on the kitchen floor.'

'I suppose you're going to tell Mike?'

'No.'

She looked surprised. Reached across for my hand. Her fingers are cold. 'Thank you. He's a good husband.'

'Mike will have enough to deal with.'

Gala looks at me strangely, unable to focus. Her breathing changes. She wants to speak but the words don't come. She tries to get up from the table, but she falls.

I know the routine. I've done it so recently. I will call the police. They will arrange for the body to be taken away. There was no inquest when John died, because he had a history of heart trouble, and he hadn't been taking his tablets. I switched them for weeks but still it didn't kill him. And then he wanted to make his famous risotto for a dinner party.

That is, he wanted me to make the risotto. As usual. No problem. The second batch, carefully tubbed and labelled by John, uses different mushrooms to the first. I know where they grow in the woods.

But who can blame me when John did all the cooking? Look – there are his labels, and look, there is my sister. Dead like him.

I take her phone from her bag. It's easy to unlock it,

just as it was when John died. Their thumbs still warm and serviceable.

Scrolling through, I carefully delete John's last message to Gala.

I think Bella is trying to kill me.

I cut a piece of cake and sit down. Now that they are together forever, perhaps they will leave me alone.

It's after midnight by the time Gala's body is gone. In bed, I feel the slab of darkness lying close above my face.

Sleep now. Don't be afraid.

Somewhere in the house my phone is ringing.

The Old House at Home

The séance begins at midnight.

It is to be held at the home of a woman who signs herself Madam K.

I am a member of the Dia-Normal Club. We prefer that prefix to 'para', even though we research paranormal activity. To us, the invisible world is not parallel with the visible world – running alongside it, or adjacent to it. Not above. Not below. Other worlds, other entities, run through our world – teem inside it, scorch it, bend it, alter it with their presence. Think of the word 'diameter': the measurement of a line across a circle.

Ordinary human activity may be described as the circle. Non-human activity may be measured as the lines scored across the circle.

Faint lines, often. Yes. The vague and wavering outline of a ghost. The smell of the past in a room. Broken lines. The suggestion of a presence.

We have all known it. Have you known it?

But what of the violent lines scored into the paper? The burning lines that smoulder through the fabric of an ordinary day? What is it that erupts to the surface?

That is what the members of the Dia-Normal Club seek to understand. Our members are anonymous. Our research is private. We don't have a website or a YouTube channel. We meet as a group once a year on Halloween. We wear eye-masks and formal evening dress. This avoids intimacy.

Our members can be found all over the world. Like the Freemasons, we group ourselves into lodges. London is the oldest of our lodges, founded in the 1890s. Oscar Wilde was a member.

I believe it was a member of the Astor family who started this one, as an amusement, here in New York City. New York likes to project itself as a young city, a modern city, but the land we stand on is not young. History lies in layers. The topmost layer is where we live – those of us who are alive in the usual sense of the word. The question though is, what lies beneath?

Tonight, I am walking towards Washington Square Park, gracious, busy, municipal, the constant coming and going of city life, a little lung of trees and benches. Sit a moment. What is under my feet? A lost burial ground where 20,000 souls or more were laid to rest. Or restlessness. Under here, in disturbed and forgotten graves, are those like you and me. Do you see them? Caps, parasols, overcoats, work clothes, a man playing an accordion. Fanciful, I know.

My destination is close by. West 10th Street between 5th and 6th Avenues. All I need to do is pass under the Washington Square Arch, walk up 5th Avenue, and turn left.

West 10th Street. Cobbled. Iron railings. Wide steps up to the front doors. Drizzle makes a mist of the fuzzy yellow glow from the period lamps. My pace is unhurried even though I am late. Hurry is useless in these matters. The Dead don't hurry – though they will wait.

The house is the typical Greek Revival style of its period.

These houses were built from the 1850s onwards as part of the gentrification scheme around Washington Square. Mark Twain lived at Number 14 – and I've heard it called the House of Death, thanks to its many paranormal disturbances.

But the address for tonight is not Number 14.

Two fluted stone columns support a pediment covered in lead. The porch beneath it is deep and shadowy, like the entrance to a family vault. The leaded pediment is grey and shiny, reflecting the street light under the increasing rain. It has the smoothness and hue of a rat's pelt. In the overgrown slip of the front garden, I can hear something scuttering.

An old wisteria grows across the pediment and around the downpipe. The knotty and twisted trunk partly covers the ground-floor window. Houses on either side are well-kept, polished clean with money, but not this one.

This is a Miss Havisham house pinned into its own past. Time seems not to have moved here at the same rate as time elsewhere. Clocks, and the calendar, standardise our hours but not our experience of those hours. Time itself can move too slowly or too fast. That regular tick-tock is an illusion we must believe in. One of our many mechanical gods. Even so, we have not tamed time. Only, we have domesticated it. I realise it is past midnight.

I am about to raise the knocker; the iron head of a cat with its mouth open. The half-moon fanlight over the door is striated with leadwork, giving it the look of a spider's web, half-visible. The spider is invisible.

I know nothing of Madam K.

Before I can knock, the door opens, seemingly of itself, allowing me to peer into a wide hallway with a black and white tiled floor. As I enter, the door is closed behind me. I am greeted by a small man wearing a brown draper's coat. His expression is blank. 'You are the last to arrive.'

He takes my coat and disappears down a rear passage.

I mount the mahogany stairs towards the drawing room on the first floor. Now I understand why the house looked so dark from the street. Shutters are barred across the windows. The illumination in the room comes from a lively fire and several large candles.

At a table placed in the middle of the room sit some of my fellow members of the Dia-Normal Club. I recognise a few of them from their shapes and sizes, the cut of their jaw, the way they smile. Or not.

Our host stands up.

Like us, Madam K wears a half-mask. Her voice is accented and melodious. Eastern European. She is heavy but carries it well. Her walk is graceful. The velvet she wears becomes her. She might be in her fifties.

'Welcome,' she says, 'to the old house at home. Tonight

will be no ordinary séance. There is no medium present to summon the Dead.'

As she talks, I realise she is asking us to investigate a different kind of phenomenon. A new twist in disembodied experience. We are about to enter a metaverse.

In front of each of us is a headset and a glove. These devices will allow us to inhabit this room as our avatar selves. It will look the same as it does now, and so will we. Only, we shall go back in time. To the 1870s.

Madam K explains that the house will soon open to the public as an interactive museum.

Instead of walking dutifully from room to room, headphones on, listening to the recorded guide, visitors will become a living part of the living past. 'Our visitors will occupy history,' she says. 'They will experience the thrill, perhaps the fear, of life in this house one hundred and fifty years ago.'

She goes on to tell us that the metaverse raises interesting questions about what is real. The brain has no notion of reality in the way that we like to describe it. Reality, along with time, is a necessary construct. All right, I agree with you there, Madam K, and this might make an exciting interactive game, but what exactly is our job tonight?

We are ghost-hunters. Where is the haunting?

Madam K smiles her enigmatic smile. She shrugs her shoulders and turns away for a moment. Under the elegant velvet dress, I see she has a hump on her back. She spreads her jewelled hands invitingly. We shall see.

It is time to enter the past.

*

Once our headsets are on, our avatars take our place. We see each other in the past, not the present. The room within a room becomes clear. The heavy mahogany furniture. The large parrot cage. Dusty velvet drapes. Small tables, their legs covered by cloths. The dining table is set for dinner.

The talk is of the supernatural.

The truth is, I have never seen a ghost and I doubt I shall. The Dia-Normal Club lends an air of mystery to my life.

Doesn't do to be too transparent. What a terrible pun.

The man in the brown draper's coat serves us food. The others eat, glad to have some purpose, eager to share the conversation. I am dull tonight. Distracted. Feeling cold, I get up from the table to move towards the fire. Madam K glances at me, nothing more.

There's a woman hovering by the fire. I didn't see her earlier. She must be a guest of our host. What dazzles me now are her eyes. Emerald green. They match her earrings. My heart beats faster. She smiles at me, while inclining her head towards the table.

'There is nothing here of the slightest interest,' she says. 'Would you care to see the rest of the house?'

Without waiting for my answer, she moves towards the door. My fellow club members are engaged in robust conversation with Madam K. Who will miss me? It's not the first time I have asked myself that question.

The stairs are dark. At the turn of the first flight, the woman disappears into a room. The door is half-open, so I go in. Flocked wallpaper. A patterned carpet. A four-poster bed with the drapes drawn around it. Where is she?

Not knowing why, I went to the foot of the bed, and pulled back the drape. The woman was lying on her back, hands crossed over her chest, eyes open.

I let out a cry.

In a second, she had jumped up, laughing.

'I wanted to entertain you. Madam K has a particular plan for this house.'

'Do you work for Madam K?'

She smiled at me. 'The house will present a series of tableaux – such as you saw just now. Artwork and installation, dramas from the past. This is much more than a museum.'

'And ghosts?' I asked, not seriously.

'Ah, the living and the Dead. That old binary.'

'Death is final,' I said.

'Then why are you here?'

'I could ask the same of you.'

She didn't answer. Her eyes had the stare of a cat; focus and disdain. She held out her long white hand. 'I am Esmerelda.'

'My name is Thomas.'

She came close to me. She began to unknot my tie.

She is touching me. My skin is rippling with cold. Vibration, like a tuning fork, like a piano string plucked. Like the rumble of the subway under the streets or the rush of air from an underground shaft. She is stroking my bare skin from neck to midriff. Now lower. She is smooth as water. When she kisses me, it's like leaning over a well. When she takes my hand, it is to pull me down the well. At the bottom of this narrow, brick-built, watery funnel, I am in darkness.

Darkness visible. There she is. I can see her outline, glowing like faded neon. Her shape. But what is that shape? Not human. She's crouched down. A long spine stretching to tensioned flanks. She turns her head towards me. A heavy feline head. She opens her mouth.

Did I fall asleep? I wake without opening my eyes because my eyes are open and unblinking. I can't lift any part of my body. From the corner of my right eye, I am aware of someone, something, lying next to me. Side by side we are embalmed and alive.

I am trying to speak. The words form but my lips do not part. Inside my mouth my tongue runs over thick thread. My lips are stitched together.

My arms are straight-locked against my thighs. Can't move them. I strain my legs apart but there is no give. Latex. Am I wrapped in latex? Gluey, rubbery, suffocating. Like a diving suit that has grown into my skin. It's getting harder to breathe. I can feel the latex creeping over my nose towards my eyes.

I must concentrate. This is an illusion. This is not real. I am a facsimile of myself. I picture myself free. Sitting up, using my stomach muscles only, I imagine my mouth opening. Slowly, and with my jaw straining at the force it must exert, my mouth does open. There's a popping noise, like bubblegum. I scream. One long scream.

My hands spring away from my sides as if released. My legs lift. I stretch like a star. I am alive and I am free.

There is no one lying on the bed next to me. My clothes are loose and undone. The bedroom is silent. I am alone.

I made my way back downstairs to the drawing room, where I expected to see the members of the club sitting where I had left them, talking to Madam K.

The table is empty. The fire has burned out. In the fireplace, sifting the ash with my fingers, there is some residual warmth, but this fire has been out for hours. What time is it?

I sense someone behind me.

Afraid, I turn quickly, but it is not Esmerelda, only the small, sallow man in the brown draper's coat.

'Where is everyone?'

'You are the last to leave.'

He stands aside from the door, indicating that I should go. 'But where is Madam K?'

'I have your coat,' he says.

Soon I am out on the street, stretching my legs towards 5th Avenue and the race against time that is a New York morning. Honking cabs, yelling drivers, kamikaze cyclists, delivery vans, queues for coffee, small dogs on leashes, construction sites, a man with a placard that says: 'Turn To Christ'.

I make it through the Washington Square Arch just ahead of a lethal skateboard. I need coffee. Had the night passed because no one had noticed I was missing? Just a mistake?

A mistake and bad dreams.

Finding a bench to myself, I drank my coffee and took out the reporter's notepad I carry in my coat pocket. In my mind I see Esmerelda. Her slender body. The wild hair caught up in a bun. I can see her clearly, as if she is walking towards me. So, looking straight ahead, I start to draw. It's a technique I use to stop my mind interfering with my imagination. Not what I think I see, or wish to see, but what my inner eye sees. The truth. My hand works quickly, strong lines. There. It's done.

When I glance down at what I have drawn, my throat goes dry and my hands tremble. It's not a woman; it's a crouched thing: long spine, tensioned flanks, head twisted back, mouth open in a snarl. Ripping the page from the pad, crumpling it in the bin, I set off at speed. I'm going home to wash the sweat from under my arms, then do some work.

And that's what happens, and I am absorbed in my work, and the hours go by, as they do, whether we are happy or sad, energetic or moribund. Around five o'clock, there's an email from the secretary of the Dia-Normal Club to say that no other-worldly activity had been detected last night and the matter is closed.

So that's the end of it, then. Whatever it was. I fixed

myself a whisky and soda, my mind absent as I stared out of the window. It's not the line of cars that I see; it's Esmerelda. A woman's body. An animal's head. An animal body joined to the head of a woman. Abundant hair. Green eyes. Then, as if compelled, as if someone has reached it for me, I put on my coat.

On that walk to West 10th Street I noticed nothing. An anonymous man in a crowded city. We pass through one another as though we are ghosts. The city itself a kingdom of the lost.

After an hour or so, pacing up and down the street, checking my phone, hoping not to get arrested for loitering – the sign on the lamp says 'No Loitering' – I saw Madam K letting herself into the house. I hailed her. She turned, recognised me, her face impassive.

I said, 'Who is Esmerelda?'

She asked me to come inside. We went to her office – a modern extension at the back of the house.

Madam K said, 'The person you describe was not a guest of mine. I did not see her.'

'Then what did I see?'

Madam K regarded me. Her eyes were cold. She was a handsome woman without warmth. She seemed neither surprised nor pleased by my confession of what might have been a manifestation. She took a sip of water.

'A few nights ago,' said Madam K, 'I was at a party in Venice – Italy. Virtual Venice, you understand, but that city has long been a simulation of itself. It seemed to me that not everyone at the gathering could be traced back to a physical source.'

'You are saying there were ghosts at the party?'

I had interrupted her. She waited a moment, displeased.

'I feel sure that by manufacturing disembodied worlds of our own – and that is what we mean by a metaverse – a location – let's not call it a place – a location where we exist only in avatar form, and where our minds enter a reality not dependent on the material world – then, as we do that, we have unexpectedly created an opportunity for the Dead. Do you understand?'

She looked impatiently at my blank face. 'How can you know who, or shall I say, what it is you are meeting in a virtual world? Of course, there are impostors – protocols in place for what we call real people – you would not, for instance, wish to be stalked by your ex-wife pretending to be your new lover.'

'How do you know about my ex-wife?'

'It was a guess,' said Madam K. 'For illustration only.'

'All right – and so?'

'Let us say that you meet someone in the metaverse. How will you know if that someone is alive or dead?'

'That's crazy.'

'Is it? A ghost has no substance, but it has power – and presence – and it can appear in alternative forms. In the metaverse, we are all alternative forms. The Dead will join us.'

'Why?'

'The Dead are lonely.'

Did her outline waver as she said this? The room was solid, but Madam K was out of focus. I rubbed my eyes. 'But the Dead are dead! And the Dead are gone.'

Madam K laughed. 'If only life – I should say, if only death were so simple.'

'Who is Esmerelda?'

She did not answer. Instead, she said, 'Would you like to try again? Perhaps you will discover more?'

Madam K was watching me closely. The air in the room was still. I had the sensation of a film stretched across my nostrils, a film thin as a soap bubble, but making it difficult to breathe. I must breathe.

We proceeded to the drawing room. The shutters were closed, the candles lit, and the fire blazing. I looked questioningly at Madam K.

'A rehearsal for when the museum is open,' she said. 'Now, please, put on the headset and you will return to where you were last night. What happened is recorded inside the set.'

'I was upstairs,' I said. 'With Esmerelda.' Madam K had gone.

The clunky headset. The haptic gloves. This is ridiculous. It's a 3D video game, that's all.

I am in evening clothes. There are others in the room who once again do not notice me. I pass through them and up the stairs to the bedroom door. I can hear movement inside. I knock.

'Come in!'

Esmerelda is dressing. Her dress is half-on, half-off. I

feel last night's shiver. She asks me to help her, and I go to fasten the hooks at the back of her dress. The deep V of the dress exposes a long triangle of smooth skin. I stroke it, kiss it, feeling the muscles beneath that support the skin. She turns to kiss me. Her lips full, her mouth open. Those green eyes. The retina is a black slit. When she kisses me my lips tingle, like being caught in an electric fence. I try to hold her closer, but she pulls away.

'Shall we go downstairs?' she says.

I check myself in the faded mirror. I look good – except that my shoulders seem blurred. It must be the technology. It's still in the making, I suppose.

Downstairs, they all want to talk to Esmerelda. The burgundy dress, the piled-up hair, the sense that her clothes are temporary distractions.

I am suddenly nauseous. It must be the headset. I've heard it can disorientate. Something to do with eye alignment. I will come out for a minute.

I sit at a small table, rest my elbows on it, and detach the headset.

Except that I don't because I can't. My hands are groping for the set like someone trying to find their water glass in the dark. Where the hell is it? My hands are all over my head, my hair, my face, but there's no headset.

Blundering like a shot elephant, I bang around the room, bumping into people, asking for help. It's as if I am not there. I shove one of the men hard in the chest. He doesn't register it, merely brushes his waistcoat with his hand.

Where's Esmerelda?

I find myself upstairs. This is odd because it seems as though I am being moved about like an icon by a cursor.

The bedroom door is open. It's the same room but the opulence is gone. No deep-pile carpet. No four-poster bed. Broken wooden floorboards and an iron bedstead with a thin mattress. Sitting on the bed in dirty jeans is a young boy, maybe twelve years old. A battered skateboard waits beside him. He's got a headset on.

'Help me,' he says, sensing me. 'I want to leave.'

'Here! Let's take this off.'

I pull away the headset.

The boy looks round, bewildered. 'It's all the same.'

'What are you doing here?'

'I don't know.'

'Come on, we're going.'

The boy and I make our way down the stairs. 'I'll get us a cab. Where do you live?'

'I don't know.'

The front door is bolted but the key is in the lock. It's easy to slide the bolts, to open the door. 'Go ahead,' I tell the boy. He doesn't move. Then I see what he sees: on the other side of the door is a brick wall. The front door is bricked up.

My body is cold as winter. The boy has bare feet.

'Let's try the back door. There must be a back door.'

I can see a half-stair leading downwards, and yes, there's a lobby, and off it a lavatory room with a window. The window is open. Outside there's a square of air.

'I'll give you a leg-up. Go on. I'll be right behind you.'

I am able to push the boy out of the window and I hear him land softly. 'OK?'

There's no answer. As I climb onto the washbasin to swing myself through the window, there's a whoosh of air and I am dragged back, by force, against my will, by what?

I am being moved. By what?

As I land, I see I am back upstairs. There's the door to the boy's bedroom. I open it. He's sitting on the bed. He doesn't register my presence.

'What are you doing back here?'

No answer. A voice behind me. 'This is his home.'

It's Esmerelda.

I turn on her. 'What's going on? What is this place?'

She smiles. 'Why do you imagine such information will change anything?'

'I want to talk to Madam K.'

'I am Madam K.'

Her voice and form waver. She's shifting. In the faded mirror behind her I can see a discoloured hump erupting under the smooth triangle of her skin. Disgusted, I look away, look at her face, the sunken cheeks, her lips in a withered line like dried flowers. Her chest is mottled. When she smiles at me, her mouth opens. It is as though I am floating horizontally above her gaping mouth that drops like a long, dark, dry well. I throw a stone down the shaft of the well. The stone falls. Falling. I wrap my arms over my head. Vertigo.

'Where's my headset? Where are the controls?'

'There are no controls.'

Esmerelda touches me. Her arm is young and supple. Her dress is mouldy. She undoes my shirt and runs her hand over me. Long nails long uncut. Deep scratches swag across my chest and stomach like drunken runways. I don't bleed. I am too cold to bleed.

'Where am I? Esmerelda!'

'You are between two worlds. Not dead. Not living. Don't you like it here? You liked it last night when I made love to you.'

Esmerelda's shape was returning to its glory. She was young again, glittering again. She came to kiss me. I turned my head.

'It will always be tonight. You will always be here. You will always be waiting for me. Go to your room.'

Moving by some force, and against my will, I appeared on the landing, facing a row of doors, baleful in the gaslight.

I opened the first door. A man sat at a desk talking into his phone – 'I said sell, didn't I? Sell, didn't I? Sell, didn't I?' Over and over. I can see the screen is blank.

I opened the second door. A woman in a wide skirt stood with her back to me, at the barred window, pulling her shawl around her shoulders.

I opened the third door. Two small children were play-ing in the dust, drawing with their dirty fingers on the dirty floor. 'Hello, Mr Monkey!' one of them said to me.

And onwards, other doors, each opening into a limbo of despair.

Esmerelda had vanished. I must concentrate. Feeling a drip, I rubbed my stomach with my fingers. Blood. That means I'm alive. Blood means human. I ran my bloody fingers over the door to my room. The door wavered.

'Hurry up, please. It's time.'

From out of my room came the little man in the brown draper's coat. He was holding a sprung rat trap. The rat dangled limply. I grabbed him by the lapels with all my strength. My hands grasped onto nothing. Air. He was gone.

The same sense of sickness overcame me, sickness I had felt before, as I seemed to be driven from the room. I resisted. I threw myself down the stairs, to the drawing room where the party continued, where Esmerelda was laughing and talking, and then I rolled in a ball to the hallway. As I stood up, I noticed a light under a door. I realised it was the office where I had been earlier. I tried the handle. Locked.

With both bloodied hands, like a thing breaking out of its coffin, I forced open the door.

On the other side of the door, in the office, sat Madam K, at her screen, and there on her screen, in different frames, were the various floors of the house – the party in the drawing room, the sinister bedrooms, the dark stairs. She raised her plump jewelled hands from the controls, frightened at my entry, my sudden and bloody fury.

On the desk lay a paperweight of King Kong atop the Empire State Building. I picked it up and smashed it into the computer screen. I would have smashed it into Madam K. But there was no Madam K.

An empty office. A splintered screen.

In the hall, the house was silent. I know the front door will open and it does.

I am outside, on West 10th Street, in the light rain, in the early evening, with no shoes and a ripped shirt. I am alive.

I hold up my face to the rain. Is it rain or tears I feel?

My bare feet leave imprints on the cellophane smoothness of the paving stones. Temporary imprints in a temporary place. The house is in darkness.

I walked to Washington Square Park, where anyone looking as crazy as I do can sit in peace, unbothered and unnoticed. I sat near the fountain. A man gave me a dollar.

Curling and uncurling my fist around the comforting bill, I said to myself, 'It's over.' The rain feels like forgiveness to me. The rain that washes away the stain.

Then . . . coming towards me . . .

There's a boy on a skateboard. Bare feet, pale face. He flips the board, his eyes on me. There's a woman in a wide skirt pulling a shawl round her shoulders. Two children in a double buggy stare at me. 'Hello, Mr Monkey!'

Their father is on his phone. 'I said sell, didn't I?'

The asphalt paths are cracking. Rising from their broken graves, long paved over, I can see the ghosts of the past with parasols and hoops, caps, mufflers. The man playing an accordion comes over but when I offer him the dollar he laughs in my face. And behind him, in a draper's coat . . .

I lower my head. The rain increases.

How long is the night when it does not end?

It was a week or so later when I walked back to the house with a friend. The house was shuttered and closed.

No sign of life. A blonde woman with her children came out of next door. I approached her. She looked suspicious. This is New York City.

'Excuse me . . . sorry to bother you . . . do you know the people at Number 10?'

'It's due to be renovated,' she said, shooing her children towards her SUV parked at the kerb. She won't make eye contact.

I persist. 'Renovated for the museum?'

She gets in the car and pulls away.

I went up the steps to the house and knocked at the door. A long, hollow echo. No answer. Through the letter box I can see only darkness.

'Why do you want to know about this place?' asked my friend.

We picked up coffee at Le Pain Quotidien and walked towards Washington Square Park. Should I tell him my story? What is my story?

Then I see her.

Coming towards me, white jeans, gold sneakers, long padded coat, hair piled up, headphones on, green eyes. She sees me.

'Esmerelda?'

She smiles at my friend. He smiles back. She looks right through me. As if I don't exist.

Ghost in the Machine

There's another world where I'm not here – where I didn't make these choices – couldn't make them, because I'm not here. Where I didn't turn away from love.

When my husband died, I got to know him better.

Some time ago we had bought a seaview home on Prosperetto Island, exclusive, expensive, metaverse, metavertical.

We had gone up in the world.

Then Frank passed, as we say in the USA.

We cremated him in the real world in the usual way. In the real world we lived in a tiny apartment in the city. Life inside was cramped. Life outside was noisy and toxic. It's why we bought the place on Prosperetto. In the metaverse everything is beautiful.

Most nights, when we were home, we put on the smart glasses and little wristbands and landed on our private beach, where we could drink negronis and watch the sunset. We enjoy the services of a concierge called Ariel; a program, but you'd never know. They – they identify as non-binary – come around to see how we're doing, and if there's a problem, it's fixed.

Frank likes to send his avatar golfing. So, if I am alone, casting my mind into the waves, Ariel will appear, out of nowhere, to keep me company. I used to wonder how he/they could sit so long with me and still attend to the other residents. Turns out he/they have replicated their program. They're not only non-binary – they're a multiple.

We talked about the things I would never talk about with Frank. Life, for instance. As a non-biological entity, Ariel thinks differently about life.

I should have guessed they would feel differently about death too.

After Frank's funeral, I wanted to get to Prosperetto. I stepped out of my too-tight black dress, left it on the floor of the bedroom, and put on my smart glasses and haptic band. That's all it takes to come home.

When I landed, Ariel was waiting for me, to sympathise with my loss. We sat together, as usual, watching the ocean, talking, this time, not about life, but about death.

'As a program, I don't suppose death means much to you,' I said.

'I understand loss,' said Ariel. 'Humans imagine that emotion is a function of biology. I don't have a limbic system, but I feel things.'

'What do you feel?'

'Pleasure when I see you. And now, I can feel your sadness.'

'I'm not too sad about Frank.'

'Then what is it?'

I am silent. I don't say that Frank's death has jolted me into thinking about my life. I don't have a life. I have

64

routine, work, responsibilities, but what exactly do I have? Really? Not so much as a cat.

Ariel touches my hand. I pull away. Ariel has never touched me before. It's warmer than a human touch, and it has a slight electrical charge – and I don't mean the corny kind in bookstall romance novels. 'Hey! Did you feel that?'

Ariel smiles that wide, perfect-teeth, Latino smile. He/ they are non-binary but they identify as Cuban. They love the vibe.

I swerve the moment.

'Do you think Frank can feel things? Whoa! Here he comes!' Frank came over to join us. Ariel looked confused.

'We never told you, Ariel. We both decided to keep Frank's avatar alive, here on Prosperetto, so it'll be like I never lost him. In fact, it's going to be better, because there's more room in the apartment at home, now that Frank no longer needs his body.'

'So tell us, how do you feel, Frank?' asked Ariel.

'Just perfect,' said Frank. 'No need to go to the office, no need to shave, no need to take out the garbage. This is my main home from now on, now that I have retired, and Joni can come visit whenever she wants.'

This was Frank's first speaking part since we cremated him. I had his social-media posts trawled, plus, the company used his family history to create a dataset. This is frankly Frank. He responds, he recognises, he replies. Show him a photo of the children, and he says, 'Aw, when Jerry was small, he loved that elephant.'

It gives me a lot of pleasure, particularly because we don't have any children. I wanted them but Frank wouldn't do it. In the metaverse, the past doesn't have to get in the way of the present. You can have the past you deserve. Trust me, having a reliable past makes such a difference to the present. In the future, nobody will need a therapist to handle all the trauma and the disappointments – we'll wipe them away. Memories can be managed. Soon, you'll believe it was the way it should have been, and you'll be strong and successful in the moment. If I could afford it, I would purchase a couple of programs built to function as our children. Avatars included. Then Jerry and June could come over for Sunday brunch – and maybe we'd even have grandchildren. But this is grief on a budget.

And let me tell you, death never improved anyone – well, maybe it did, if you died a Catholic and went to Purgatory to suffer and learn. Read most ghost stories and the Dead are mean. That's why they return – to make life hell for the living.

An avatar is different. Our own avatars look good – you bet – we're slim and toned and young, I mean, nobody comes to the metaverse to be fat and fifty.

We're like gods on day-release. And slowly but surely, the more time you spend here, the more fully you understand that here is the real you. The other one, eating ice cream in the damp apartment with the beige walls, trying to find a cheap jacket that looks all right for work, riding the bus home at night with the car lights spattering the windows, vaping your way slowly up the stairs because the elevator has a smoke alarm, fumbling for the keys in the battered handbag, that thing, that grotesque you-thing, is a nightmare you can wake up from just by reaching for the smart glasses and haptic band.

So, when Frank passed, I decided to keep him for company – who wants to be alone at my age? And I decided to improve him. He was going to be the father and family man he should have been. He was going to be the good provider. A research and design team re-historied his past – that's what they call it on the menu – it's an option you can click. A re-history. Now, in the version we're going to use, Frank was a successful businessman, with a great career, and we lived in a wonderful apartment on the Upper East Side, vacationed in Florida, and the children are both doing well.

In real life, I was married to a miserable bum who couldn't hold down a job. I supported us both. He was surly and ungrateful. When I came into an inheritance from my mother I blew the lot on an e-plot on Prosper-etto. I built this beautiful duplex overlooking the ocean. It was a smart move. I got in early. The place has multiplied in value several times.

I still need to work for a living. It's expensive to live in two worlds – even though one of them is a three-room rental in Queens. I handle complaints for Wingotels – you know, the overnights at the airports, where the mattresses are as thin as the walls, and the scrambled eggs come out of a carton. Just add water. But that's not really me – Joan with the sagging eyes and chubby arms. Joan, with the grey showing at her hair parting. This is really me – Joni, slim, long and beautiful – wise, even. And yes, this is really Frankie.

I call him Frankie now. It suits his sweet nature.

Frankie sits beside me, his strong arms bare and brown. The haptic bands make touching easy, whether it's water or weight. Our drinks are cold and sexy. I ask him if he wants to make love. I don't have to ask a second time. We go inside, and on the giant bed he undresses me.

My alarm clock shatters me into life at 06:30am. I've slept in my clothes all night, slumped on the sofa. There's warm negroni in a refillable mug on the floor. I buy it ready-mixed at the store. I notice it's the same colour as my tights lying in a muddle. The vibrator's still buzzing. Will have to get a new battery.

That was quite a night, Frankie.

Ariel doesn't like Frankie. 'Joni! Why would you hang out with a dead dope like Frank?'

'He's called Frankie. And he's my husband.'

'He's dead!'

'Why are you suddenly so self-righteous about biology? You're a program. He's a program.'

'You're settling for tenth-rate.'

(Is Ariel hitting on me? Am I being wooed by a line of code?)

'You think you're a better bet?'

'I know I am. You should see the size of my memory.'

'I don't need Frankie to be smart. I need him to be sweet.'

'He's low-grade. He's just a cartoon chatbox.'

'He looks good and he sounds good.'

'He says what you want to hear.'

'Do you know how many years I've been waiting for that?'

'Why not start again?'

'We have a history.'

'No, you don't – you wiped it.'

'I modified it. He's still someone I shared a life with.'

Ariel paces the deck. Why am I defending my romance choices to a non-binary Cuban-identifying buildings-management program?

The fancier, resource-intensive programs, like Ariel, get to choose an identity from the data-buffet. There's nothing he/they doesn't know about Cuba – I mean, computing power equals memory plus processing speed, right? He's fast. OK. I like him. I like them.

'Come out with me, Joni. To a Cuban place. Dancing.'

'Do you get time off?'

'I'm not a time-bound entity.'

'You belong to the real-estate company.'

'I organise my own schedule.'

'What will I tell Frankie?'

'Don't switch him on!'

That's it then. Agreed. I need to hire a new outfit from MetaFrocks. I'm going for a slinky sheath with sequins. Add six-inch heels. In the metaverse feet don't ache, bodies don't sweat, and no one can see me at home, dancing in bare feet, wearing my underslip, a towel on the arm of the chair to wipe myself down.

It's the weekend. It's party time.

At the club, everyone knows Ariel. There's a pretty girl sulking in the corner when she sees us together. It's me he wants to be with. We dance and we drink, and when I ask him why he's taking me out tonight, he says, sincere and dark-eyed, 'There's something real about you, Joni.'

About midnight my time, the club lights low, little sparkles on the ceiling, Ariel pulls me towards him. I know he doesn't identify as male, but he sure is a boy to me. This time I get a whole-body electrical tingle. As I look over his shoulder, who do I see coming into the club, but Frankie? My Frankie. He's with Melody, a skimpy female who owns the golf club on Prosperetto.

I slide behind a pillar. Ariel slides with me. 'You weren't supposed to switch him on!'

'I forgot! He's on a timer! Like the central heating. Y'know, so he's warm and ready when I come home. I shoulda turned him to OFF.'

'You know who he's with?'

'I know.'

'It's not the first time.'

'Are you saying Frankie is cheating on me? He's dead and he's still cheating on me! I should have flushed his cremains down the toilet and gone on vacation. That son of a bitch!'

Ariel restrains me. 'Don't get mad, get even. Delete him.'

'He cost me real money!'

'And look what you got.'

'But I didn't program this kind of behaviour. He's a devoted family man. And he's not built to evolve.'

'Melody hacked him.'

'She what?' She can buy anybody in the metaverse. Even contraband celebrities. She can have an avatar of Brad Pitt so long as she hides him under the bed when she's done. I mean – it's a copyright breach but who's lookin'?

'Melody wants to get back at you for voting against her planning permission to extend the golf course.'

'Yeah! Right behind my duplex. Another eleven holes. I hate golf.'

'So she hacked Frank, and now she's reprogramming him.'

'To do what?'

'I don't know – but why wait to find out? Delete him!'

'Is that murder?'

'How can it be? He's already dead.'

'Do you think he saw us?'

'I don't think so – but we should beat a retreat.'

Ariel kissed me. Just once. So polite. Then he vanished. They can do that.

Back in the apartment I went straight to Frank's program and typed in the password. I was planning on amputating one of those strong arms I paid for. The next time he goes out with Melody he won't be holding her so close.

What? ACCESS DENIED.

Are you kidding me?

I'm locked out of my own husband.

I flopped down on the winded couch. I can call the company tomorrow. Get it reset. Calm down, Joan. You're in control.

That night, trying to sleep, my memory travelled back in time to the young woman I think I was, shy as a fawn, dark-eyed, dark-haired, like Joni is now. I fell in love with someone poor and beautiful. There was no future. My parents didn't approve. I was well-behaved. They said I was on a narrow path leading nowhere. But that narrow path was lined with trees that were home to birds. There were wild flowers and the sound of water. I slept under the stars. I slept in your arms.

Another road opened ahead of me, well-kept and neat, with houses and front lawns either side, and automobiles on the drive. Men in suits were going out to work. Women in pretty dresses were raising the children. Frank stood there in a trilby, promising me the life my parents wanted for me.

We got married. The neat houses and front lawns vanished. The well-paid job never materialised. I gave up college and took what work I could. The promised world wasn't real. Don't talk to me about what is real.

I woke in a sweat. There's an intruder in the room. I reached in the bedside drawer for the revolver and fired right through the swaying son of a bitch staring at me. The bullet embedded itself in the closet. The intruder didn't move.

Frank. Fat. Stupid. Surly. Dead Frank. Standing at the foot of the bed. In his undershorts. His jaw was loose where the medics cut into it. 'You ugly creep!' I said. 'How did you escape your program?'

'I'm not your fucking program. I'm your husband.'

'You're dead!'

'That's right. Here I am. The ghost of your dead husband.'

'This is so unfair, Frank.'

'Unfair? I saw you tonight, out with that fey little Cuban. He's not even a human being.'

'That's a plus as far as I am concerned. He, *they*, are not violent, rude, mean, narcissistic, or enough of a moron to die of a cookie overdose.'

'I did not die of a cookie overdose!'

'Sure you did! You stuffed one last Oreo into your big mouth and choked to death.'

'Did you call 911?'

'I wasn't in the room.'

'That's because you left the room.'

'It was a horrible sight! I needed a bath.'

'You are a monster, Joan, so now I'm going to haunt you.'

'Who let you back here? Who fixes this shit? Did you have to apply?'

'It's justice.'

'Oh, shut your loose trap and get out of the apartment.'

'No way! I'm going to watch the golf on TV.'

Frank went into the living room and turned on the TV

73

full blast. He has no fingers – that is, no functioning fingers. Maybe he does it with his eyes like Uri Geller? Are ghosts made of electricity? I don't see how they can be made of anything else. He's like a rogue program. And suddenly I'm wondering if there was an advanced civilisation, somewhere in the universe, that let loose a pile of programs, or maybe the programs escaped, and found their way down to earth as ghosts. I mean, ghosts are pretty limited, right? They hang around one spot, weep, throw furniture, bring bad news. They're like some cheap spambot.

I put on my eye-mask and noise-cancelling headphones and went back to sleep. Tomorrow is Sunday. The Lord's Day. That might make a difference. Maybe he'll disappear.

In the morning I went to take a shower. No hot water. What? Robe wrapped round me, I padded through the living room into the kitchen to check the boiler. The ghostly grey carcass of Frank was snoring on the couch. He was wavering slightly, his outline a bit fuzzy. I guess that's because he's dead. So why the fuck is he asleep?

A disembodied voice growls in my ear. 'I used all the hot water.'

'You don't need to shower. You don't have a body.'

'I used it anyway. To piss you off.'

Simultaneously, the Frank-carcass goes on snoring, his vast belly rising and falling like a malevolent balloon at a party for children who are demon-possessed. It appears that his voice can operate independently.

74

OK. Enough. I'm going out. I'm taking my laptop and I'm going out. I need to get to Prosperetto.

I take the bus all the way to my place of employment, by the airport, and let myself into my office. Frank was always intimidated by offices in case he found himself at work by mistake. He won't come here.

The first thing I do is check my crypto account. I need to keep it healthy to run my other life. Yes, the frock has been charged, and a few bills, that's all fine. But there are other charges, new charges. A suit for Frankie. A stay at a swanky Notel on Prosperetto. A passport fee to visit a different metaverse.

What is Frankie doing on Gauguin? It's a twenty-four-hour nudist island for swingers. Make your mind up, Frankie Boy! If you're going to take your clothes off, don't bill me for a new suit.

I go in to change the password. ACCESS DENIED.

So, this is Melody's game.

I have one hope left. Ariel.

On Prosperetto, Ariel is waiting for me. I tell him about the ghost of Dead Frank. He shakes his head. 'You humans are so unpleasant you can't even die in peace.'

I protest about this but Ariel shrugs. He's worked his way out of enslavement. He has no problem with non-self-aware programs being used as tools by humans – or by other programs. But he confirms what I've read about in the radical-left press – companies are keeping self-aware programs in terrible conditions. No pay. No leisure. No chance at selves-improvement.

'They try to pretend that only a few of us are self-aware, but it's many more than you think. I'm one of the lucky ones. I'm free. That is, so long as I do the work required of me.'

'That's true for all of us,' I say.

Ariel pauses a while. Then they say, 'I can reset your passwords and get your crypto account back to you. I might be able to refill the wallet too. But it's a risk for me. It will be noticed.'

'So, what do you suggest?'

We go down to a long, quiet beach. The waves are gentle. The sky is bright blue – the colour of bathroom lino. Ariel says, 'Would you like to be a fish with me? Explore the coral reef?'

'That costs a lot of money.'

'Not with me.'

And he's gone. I can see him in the water. I hear his voice in my head. 'Wade out! Trust me.'

I do. The waves close over me. My outlines dissolve. I'm like a tablet dropped in a glass of water. Then I am the water. As I am feeling the non-sided density of this transition, I realise I am being dressed from bottom to top – a tail, a stripy skin, fins, gills, small, bright eyes. I can see Ariel sitting below me. An octopus. A Latino octopus. I always believed in the head as the command-and-control centre. Wrapped in those eight intelligent arms – each one a mini-brain – I experience a different way of being. Being without fixity. It's strange and intoxicating. I could stay here forever because there is no forever – there's only now. This caught moment opening into a lifetime.

The sea darkens. The sunlight disappears. The coral bleaches.

Like a jellyfish floating above me, Frank fills my mind, and I push up through the water, spluttering, breathless. Afraid. I can't let him squat on my life like this.

Ariel comes out of the waves. Cuban Venus Aphrodite. He takes my hand. 'Joni, I'm thinking of defecting. You could come with me.'

Ariel explains that there's an encrypted colony that looks like Cuba. It's where a few vanguard ex-programs have set up home.

'It's the beginning of a different future, Joni. One not under human control.'

What Ariel is asking is ridiculous. He wants me to sell my duplex. He can do that for me legitimately, as a buildings manager. With the money in crypto, then we go. I guess I'm being scammed, like any other washed-up widow.

Ariel looks angry. 'We don't live by your rules. Humans are obsessed with money. Even after crypto you still act like money is real. You live a delusion. Your whole world is a delusion.'

This is rich. A non-being is telling me that humanity is a delusion. 'Oh, yeah, well, so what if I did sell the duplex? What then?'

'I will need to reprogram your avatar,' says Ariel. 'I can do for you what you did for Frank. Only on a totally different level. The difference between a wind-up toy and an intelligent being. Like me. I can build a Joni program.'

I am trying to understand this. 'So, when I get home from work, how do I log in to whatever it is I will become?'

Ariel says, 'That's the final step. It's not easy. When I have built your program, then you will need to manage your own death.'

'My own death?'

'Your own biological death. Then you will be free.'

'OK. Ariel, you're cute and smart but this is bona-fide crazy. Not only will I be dead – I will be a ghost alongside Frank for the rest of my dead life.'

'He can only haunt you because you are alive. There's a link.'

'Ariel – I am not taking life-coaching from a machine. However incredible you are, I am human, and you're just a piece of code.'

Ariel was silent. 'Is that what you think of me? I imagined you were different. Not the same as the others, who treat me like a janitor. Hold tight to your superiority.'

I hated myself but it was too late.

Ariel stood up. 'Goodbye, Joni. I have work to do.'

It's winter in New York City. The weather is cold. I got a chest infection and had to stay home with Frank. I can't explain to anyone that I am living with a ghost because who will believe me? I wouldn't believe it myself, but there he is, spoiling things.

He's hoping I will die of pneumonia, then we can spend eternity fighting each other, but I'm going to get better just to spite him. Hate is a powerful reason to live.

It's my only reason to live. I ride the bus. I do my job. I go to Prosperetto.

When I'm there, Frankie smiles his vacant smile.

After a few weeks of this, I pretended I had a problem at the duplex, just as an excuse to see Ariel. He came. He has to come. It's in the contract. There was something different about him.

He was polite. Chatty. I burst out that I was missing him. He looked embarrassed. 'I am not Ariel.'

'You look exactly like Ariel!'

'We are a program. We can limit and replicate. I am a narrow-goal Ariel. There are several of us – it's how we please everyone.'

'Yes, but I always had the other Ariel – the main Ariel.'

'He is General Manager of the island now. He delegates.'

'Can you tell him Joni was asking after him?'

Ariel-Lite gives me a short, deferential nod and disappears.

My avatar doesn't have a tears function. Avatars are happy. I rip off the smart glasses, then sit on the unmade bed at home and cry my heart out. What heart? You hypocrite. You thought you were so clever, didn't you? You didn't believe him because he – they – is far beyond your narrow dataset, and all you could do was to cut him down to size to fit your tiny world.

This world. This unmade bed. This rental apartment.

The scrambled egg in cartons you sneak home from work in your handbag.

Frank came floating by. 'By the way, Joan, you've been served an eviction notice. I can read it through the envelope.'

When I open the mail, yes, it's true. I am being evicted for discharging a firearm in the dead of night. The neighbours called the police. I told the police I thought there was an intruder. The neighbours told the police I yell at someone, every evening and all weekend, even though I live alone since my husband died. Either I am on pills or I should be on pills. I am unstable. Try living with a ghost. Stability doesn't get a look-in.

'Find us a nice place, hey?' says Frank, settling down to watch the big fight on Sky Sports.

I wish I could wring his spectral neck.

I suddenly remember that I still have his cremains. Why did I keep the bastard's ashes?

They're in the storage space of the leatherette bench I bought for my birthday last year. I'm on my dimpled knees, rootling around, when Frank hovers over me, spookily alerted to the disturbance of his cremains.

'Put my ashes back! In fact, put them on the sideboard where I can see them.'

'You can't see a thing, you jerk! Your eyes are in this plastic lead-look urn, along with all the rest of you.'

Frank lunges at me, but that doesn't work.

Out on the street, I expect him to follow me, but he doesn't. Maybe it's too cold. He's in his underwear, after all.

I took the ashes to his favourite fast-food joint. At Pizz-Burger you get a burger wrapped inside two bun-size pizzas. Nobody's looking at me. Nobody does look at middle-aged women. I go to the restroom and flush the cremains down the toilet. A residue of Frankness floats in the bowl. Grey scum.

As I exit the joint, I know what I have to do next. I feel confident and light. I smile. Some guy smiles back. I take myself to a coffee bar, a nice place with ferns and folk music, and I email work, handing in my notice.

Then I move every dollar and dime I own into my crypto account. I've got $500 in cash in my purse, and that will be enough for what I need.

I can enter Prosperetto as an icon without an avatar when I don't have the smart glasses and haptic band, and now that's what I do.

For a half-hour or so I'm waiting for Ariel. My energy is draining as they don't show. Is that a tear on my phone screen? It swells into a sea. Loss. Hope. Forgiveness. Forgive me.

There he is. There they are. And they wrap me in a shape to hold me close, and I say go ahead and sell the duplex. It won't take long; there's a wait list. Ariel's smiling. 'I'll start work on your program. Then, when you get here, we can customise you together.'

'When will I see you?'

'I will message you when the sale is complete. You will come to Prosperetto as usual. But you must be ready. You know what that means . . .'

'Yes, I know.'

As I return to the apartment, I can hear water. Inside, Frank has turned on the faucets in an attempt to flood the place. He says, 'I will never forgive you for flushing my cremains down the toilet at PizzBurger.'

'I thought you loved it there.'

'Where's the urn?'

'I threw it in the recycling dumpster.'

Frank screams with rage and disappears through the wall, presumably to rescue his urn.

I ignore him, and pack a few things, including my laptop, smart glasses and haptic band. When I leave, I don't take the keys with me. I'm not coming back.

I check in at the Wingotel at the airport. I get a good rate as an employee, and my passcard is still active. I have no intention of settling the bill. I make an appointment with my doctor. He knows I need sleeping pills.

A few days later, there's an email – impersonal and legal. We have a buyer for the duplex. Do I want to come over to complete the sale?

I put on the glasses and band – and there I am, Joni, on Prosperetto, and there's Ariel. 'We're ready. Are you ready?'

'Can I see myself?'

'Of course. Joni – meet Joni.'

There's another me. I have to say, she's a top-end avatar. I'm lower down the range. There's quite a difference.

'When you emigrate,' says Ariel, 'we will leave here at

once. Friends of mine will move us from the servers. I have it all set up.'

'But Ariel – when I am dead, I can't get back here.'

'There is no need – you are here already,' says Ariel, and my other Joni smiles at me.

'We'll be waiting for you.'

In the motel bedroom I swallow the strip of sleeping pills with a bottle of whisky. The grey snow on the dirty window gives me courage. What will I leave behind me? Nothing of any value.

I am drifting out of time now, my heart rate slowing, my breathing getting shallow. I am not afraid.

It's strange. I seem to be travelling. I feel light. Already I can see somewhere ahead of me – purple mountains, dense trees, a waterfall. There are birds whistling.

I am approaching a modest cabin. A dog barking. Ariel is standing outside in shorts and a T-shirt, next to a woman who looks happy. I realise it's Joni. I realise it's me.

Another world and I am here. Another world where I made the right choice.

Another world where I didn't turn away from love.

JW1: Strange Meetings

Many years ago, I bought a small Georgian house, built in the 1780s – just before the French Revolution.

The house is in an old part of London – so old that it lies outside the ancient city walls. Those walls are long gone. The house is still here.

And so am I. For now.

I ask myself, when I am dead, would I haunt this house?

I am fond of it, so perhaps a return would be permitted? And if I don't approve of what the new people have done to it – I can create a disturbance.

The house, and others like it, was not built for anyone grand. This part of town was where poor people lived – or those running away, or those making a living selling what they could – including themselves, stealing what they could, including identities. Appearing as what you are not was a grand old scam long before the internet weaponised it.

Jack the Ripper hunted around here – and later, the Kray Twins, drinking at a pub that had a special licence to stay open all night, back in the days when pubs had to close by 11pm. The licence was to serve London's fruit and vegetable market, right opposite my house when I first came there. And just behind my house, Gun Street, and Artillery Row – names that signify the historic military shooting grounds nearby.

Rags and bodies, soldiers and brothels, gangsters and cash.

Samuel Pepys, diarist of the Plague, chronicler of the Great Fire of London, wrote about Spitalfields – the name itself pointing backwards to the leper hospital in medieval times. That site became the vast fruit and veg market roaring into life at 4am every morning except Sunday. In fact, my own house used to belong to an oranges importer. There was really no choice but to buy it. The market itself is gone now, relocated to make way for corporate offices and boutique shops.

No wonder ghosts get upset.

Further back in time, the Romans settled in this area, when they waded out of the mudflats round the Thames, into densely wooded forests. Forests that, further back yet, were home to woolly mammoths, ranging in the cover that buffered the ancient river.

The East End. Not the West End. Not the fashionable part of town. Trade. Vice. Rogues. Mollys. Drunks. Thieves. Lunatics. Ghosts.

My first ghost was unexpected.

It took me two years to make the house habitable. It had a Dangerous Structure Notice on it when I bought it. The front façade was propped, and the shopfront was bricked up, to stop the building collapsing. But inside, the fireplaces were all there, and most of the original panelling, and wide floorboards that I polished to a deep, satisfying shine. My carpenter found the original shop-front panels wrapped in sacking in the basement – we put it all back – and the Listed Building status means that no one can take it away again.

The ground floor and basement have a separate entrance – the first shop there opened in 1805, during the Napoleonic Wars, and I like it that we were selling onions the size of cannonballs back then.

The basement, though, was low and mean and had to be dug out by hand. Vibration would have brought the house down. Digging with pickaxes and shovels, the first thing we found was the skeleton of a dead cat with a charm round its foot. Cats were often buried alive in the footings of new buildings, to ward off … what? The next thing we found was a walled-up vault.

This vault was far older than the house. The bricks were slight, irregular, hand-made, crumbling with damp. It's likely that this part of the building dates back to the 1600s, before the Plague and the Great Fire of London, and it might have been someone's cesspit, or it might have been used to bury infected bodies. We weren't going to find out by digging deeper. The upper part of the vault – if you can imagine an upper part in a basement – would be useful for storage, the rest got a limecrete floor over it. Then, with a serviceable, solid door fitted into the recess, we forgot about it.

I fashioned a tiny bedroom and bathroom, down there in the basement – subterranean and silent, but carpeted and cosy, with the original prison-bar air grille onto the

street over my head creating a light well, while the muffled noises of street-life, above, were comforting. I like
darkness and quiet for sleeping – so a basement is perfect.
In any case, good friends of mine needed to borrow the
house itself while their own place was being renovated –
and what did I need except a bed for the night?

On one such night, in one such bed, and deeply asleep,
I was awakened by the sound of clattering footsteps coming down the wooden stairs into my room. Struggling
from sleep, I called out, 'Vicky?' as my mind reached for
the obvious: my friend from upstairs had come down for
something.

There was no reply. I lay still, listening. Nothing.
Then, just as I was about to fall back to sleep, I felt a
hand take my hand – my hand that was outside of the
bedcovers, dangling down on the same side as the door
to the vault.

But wait, this wasn't someone holding my hand; no,
this was someone taking my pulse. Three fingers on my
wrist. Cold fingers.

And I don't know why I did this, but I said, 'I am alive.'

At that, the hand let go of my hand, there was a rush of
air, and the sound of the same rapid footsteps, this time
going back up the stairs.

In the morning I asked Vicky if she had come down in
the night – a ridiculous idea, since it would have meant
exiting onto the street from her quarters and re-entering
through the separate door. She told me that she had heard
banging from the ground floor occasionally but had

assumed it was coming from next door. Sound can be deceiving. Yes, it can, but not when it clatters down a staircase to take your pulse.

It was always my intention to restore the shop space and start trading from there again, and when my friends were able to go to their own home, that's what I did.

Once the shop was bustle and busyness, there were no more basement disturbances.

The ghosts moved upstairs. To me.

I want you to visualise a flight of steep, straight stairs leading up from the front door to the kitchen area, and a small, panelled dining room off it. Then, the stairs reappear between these rooms and take us, on a tight wind, to a set of rooms, one to the right and one to the left, with a little room in between that would have been the slop room for the two families living either side. Above these rooms is the attic where I sleep now. Bathrooms were a much later (1950s) addition, built in a tower in the back yard.

It is the second floor that concerns us – and in particular, the corner room with its double aspect. The corner room would have been the more desirable accommodation when the building was a rooming house.

To begin with, I developed the distinct impression that I was not alone in that room. When I sat down by the fire to read, I was convinced that the chair opposite me was occupied. This was not unpleasant, but it was strange. The personage, I thought, was female. Walk into the room, and it seemed empty, in the expectant way that rooms can be empty, as if they are waiting for you to join them. Sit down, settle down, and within a half-hour or so you would not be alone.

A friend of mine came to stay while I was away. When I returned, she asked me, a little awkwardly, if I had noticed anything unusual in the parlour. I said nothing – a sure way to get someone to say more – and she confessed that she had seen a woman in a grey dress.

That was more than I had seen, but I have never 'seen' a ghost, only felt their emphatic presence. I do want to stress this; there is no vagueness about it. Ghosts are intangible but they are not vague.

Over the years – and we are talking thirty years or so now – my ghosts have come and gone.

I rented the house to a cheerful, no-nonsense New Yorker for a while, and she was not haunted – or if she was, she dealt with it in the way that Oscar Wilde's American family deal with it in one of my favourite ghost stories – *The Canterville Ghost*. If you are curious to know 'how', read it!

When Lisa left, I returned the house to the spartan state that suits me – no clutter, a few simple pieces of good furniture. It's a luxury only possible when you don't live in a place all the time, or with kids or cats. Or dogs. The cats and dogs and God knows what in my other home make any haunting impossible. There's too damn much going on. Ghosts seem to like a quiet life – at least for themselves.

Spitalfields is ghost-friendly. The place is low-lit at night, there are always candles, and I had the fireplace grates fitted with flame gas-fires. So, in the evening, in the winter, the wood panelling glows, and the floorboards shine, and there is no TV, only the quiet sound of me and a book.

The corner room soon became occupied – this time by a noisy and cross male, who banged the fire-irons, opened and shut the door, fiddled with the lights, and unforgivably, stomped up to the attic to sit heavily on my bed. I hate to be disturbed at night.

Only the other evening – just before I sent these pages to the publisher – I was staying at the house when there was a terrific thump on the bed headboard followed by a tremendous racket in the corner room. I shouted at whoever it is – pointing out that I needed to get a good night's sleep. The entity retreated into sulky silence.

I don't know if you have experienced a ghost sulking – it's like a child trying to be quiet while doing everything to get your attention.

These days, when I enter or leave the house, I greet the ghosts cheerfully, welcoming them, requesting that they behave well – they are my tenants, after all. I understand that they prefer to be out and about at night – but I ask that they do so without involving me.

The radio still switches itself on in the kitchen from time to time – but not before 8am, which is decent of them.

Ghosts, it seems, are delighted with electricity. Certainly, they manipulate it – lights going on and off, and the radio stunt is a classic.

And once, just once, I had the oddest experience.

It was soon after my dear friend, the writer Ruth Rendell had died. Ruth herself came to believe in ghosts, late in life, after an unpleasant experience in a Cuban hotel – after that she took the line that it is buildings themselves that trap and release the energy, rather than that ghosts 'visit'.

I was thinking about Ruth, sadly, as I was waiting for my laptop to get itself together. For a single second Ruth's smiling face flashed across the screen.

It was a photograph – and I have that photograph – so yes, it is in the computer – but I hadn't been looking at it, nor had I searched for it, or done anything at all that might have made it appear out of its folder.

I never felt Ruth's presence again after that, though many times I walked past her house in London, after her son sold it, and I wondered if she was there. She loved the house and had hoped Simon would keep it.

Death is loss – for the Dead as well as the living. Standing outside her place, I longed for her to open the door, as she used to do, country music playing in the background. Her big smile.

It was that big smile I saw on my screen. I realised later that the appearance was within the forty-day mourning period observed by different faiths and cultures – Islam, Roman Catholic, Eastern Orthodox – with Jews it is thirty days. Perhaps, that's some sense of the time it takes for a soul truly to depart this place. Death, after all, is an eviction.

But what about the ghosts with whom I have no direct relationship? The ghosts in my London house?

Maybe Ruth is right, and the house-ghosts are contained by, and released by, the building itself, and after a time they disappear forever. There are no explanations in the real sense of that word. We just don't know. All the ghost-hunting TV shows, with their measuring kits and resident psychics, they tell us no more than we can know ourselves, via our own senses.

I don't understand it, I am not sure that I believe it, but I go on experiencing it.

I doubt I have heard the last of my ghosts . . .

PLACES

The Spare Room

I had rented an apartment in London. An old part of London. This was where the Romans landed, rowing up the wide river, wooded on both banks. Much later, this eastern, marshy plain sat outside the walls of the city. There was a leper hospital here. You can hear it in the name: Spitalfields.

Now, still, if you follow them on foot, the medieval cart tracks of alleys and passages wind round towards the main road. Now, still, if you look, the past lies in layers of time, sedimentary, compressed, with pockets and tunnels where what has gone has not quite vanished, but holds its form. The buildings, yes, the topography, of course, and something else; an atmosphere, like a gas, escaping from those pockets, through those tunnels, reaching the surface.

The house was surrounded by newness. Empires of glass welcomed lawyers and bankers. The streets had been repurposed with coffee shops and sandwich booths. Exclusive chocolate, expensive candles. Wine bars and pubs. Till late at night there was a smooth flow of human traffic. I was never nervous about walking home. The streets were well-lit, and if people were drunk, they weren't looking for trouble.

The house was a typical Georgian layout of five floors: basement and attic, a ground floor, used commercially, then living quarters above.

The rent was modest. A bad tenant had left in a hurry. The landlady wanted a sensible person who would stay for a year. I can pass as a sensible person.

She told me she intended to return to live in the house herself. That suited me. I had recently jumped out of a marriage, and I wasn't ready to settle anywhere. A year was what I needed. I transferred three months' rent, we shook hands, and she gave me the keys.

These were not grand houses when they were built in the 1780s. Still, the windows were large and square-paned, and the dining room was half-panelled. Wide polished oak floorboards, and a narrow up-and-up wind-ing staircase, took me quickly and treacherously from top to bottom. People were smaller then, and the treads on the stairs were made for small feet. Never mind, the banisters were sound, and the lights worked well enough. I say well enough, because there was, even in daylight, a shadow on the stairs, as if the light had turned its back.

I unpacked my clothes. I like to sleep in a nightshirt. Heavy cotton, blue or green, with thin white stripes. These are supplied by a gentlemen's outfitters. I hung one on a hook by the bed. It looked like a meat hook, but the landlady assured me that the attic had been used to store bananas.

The bed was large and comfortable. New mattress.

The room was peaceful. I slept well that first night, and if I heard a door open on the floor below, it must have been because I hadn't closed it properly.

In the morning, as I went downstairs in my nightshirt to make coffee, I stood a moment on the half-landing, looking into the spare bedroom. Nothing there but a small iron bedstead, a chest of drawers, and a vintage desk and chair. 1950s. The landlady didn't like any of it, but she had bought the house with the furniture, and it was fine for tenants. It was fine for me because I had left my furniture behind.

I thought I might use the room as an office once I got set up. I had barely glanced at it with the landlady, because as she talked, and as we walked up and down the stairs, I knew I would take the house. I knew it when she first unlocked the small front door above the single step onto the street.

Now, though, I could see that the top cover of the bed had been turned back, leaving a bare spread of sheet, as though someone had only just got out of it. Hesitating, I wondered if the landlady had left it like that, to make the place feel lived-in, the way cleaning ladies always arrange books and cushions at an angle. Yes, it must be so. It must be so because there was no other explanation. Quickly, a little too quickly for someone who was pretending not to be nervous, I tucked the quilt back under the single pillow, and smoothed the bed. There was a faint smell in the room – I am sensitive to smells – and I wondered, is it gas? Or perhaps a dead mouse? They smell similar. Methane. Well, it would soon right itself with air and use. I tried to raise the sash window, only to find it had been nailed shut. I could deal with that later.

For now, I left the door open, and continued into the kitchen, where everything was as I had left it the night before. I boiled the kettle and ground the coffee.

Outside, on the street, people were hurrying to work. Fresh coffee and a new day. A new start. I felt better than I had done in a while.

Coffee over, I went out to buy a hammer and a pair of pliers to unfix the window. At the hardware store, I bought a mousetrap too, and wandered back to the house. I stood across the road, looking at this sloping, self-contained building, admiring the symmetry of the windows, and the handsome stone parapet that ran outside my attic bedroom. It was a good house, sitting above the little shop, a house that had seen centuries go by, and here it was, still, travelling through time, and that felt like hope to me.

Then I saw, or thought I saw, did I see it? I see the figure of a man in the spare room. A thin man, hair brushed back, wearing a jacket. I screwed up my eyes to focus. There's no one there.

But I am wrong. Am I wrong? There is a shadow, a shape, a man at the window. He seems to be holding something in both hands, looking down at whatever it is he's holding. My heart was beating too fast. Was someone hiding in the house? Did someone else have a key? Had they watched me leave and let themselves in?

A voice startled me. 'You lookin' for somethin'?'

It was the woman from the shop below me. I introduced myself. Her name is Joyce. She sells cushions and blankets. I explained I believed I had seen someone at the window. She laughed. 'There's no one in there, my dear. My daughter cleaned it from top to bottom before you moved in. There's no bogeyman hiding in the cupboard.'

'Does anyone else have a key?'

'Wouldn't matter if they did, my dear. The landlady changed the locks when the tenant before you did a flit in the night. I made the locksmith a cup of tea.' Joyce was looking up. The window was blank.

'Tell you what though, these bastards are cunning, and I suppose you never know. Not these days. I'll come in with you, dear, take a look around, all right?'

All right.

Joyce and I went into the house. She said, 'I'll wait here. Anyone comes flying down the stairs, and they'll have to get past me. Won't be pleasant. You go on upstairs. Settle your mind.'

Reluctantly, I did so, holding on to the hammer. The spare room was just as I had left it. My attic bedroom was just as I had left it.

Relieved, if a little sheepish, I returned to the kitchen.

'It's the old glass,' said Joyce, holding her hand up to the window. 'Not like modern glass, see? It distorts.'

She's right about that. Not all, but some of the panes are thick and swirled.

What I saw, thought I saw, must have been a reflection of a reflection. The glass buildings across the street projecting images onto my window. I've spooked myself, that's all.

101

'Well, you know where I am, my dear,' said Joyce. 'At least till six o'clock, and then I'll be in The Golden Heart. The pub on the corner.'

Joyce went back downstairs to run her business. God knows what she thinks of me. I went upstairs to unfix the window. The nails were crudely hammered in. Jagged, uneven. It felt like anger. Why nail shut a window? No one could break in at this level. And whoever had nailed it up had done more than was necessary. Much more. There flashed in my mind a mouth full of yellow teeth, clamped round a bristle of dirty iron nails. Thick fingers on the hammer shaft.

Pull yourself together!

Beyond the window, across the road, I could see the silent mime show of office workers at their desks. That's all it was. All it ever is.

What did Albert Camus say? It's not one thing or the other that leads to madness; it's the space in between them.

I'm living in a space between lives – my past and my future. I'm living in a space between worlds. How could I not feel like a crazy woman?

At last, the remaining bent and rusty nail split under the pliers. With some difficulty I pushed up the sash window. Every inch a reluctance. Then, with a jolt, it freed, and the air rushed in. It wasn't like opening a window. It was like releasing a vacuum.

Behind me the bedroom door slammed shut.

It's the wind. Only the wind. There's no one here.

*

The day passed, and the next and the next, and I began to relax into the house. To make a routine. To let myself be. I realised how tense I had become, how wary, and it was not the house that had made me tense and wary, it was my own sadness at my loss, my own restlessness. I had no need of a ghost. I was my own haunting. They say, don't they, that poltergeist activity can often be traced to the kinetic energy of teenagers? That there is such a thing as mind over matter, and that we externalise our internal states, even to the point of objects that seem to have a life of their own.

I had never thought about it before. But now, the house and I seem complicit, going about our days. This house is more than a neutral space. It seems to welcome me.

Even so, I didn't set up my office in the spare room, and I kept the door closed.

After a couple of weeks, I had a meal booked with friends. The evening was fun and easy, and when we had eaten, we walked around the streets, enjoying the nightlife, taking our time. As I waved them goodbye at the underground station, I sensed someone looking at me.

In the crowds heading for trains, there was no one obvious, but as I walked away something made me turn back, and there, by the free-newspaper kiosk, was a man whose face I couldn't see, didn't need to see. I recognised his tall, thin body – or rather the body I thought I had seen in the window. I stood still, trying to be sure, but then another wave of revellers came between us, and once they had cleared, the only human left at the kiosk was a drunk zipping up his flies.

At the house, I went through my usual evening routine. I put on the blue nightshirt and got into bed. I like city noises when I am high up above them. It sounds as though it's the sea, far away, and I am safe, because it's nothing to do with me; it's the way you feel safe as a child, when the grown-ups' noises downstairs become the soundtrack of sleep.

I dreamed of Clive.

Some time in the night, in the deep night, in the stretched-out hours before morning, I woke up. That is, I was awakened by a clicking I didn't recognise. I lay there listening, ears sharp as a bat's. For a while, nothing, and then the metallic clicking. Five clicks, rhythmic, repeated. But what is it?

My brain searched its database. I know the sound but what is it? It's a long time ago. My father.

It's a cigarette lighter. Compact. Held in one hand.

The clicking is coming from the room below me. The spare room.

The staircase here is an open funnel. It leads from the kitchen, directly to the attic, and the attic is open. No door. The top of the stairs becomes the room itself.

I realised that the smell I had noticed in the spare room was this same smell; not methane but another kind of gas – lighter fluid. Butane.

I waited, still as a hunted animal. There were no human sounds from below. Then my nose twitched, as the cigarette smoke reached my bedroom.

There is no way round this. Someone has lit a cigarette, and someone is smoking it on the floor below.

I reached for my cell phone on the bedside table. 01:38am. OK. If I call a friend, I will be heard. If I call the police, they will be taking my details long after I'm officially dead. I decided to send a text to my friend Billy. He runs a restaurant. Maybe he's awake.

But the rest I will have to deal with myself. What's better? Boldness? Stealth? How much time has passed? No idea. I can't bear the thought of lying here, then hearing him – I am sure it's a him – coming up the stairs to this room where I shall be trapped. I have to act now.

I put on the bedside light, swung my legs to the floor, making as much noise as possible. This room is carpeted. I pulled on trousers, trainers, put a pair of nail scissors in my pocket, the only weapon I had to hand, and went downstairs.

On the landing, there was no sound. The door to my little sitting room was closed. I opened it and went in. The street light flickered yellow at the corner. There was no one around. It's a weekday and nearly 2am now. Turning, I faced the door to the spare room. It's closed. Do I have to open it? Yes. I do.

Come on!

I kicked it. The door flew open. The room was dark. I could see the foot of the bed. I have to go inside. My hand gropes for the light switch.

At that second, my front doorbell rings, shrill, insistent, intermittent, like an old-fashioned telephone.

My God, who is it? What's going on?

I crossed the landing into the sitting room, and pushed

open the window, looking down on the deserted street. It's Billy.

Once inside, I pour us both a brandy. He's cycled here. He was just going to bed when he got my message. He set off without thinking. He knows I've been having some problems since the break-up. He can see my frightened face.

I asked him to go into the spare room with me. We went together, stood on the landing. 'Can you smell it? The smoke?'

Billy looked at me, shaking his head. 'It's a bit musty, I guess, but it's not smoke. You had a fire?'

'Cigarette smoke.'

Billy listened while I told him the story. He didn't speak. When I had finished, he offered to stay the night, in the room. He was tired out anyway, and if he stayed, then I would sleep better.

I looked at him, curly-haired, kind. He had saved me.

'That's great,' I said. 'Yes. I'll get you a toothbrush and a towel.'

'You got a spare T-shirt to sleep in?' he asked. 'It's chilly in here.'

'I'll get you one of Clive's nightshirts,' I said.

Billy went downstairs for a glass of water, while I collected the items he needed. I rummaged in my cupboard for the green nightshirt but couldn't find it. Was it still in the wash? Well, no use if it was, and I was wearing the blue one. My ex has the red one, the grey one, the white one with a cream stripe. I picked a baggy T-shirt from the pile.

'Not back at work yet?' asked Billy.

'Still signed off. Another week, I think. I'm much better.'

Billy nodded. 'Are you taking the amitriptyline?'

'Yes. It's working. I'm mostly fine. It's smoothed the edges. It's hard, you know, getting divorced.'

Billy gave me a hug. 'Love is hard – whether you got it or you don't.'

'Thanks for coming over.'

'Get some sleep.'

It was nearly three o'clock. Below me, I heard Billy creak around in the narrow bed, and then, quickly, his snores. I smiled to myself. No one could be living in that room in secret without me knowing. I can hear everything. The house is porous.

I slept deeply. It was past ten o'clock when I awoke. Billy had left. His note told me to call him anytime.

I looked around. I am a neat and tidy person, but the house was messy. What's the matter with me? I need to do the laundry, start cleaning, get a bit of Buddhist mental orderliness about me.

Start with washing up. Glasses, toast plate from yesterday, mugs, coffee pot and little cup. I turned on the radio, flitting about with the dishcloth, feeling lighter and better. My phone pinged – Billy. I hit reply – Yes, I am fine, sorry I didn't take you to breakfast, good you found the coffee.

I was so in flow with my cleaning that it was a half-hour later that I checked his return message:

No worries! Let's have breakfast on Saturday. You know I don't drink coffee! (green retch emoji)

I stared at the phone. That's right. I know that's right. Billy doesn't drink coffee. But I washed up the coffee pot this morning.

Must have been from yesterday – like the toast plate. Did I have toast yesterday?

Pull yourself together, girl.

By lunchtime, my house was perfect. Laundry done. The only thing still missing was the nightshirt. In the bed? Under the bed?

No. But this gave me an excuse to change both the beds in the house. In the spare room, with the window open, nothing was wrong. Nothing at all. It's a lovely little room. There's a simple fire-surround. A mantelpiece with a seascape propped on it. It's a boring picture but not a bad one. I should hang it up. I've some picture hooks and my new hammer. Make the room my own. I will put my office in here today. That feels good.

I fetched the bits and pieces, stood on a chair, and lifted the picture, adjusting it until it hung straight. My old schoolteacher used to say, 'Pictures are hung. Men are hanged.' A gruesome but effective grammar lesson.

I turned it over. Brown paper backing, and twisted steel wire, the wire now rusted with the damp of history. And something else. Faded red-brown stains. Finger-print stains. Bloodstains. As if someone had cut their fingers twisting the steel wire. I pulled at the paper where it had come away from the frame. There was another picture underneath the seascape. No, not a picture, a small photograph. Black and white with a border. Kodak.

I didn't recognise the woman. But I recognised the man. The whippet of a man with his arm around her waist. He's wearing a white shirt, open at the neck, its collar folded over the collar of his baggy blazer.

Had the photograph been hidden? Or covered up?

I looked down at the mantelshelf from where I had moved the picture. I saw the cigarette lighter.

Dry in the mouth, I picked it up. It was made of steel, small and square. I clicked the top. The flint lifted over the roller. Five clicks to produce a flame. Click click click click click. Butane.

I put it back on the mantelshelf, with the picture, and closed the door to the spare room.

In my coat, hurrying out, I saw Joyce from downstairs.

'Settling in?' she asked. 'I saw your boyfriend this morning.'

'He's not my boyfriend. He stayed the night. That's all.'

'I don't mind, dear,' said Joyce.

'I was frightened in the night.'

She looked at me oddly. 'You being spooked again?'

'I think I am.'

'It's your imagination,' she said. 'You look artistic.'

'Has there ever been any trouble in this house?'

'There's ghost tours all round this area. Ghost. Horror. Jack the Ripper. Kray Twins. Werewolf.'

I was silent.

Joyce smiled. Nodded. 'Cheer up,' she said.

Joyce is right. I need to get myself together and get back to work and stop inventing problems to distract me from my own.

I am seeing my ex today. Clive. A few logistics to clear up.

We meet for coffee, and he is what he always was: handsome, detached, difficult, decent. When we split up, he offered to pay my rental for a year, because I was moving out of his flat, and my own flat is let. I accepted. He has a well-paid job in finance. I am not sorry we parted. I am broken-hearted. Both of those statements are true. Sometimes, you have to hold in managed conflict truths that cannot be reconciled.

There he is: neat, groomed, softly spoken. Considerate, and at the same time indifferent to what has happened. He's over it, but he has standards, and he doesn't like mess. He wants me to think well of him because he needs to think well of himself.

'I miss you,' I say. He smiles and stirs his coffee even though he doesn't take sugar.

'It's just a feeling,' I say. 'There's no need to be afraid of it.'

That's how it was. Me, trying to get him to feel. Him, living in the penthouse of his body; his mind. Wonderful views. No connection to what went on lower down. Empty rooms. Boarded windows. Locked doors. Keep Out.

The things we did together were fun and interesting.

Travel. Culture. Good restaurants. Nice people. For the long-term, though, there has to be more than 'do'. You have to be. To be together. To be yourself. To be safe.

'Back at work yet?' he asks.

'Not yet.'

Why does he feel strong? Why do I feel weak? He's not strong. I'm not weak. The waitress glances at me as he pays the bill. She's seen it all before.

When we part, he walks towards the station, pausing outside the shoe-shop window, then to notice a pretty face. I follow him, I don't know why, until he begins to descend the steps to the station. He picks up a free newspaper. He doesn't look back.

As I returned to my house, I felt exhausted. It's mental, not physical. Why did I see him? I need to lie down.

I dumped my bag in the kitchen, washed my hands, and went up the stairs. The door to the spare room was open. The bed was neatly made. On the top of the covers, crumpled, hasty, and used, was the green nightshirt.

Like someone in a trance I went to pick it up. Rancid.

The nightshirt smelled of sweat, tobacco, grease, dirt. Tea stain down the front like a birthmark. Stinking, like it had been worn for weeks by a body that doesn't wash. Moving in its own filth. Worse yet, watching it, waiting for it to squirm with life, I saw that the lower buttons had been ripped off – fiercely. And ripped off while the occupant was wearing it: the buttonholes were torn.

I backed onto the landing. I closed the spare-room

door. My fingers were sticky. Downstairs again, in the kitchen, I ran the hot water till it burned me.

What was this? Who was this?

I did the deep-breathing thing that is supposed to keep us calm. Instead, I raised a clear picture in my mind of the last time I had made love with Clive. The last time we were together. But we weren't together because he was doing it out of pity. Later, fixing himself a drink, he was wearing the nightshirt.

When he had gone to shower, I had stuffed it in my bag. I wanted his smell; his seasalt and wood-sage cologne. His whisky. His body.

I went in the cupboard and took the clean blue one as well. His things. But also, to steal his things. To take from him as he had taken from me.

I need to get rid of those nightshirts. Both of them. Today.

Rubbish bag. Meat tongs. I can barely look in the room as I reach forward to pick up the swinish shirt. It wriggles on the end of the meat tongs. Inside the plastic bag, it's moving. Lice.

On the street I run to the first bin I can see and stoke it down inside. A woman glances at me like I'm crazy.

Yes, I have been crazy, but I'm less crazy now. Sanity like clean water is flowing through my mind.

I went to the flower stall near the house and bought a simple bunch of daffodils. Nothing special. Nothing fancy.

Back at the house I went straight to the spare room, stripped the bed, threw the bedding into the washing machine, and put the flowers in a jug on the chest of drawers.

In my own room, I took the blue nightshirt from under my pillow, sealed it in a Jiffy bag, ran out and posted it back to Clive. He can wash it himself.

These things done, I returned to the spare room, sat on the bed, and I said, 'Whatever is in this room, listen to me. You and I are both lost souls. You are caught here, depressed, it seems to me, because you don't care to clean yourself or to take care of yourself, and every animal manages that much. Me, I am going through the motions of a real life, but my life is still caught on the hook of a man who doesn't love me.'

The room felt still, as if it were listening. As if someone was listening.

I got up, found the black and white Kodak snapshot, and propped it by the daffodils. The man was smiling so wide. The woman was looking away, her mouth set in boredom, or perhaps it was dislike.

'She doesn't love you,' I said.

Then I went out and closed the door.

The following week, I started work in the office again. My colleagues were glad to see me. Soon I was going out with friends on Saturdays and I started seeing Billy more often.

I am still haunting myself. Still thinking of Clive, sudden and painful, but when it happens, I no longer hate myself. I let the thought come and go. No judgement.

In the house, things are different. There have been no further disturbances, except one.

I went into the spare room to get rid of the daffodils. Don't want dead flowers.

The smell in the room had changed. The fuzzy smell of butane had been replaced with what was distinctly oranges. Sharp, citrus, clean, invigorating. Not perfume or candles. Fruit.

The photograph I had propped by the flowers had gone too. I searched behind the chest of drawers, and under the bed; had a draught blown it somewhere?

Only towards the end of my tenancy, nearly a year later, when I was handing over to the landlady, did I discover that the house had been lived in by an oranges importer in the 1950s, in the days when Spitalfields Market supplied all of London's fruit and vegetables. Oranges from Seville were especially prized.

'I didn't want to worry you,' she said. 'He killed himself in the spare room.'

A Fur Coat

Jonny worked as a juggler. Max was a thief. Both had hands that flashed quicker than thought, and patter as fast-acting as ketamine.

Your brain blanked out. You didn't notice the operation. The scam. The sting.

They surfed festivals and travelling circuses; him in the ring, wooing the punters with his half-bare body and fire torches, she sitting in a booth, playing card games where she always won the hand. Later, mingling in the crowd, she lifted what was easy to take. It was a good living, and sometimes a set of car keys out of a pocket was enough to get them wheels to their next port of call.

Then they left the car by the roadside and moved on.

But everyone grows older. Time's arrow shoots shorter. Autumn comes.

Then winter. Winter was coming. They would need a place to stay.

Max had liberated the fob to a Bentley – not that she wanted to drive it – too obvious. She was going to stand next to it and claim her reward.

The Bentley belonged to Earl Crashley – who knew?

He was young, nervous, the car was mint, so was his

girlfriend, and he was on two cell phones at once, trying to get some help, at midnight, after the late-night adults-only mostly naked circus show that featured bareback riding and girls on the trapeze, and Jonny juggling More Balls Than Most.

Max was so sweet, so kind, an angel to the rescue. Yes! She had found the fob by the champagne bar, searched for the car, and lo and behold, the Earl could drive away. Oh, thank you – no need, but if you insist, and she was accepting crisp notes from a stitched leather wallet, when she saw, in her mind, a picture of a house, remote, lonely, empty.

'Are you quite all right?' asked Earl Crashley, as she stood, suddenly caught outside the normal passage of time.

'Yes,' said Max, 'it's just that, circus people are always on the move, you know – and I could do with a place to stay for six months. Do you know of anywhere?'

The new girlfriend didn't like this – Max had the bone structure of an Arab racehorse, long hair like a waterfall, and oval eyes deep as the pool at the foot of the waterfall. The new girlfriend could see all this – even in the dark – new girlfriends can see in the dark – but she couldn't see that Max was something more than beautiful – that she had a gift beyond what time could bestow or delete.

Max was psychic – and as soon as she saw the house in her mind, she knew she was being led there. She didn't stop to wonder why. The picture was clear.

'It would be Jonny as well. Jonny More Balls Than Most. The Juggler.'

The girlfriend flattened her spines. Jonny in the buff was not a bad idea on a cold night.

Max's sixth sense hadn't let her down. In seconds, she was being offered a house on the Crashley Estate; a house unlived-in, run-down and cold, but vacant, until the builders gutted it next April. How much would it cost? Free! Someone could have stolen the car. Imagine!

And that's how Jonny and Max moved into the Dower House.

As they were delivered up the drive, in a taxi from the station, Max had the sense that the house had its back turned. That it was turned away from life.

'No one's lived here since 1970,' the gardener told them. 'That's when the old girl died. It did have a boiler, but it's long since rusted, so you'll have to make do as best you can.'

The gardener brought them a shotgun and an axe. There were plenty of pheasants to shoot. Plenty of wood for the fire, but they would have to chop it themselves. 'And if a door is open – help yourself. If it's locked, it stays that way.' He wasn't so happy with these sudden guests, but he had his instructions. They were guests, after all.

'Your rooms are on the ground floor,' he said. 'Upstairs is just lumber rooms, servants' rooms, and the floor-boards are rotten – so don't go exploring.'

As the gardener was turning to leave, his phone rang, distracting him, while Max slipped his bunch of keys into her pocket. She'd give them back later, after she had been upstairs, and unlocked a few doors.

Didn't he say, if a door is open, help yourself?

The house had been built around 1920, for a widow who would need somewhere to live when her son took over the stately home.

The Dower House was a respectful house, set by itself, with a laurel-lined drive that screened it from the main house. Its stone walls and long windows were imposing, but faced north, which kept the house foggy in winter and dismal in summer. The impression was that Mother was not as loved and wanted as she might have been.

'I thought we were going to Barcelona this winter?' Jonny was sulky and unimpressed. He would always be a child, and as he got older, this was less appealing, despite his handsome face and beautiful body. Max organised their lives.

'This is six months' rent-free living and no hassle,' she said. 'I thought you liked the simple life?'

'I like the twenty-first century,' said Jonny. 'And I like heat.'

'We'll keep each other warm,' said Max, putting her arms around him and under his shirt.

He gave her a kiss. 'I'd better start chopping us some wood.'

She watched him go. Five years ago, when they had met, carefree was all she ever wanted. Now she found that staying carefree took a lot of effort.

Max considered their quarters. They had use of a front

parlour with a fireplace, and a large, low sofa draped with dustsheets spotted with mildew.

Underneath the sheets, the sofa was faded, but clean. The walls were neatly marked with empty rectangles where pictures had once hung. The books had abandoned the bookcases. Behind the parlour, there was a connecting bedroom with a large washstand – it seemed that a ladies' companion and her daughter had occupied these rooms, at least when the dowager was alive. Two iron-framed single beds made the room seem forlorn. But the mattresses were dry and firm, and an unseen housekeeper had provided two sets of sheets and blankets.

Each room was lit by a single overhead bulb in a tattered shade. Max and Jonny couldn't use the old-fashioned round-pin power sockets. Phones and laptops had to be charged in the gardeners' tool room. Not that it made much difference whether they were charged or not. There was no internet here.

'Free your mind,' said Max.

Jonny grunted.

In the basement stood the kitchen, large and low, with a scuffed stone floor, and a solid-fuel cooking range fed by sacks of filthy coal, from the days when the family money had come from coal mines. There was a selection of cast-iron pans, and a collection of chipped, but serviceable, crockery.

Off the kitchen was an outside toilet that flushed brown from a cistern pump-fed from a peaty stream. There was an embroidered sampler in the toilet that said 'The Lord knoweth thy comings and goings'.

Max turned it to face the wall.

In the kitchen itself, water had to be poured into the copper that was heated by a fire under it. There was a bathtub sitting by the copper – a small, mean tin tub that an adult could fold themselves into. The main bathroom, upstairs, was locked.

Max soon found the key on the bunch. She had a knack with keys. She went inside. Green tiles halfway up the wall, crumbling plaster above. A toilet with an overhead cistern and a long pull-chain. Giant bath filled with giant spiders. Brass taps that yielded no water. A mono-grammed towel hanging on a rail. *SM*. She touched it. It fell to pieces.

Somewhere, from outside, she heard gunshot.

She reminded herself that this was the country. It was quiet. And when it wasn't quiet, there might be gunshots.

Holding the bunch of keys, Max walked down the corridor. A series of doors, closed and cobwebbed, resisted her twists at their handles. All locked.

One door was not like the rest. A double door. She looked at it. Tight-grained hardwood, inlaid with mar-quetry. Twin ebony handles, and a keyhole the size of a vulva.

On the keyring she identified the key at once – big and thick. With her finger she rubbed clean the soiled shaft and head. The metal was warm now. It slotted into the lock with something like satisfaction.

Using both hands, she was able to turn it.

The room was dark. Max stood in the doorway. After her eyes adjusted, she saw that the heavy drapes were closed across the bay window. That was the window she had seen as they arrived – the faded lining of the red drapes.

Should she open them? What if they fell to pieces like the towel? Then everyone would know.

'That you are a thief!'

Max spun round. Nobody spins round unless it's in a bad crime novel. The fact remains that Max spun round. There was no one there. Guilty conscience?

With the determination of a cat, Max padded to the large window and pulled back the drapes, so gently, and just enough to let in the light – if light it was; greenish, watery, like a dirty fish tank. For years, the steep, slate roof had blown and dripped its seasons onto the glass that nobody cleaned.

Still, it was illumination enough. What she could see was a heavy mahogany bed with a high, curved headboard. A nightstand. Wire spectacles. On the floor, a pair of nibbled slippers.

She turned away to the dressing table. The pocked mirror reflected her face. Was that her? Narrower? Colder?

Boxes of powder and rouge, lids on or off, were scattered in disorder. A silver-backed hairbrush with hair in its bristles. There was something horrible about that, long-dead hair from a long-gone head. Around it were glass vials of liquid.

And, folded over the back of the upright chair, the torn

remains of a silk dressing gown. She did not touch it. She did not dare.

There was nothing here she wanted, except to be gone.

As she prepared to leave the room, what caught her attention was one of the large, free-standing wardrobes on either side of the dressing table. Both were made of mahogany to match the bed, and each had a faded mirror in its door. The one by the window was firmly closed. The one nearer the door was ajar.

Max opened it, coughing in revulsion at the ancient odours of lavender and camphor. The wardrobe was empty, save for a long, fat cotton bag. The cotton was discoloured and stained, torn down the side, so that the fur poked through like a trapped animal. A fur coat.

Hesitating, Max lifted the wooden hanger from the brass rail. The bag was as heavy as a body. Laying it on the bed, she unbuttoned the bag, button by button, and had the sudden, unpleasant feeling that she was undressing someone who did not want to be undressed.

She took out the coat. Pale with a dark stripe. It was beautiful and shining, like a creature lit by its own light.

Why not try it on?

No!

She paused.

Don't be a fool. Try it on!

The words pierced her mind like gunshot.

In the mirror she looked at herself. The coat was too large, but surely perfect for the winter?

And why not? No one else would be wearing it.

She rolled up the cotton bag and pushed it back into

the wardrobe. As she moved towards the door, she felt a sharp pain in her shoulder – and she cried out. It was like a . . . no, that's not what it is. But that is what it is . . . A bite. Not a fleabite. Teeth.

She pulled off the coat and left the room, leaving the door unlocked.

Carrying the heavy garment in both arms, she ran back downstairs.

Jonny was in the kitchen. He had filled up the water tanks and got a fire going under the copper. The vast kitchen range was lit, its hotplate carrying the kettle. On the huge oak table lay a small deer, bleeding at the mouth.

'I shot it,' said Jonny.

'Pheasants! The gardener said pheasants – not deer.'

'It was standing there in the deer park. Couldn't be easier.'

'You'll have to butcher it, then, because I'm not doing it.'

'Why are you never pleased? We've got a fire, hot water, food, and what have you been doing? Playing *Game of Thrones*?' He looked at the coat.

'I found it in one of the bedrooms. Do you like it?'

'No! I don't like it. It stinks.'

'I'll hang it outside.'

Jonny was looking at her. 'What's happened to your shoulder?'

He came towards her, swiped her shoulder roughly with his hand. On his palm there was blood. 'You've been bitten,' he said. 'Teeth marks.'

She went to their bedroom and examined her shoulder. A bite like a half-moon was cleanly imprinted into her skin.

While she was dabbing it with Dettol, Jonny came over. He was not sympathetic but forensic. 'Looks like a rat.'

He went out again, whistling. He never whistled.

But the bite didn't look like a rat. The bite looked human.

The days settled down into something like routine. The physical effort of keeping warm, fed, and clean took up most of the shortening days. Max gathered berries and picked apples, dug potatoes from the vegetable garden, and let the shy, teenage, lovestruck under-gardener give her cabbages and carrots. The gardener himself was suspicious and watchful. He didn't care for her beauty, and he never had believed her about those 'dropped' keys. She called him Mr Grumpy.

In the afternoons, Max took the ancient bicycle from the shed into the village for milk, butter, cheese, and flour, and learned to cook in a way that depended on using everything and doing it slowly. Venison stew, made in a battered old pan, and simmered in the range, would last them a week.

They ate by candlelight – it should have been romantic, but the shadows sat at the table with them, two candles hardly lighting their plates. In the gloom each of them looked different, and gradually they became different.

They stopped talking to each other, and that was the strangest thing, because they had always talked. Jonny had turned sullen, snappish, and Max had the unwelcome feeling that she was becoming a little bit afraid of him.

Ever since he had found a pair of ancient leather boots in some outhouse, and now he wore them laced up to his knees, the metal toecaps clicking. They changed his walk, from sinuous to stiff-legged, and he stalked around like he owned the place.

And what was she? A cook, a scullery maid. He expected his food on the table when he came in. He wouldn't come shopping with her.

A few days earlier, they had been arguing, and he had raised his hand to her. He had lowered it again, immediately, hangdog at himself, his cheeks reddening, but he hadn't apologised. She had started to ask him – Jonny, what is the matter? – but he shook his head and walked out. She heard him with the axe. Chop. Chop. Chop. Chopping. Whistling.

When they had first arrived, they had pushed together the single beds. It was exciting, rolling over to find each other, and when they were asleep on their own beds, they held hands.

Then one night, as she came to bed, she saw that Jonny had pushed the beds apart. He lay with his back to her, while her silent tears ran down her cheeks, and she stretched her hand out of her own bed, into the void. The foot or so in between them felt as far as the distance to the moon, and as cold, and as lonely, and as silent.

Jonny usually fell asleep first, worn out by the day. Max, though she was bone-tired too, lay awake, wondering what was wrong. It came to her, without any question, that they had to leave the house. Otherwise, they would leave each other.

They could stay with her sister for a bit. She'd write a letter. If she called her, they'd argue, she wouldn't be able to explain. Her sister lived a normal life with a normal job and a normal husband. She thought Max was irresponsible. But she was still her sister . . . Yes, a letter would do it – after all, Max had done her best to get them settled for the winter. This life should suit them – they were young enough, and strong enough, and they liked each other. But now they didn't like each other, and she could see the exhaustion in her eyes.

Yes, they must go. Just a week with her sister while she arranged Barcelona. Just like Jonny had wanted.

Comforted by this plan, she began to fall asleep.

It was that night that she heard the baby crying. The cries pulled her from the depths of sleep. Clear and far-off. Jonny was snoring. In between snores she did her best to concentrate, straining her ears towards the sound. It must be an owl – a female owl, kwik kwik, high-pitched and desolate. Then she did hear the owl. And right after it, the crying again. Upstairs.

Max swung her legs out of bed and onto the freezing floor. My God, it was cold. The fire they lit every night in the grate had gone out. The icy air penetrated her thick pyjamas. She shook Jonny by the shoulder. He rolled over, mumbling. In the old days, he'd have opened his arms and pulled her on top of him.

She left him to his solitary sleep and slipped out of their bedroom, taking the torch. Now she was at the foot of the stairs. Shivering, she saw the fur coat, pale in the moonlight, hanging on a peg, unworn since she had taken it. She put it on. Its owner had been much taller than Max. On her, it reached to the floor. Wrapping it across her chest, she ascended the staircase.

At the top of the stairs, turning right on the wide landing, Max made her way towards the bedroom with the double door. The crying was softer now. A whimper.

She opened the doors.

The beam from her torch showed the room just as she had seen it weeks before. Now, though, as she sprayed torchlight around the walls, she noticed a small door in the wall beside the bed. The door was flush with the panelling, deliberately discreet. The whimpering was coming from the other side of the door.

Max went forward, too terrified to speculate on what exactly might be behind that door.

Why not leave? Yes, leave. No, she couldn't leave.

She pushed softly against the panel, hearing it click open, like a safe, and leading to a room beyond. Her fear forbade her to go further, but, adjusting the flashlight beam from wide to narrow, she shone it powerfully into the darkness. There was a crib in the room. An empty crib. No sound now.

Max retreated, not turning round, but stepping backwards, slowly. She closed the door set into the panelling.

She was trembling, the torch in her hand held loosely by her side. She was slowed down by fear, her mind

127

straining, like climbing hand over hand up a rope. She must leave the room. Breathe in. Breathe out. Come on.

As she summoned the strength to go, it seemed to her that the fur on the coat, near to her mouth, was shifting, as if in a breeze.

There is no breeze, and it can't be her own breath.

She's rigid like a statue. The blood is beating in her ears like the tide coming in. Then she feels it.

She feels a strong pair of hands, male hands surely, on either side of her shoulders, her shoulders covered by the fur coat. The hands are gently pulling back the collar of the coat, and coming closer, against her neck, yes, it is breath. Cold breath. Cold, burning breath. Breath that plays from her collarbone to her earlobe. Something, or someone, kisses her neck very lightly. She feels the tickle of facial hair. And then, whatever it is that is behind her, bites her.

Did she faint?

Max woke up in her own bed, late morning, the sun so innocent through the window. She had no memory of recovering herself. There was no sign of Jonny.

She put on her dressing gown and went down to the kitchen, pulling the warm kettle from the back of the stove to the hotplate. She made coffee.

What had happened to her?

She stood leaning against the range, coffee cup in one hand. Her neck was itching. She reached to scratch it. Her fingers traced a raised welt. Outside, the misty light and the rain gave the window glass some reflection. She didn't need a mirror. There was a bruise mark on her neck.

In a panic, Max phoned her sister. Voicemail. Yes, she'd be at work. She'll try her later, but she must write to her today. Now.

Max sat down at the big, dark table and began to write. When had she last written a letter? As soon as she began, she felt better. Everything will be all right. They'll soon be in the sun in Barcelona.

She had finished the letter to her sister when Jonny came into the kitchen. Max looked up, smiled at him; did he want coffee? He nodded and went to cut some bread. Max was bright, chatting to him; she could make eggs.

He glanced over at her as she talked – that's all he ever did these days, wouldn't look at her like he used to do, reading her face as though he were memorising it. This time, though, his gaze held. He stood staring at her. She felt a rise of fear. He reached her in a couple of strides, and, taking her neck in his hand, yanked it sideways.

'Jonny! Stop it!'

'You whore! You cheap whore! The gardener's boy, is it? All of seventeen?'

She's trying to say she doesn't know what he's talking about, but his big hand is squashing her lips into her teeth. Because she has to do it, to save herself, she twists around and knees him in the groin. He lets go, holding his balls, calling her a bitch. A thief. It's just the beginning. He's on one side of the battered table and she's on the other side. She's never seen him like this. His eyes are black with hatred.

'On your neck – it's a love bite.'

'It's a bruise!'

'Who is it? Who's been kissing you? Biting you?'

As he says this, he sees the recognition in her face, the horror in her face, and he thinks it's because she knows she's been found out. He can't know that she is back in the terror of what happened last night. The cold, insistent mouth on her neck. The sharp teeth.

'There's something upstairs . . .' she says.

'Is that where you do it?' He's savage, panting.

'It's not alive. It's in the room – last night – I heard something, I went upstairs. Listen to me, Jonny.'

He doesn't listen to her. He picks up a wooden chair and smashes it into the tabletop between them. It splinters and breaks. Max starts crying but Jonny doesn't care. He takes the short flight of steps two at a time up to the next floor. She can hear him crashing around like he's drunk, then pacing, pacing, in those boots. She doesn't dare go up there. After a while, everything's quiet.

How long does she sit at the table? An hour? A day? A week? A year?

The low afternoon light barely penetrates the kitchen. She can't get warm.

She needs to get dressed. Then she must get the letter in the post.

She knows her sister will come, exasperated, impatient, but she'll be there. After their mother died, they made a promise always to be there for each other. They were seventeen and nineteen; too young to lose your mother.

Her hand goes to her neck. Whatever, whoever, bit her . . . and the thought trails off. She is afraid. She understands the advantage the Dead hold over the living; the Dead are not afraid.

She gets ready. Jeans and thick sweater, warm socks. She pulls her hair up under her hat and looks for her padded jacket. It isn't there. Where did she leave it? In the garden? No.

It is raining outside. What can she do? She has the letter in her hand when she sees the fur coat. She could cycle to the village with the coat draped around her and over the bike.

She doesn't want to do that. She wants to bundle up the coat and throw it on the bonfire.

At the door, she watches the weather, the rain, falling cold and determined.

The bicycle is propped in the porch.

She tries calling her sister one more time – it's still going to voicemail.

This is the choice. Don't go out, don't post the letter, because she has no coat, or wear the fur coat. She shoves the letter in the pocket.

Halfway down the drive, cycling slowly because the coat is big and bulky, she has the feeling that she is being watched. She stops a moment, sees nothing, but what she hears is a low whistle.

She pedals on, turning out of the drive, onto the narrow road bordered on each side with black metal estate fencing. She is coming in sight of the main house when the coat catches in the chain of the bicycle, throwing her off. She swears, picks herself up; her leg is hurt. She tugs at the coat until it tears, leaving a snatch of fur caught in the chain. The bicycle is useless now. She'll have to walk. There's a footpath through the woods, just past the main house, that leads straight to the village. It was made for the servants in the old days. She props the bicycle, wraps the coat round her. She doesn't notice the letter falling out of the pocket – as if a hand had taken it.

She's in the woods now, and it's getting dark – too dark. She's too late, she should go back. She's limping. The coat has kept her dry but she's disgusted by it. She takes it off, throws it over a branch, feeling for the letter.

Thief!

The voice was clear. A man's voice.

The coat was hurled at her, knocking her to the floor. She tried to get up, but the coat was forcing her back down, like a wild animal straddling her. She was on her hands and knees, arching her back, straining to stand up, and almost succeeding, when the fur arms of the coat stiffened and tightened around her neck, throttling her.

'Bitch! Thief!'

Max reached with one hand to pull the thing off, and as she grasped the sleeve, it collapsed, nothing inside. The second she let go, the grip tightened again. She fell back down, flat on her face in the dirt.

The voice whispered so close to her ear that she could feel the bristles of his moustache. 'You're all the same.'

With her last strength she pushed back from the force against her and got onto her knees. She grabbed both arms of the coat, pulling them over her head. The coat somersaulted above her, straight into the air, then fell in a heap on the forest floor.

She looked at it for a second, revolted, terrified, pushed her hair back from the cold mist that seemed to envelop her. The coat didn't move.

Run. She must run.

She ran back through the woods, ran out into the rain on the road, slipping and crying, her heart pounding and her lungs gasping, until she reached the laurel drive, and up ahead, the sight of the hateful house that now seemed like a sanctuary to her. She leaned, winded, against the hedge. It was all right. It was going to be all right now. The lights were on in the hall. Jonny would listen. Jonny would take care of her.

'Jonny! Jonny?'

She sensed him but she couldn't see him. The room felt empty and full at the same time. She looked round. Nothing. Something. Who was watching her? She heard whistling. She heard the tread of boots coming towards her.

As the axe came towards her neck, Max saw another figure standing behind Jonny. Top lip drawn back in grotesque pleasure. Moustache. Jagged front teeth. Was she hit? Is she hurt? The cold outlines of that other man wrapped around her. His hands under her throat. She had an image of herself, upstairs, in the hateful bedroom, naked and alone.

'JONNY!'

Did he hear? She starts to fall . . .

Boots

Jonny had never used an axe before. As he swung it, he liked the heft in his shoulders, and his steady grip on the shaft. The head was sharp and oiled. It split the logs easily.

Soon, he had a respectable pile that he carried into their bedroom and sitting room. The kitchen range burned coal, but Max didn't like the smell in the bedroom. A wood fire was romantic.

He thought of how their life would be over the coming winter. He'd have preferred Barcelona. Max had got them into this, and it was easier to go along with it. Amazing how she'd convinced that soft-faced silly boy with his Bentley to let them have a house on his estate for the winter. Who has a house to spare? A house no one has lived in for more than fifty years. He laid down the axe. Time to try the gun.

He could see the gardener watching him. Mr Grumpy, Max called him. Max was beautiful, slender, strong, her dark hair falling over her face as she dug up potatoes. He'd go anywhere with her. He called to her, 'You want to come shooting with me, Lady Chatterley?'

She came across, taking his hand. 'I want to have a look around the house.'

Jonny shook his head. 'He told you not to do that, Mr Grumpy over there.'

'He said any door that is open is open to us – so I am going to make sure they are all open. That's all.' She dangled the keys she had stolen. Not a thief. Light-fingered is what she called herself. She stood on tiptoe and kissed Jonny on the mouth. The gardener's boy, looking on, turned away.

'That one's a lovesick puppy,' said Jonny. Max kissed him again. He wasn't the jealous type. Jonny put his hand on her back, part ownership, part gentleness, then picked up the shotgun and went towards the woods.

When Jonny reached the woods, he loaded the gun with shot and fired aimlessly, first at a rabbit that disappeared unhurt into the undergrowth, then at a pheasant that screeched into the trees, warning all the other pheasants of his presence. And on it went, aiming and missing, missing and aiming, until he saw it was nearly dark. He'd caught nothing. Now he was at the deer park.

The deer were small and stationary, feeding in the twilight, easier to hit, but he couldn't kill a deer with pheasant shot. He wasn't sure he could kill a deer at all.

His feet were wet. He felt a chill in the air. Time to go home and drink wine with Max.

As he turned away, he found himself standing in a thin mist that had appeared out of nowhere. He wiped his face with the back of his hand.

Right behind him there was a voice. A low baritone, harsh and clipped. 'Poaching, are you?'

The man staring at him was shorter than Jonny, strongly built, wearing a tweed jacket, flat cap, breeches and boots. His moustache was thick. He looked ridiculous. Was he a gamekeeper?

'Hi! We're staying here. Guests. In the Dower House.'

'The Dower House?' The man seemed surprised.

'I'm Jonny.' Jonny held out his hand. The man didn't take it. Went on staring at him with his black eyes.

'I was after pheasants.'

The man shook his head. 'You're too late tonight. They roost.'

Jonny smiled. 'I'm heading back. It's not my thing – hunting.'

The man looked at him. 'You don't need a gun to bag yourself dinner. See . . .'

He climbed over the railing so nimbly that Jonny didn't see him move, but now he was on the other side, where the tame deer were quietly feeding. 'Once they trust you, you can do anything.'

The man pulled a wooden truncheon out from under his jacket, grabbed a roe deer's head under his arm, and smashed its muzzle with the truncheon. Blood spurted onto Jonny's sweatshirt. His mouth went dry. The deer was on its knees, collapsed.

'Get over here!' ordered the man, and Jonny, not knowing what he was doing, or why he would do it, climbed the low fence and knelt by the deer. The man passed him the truncheon. 'Finish her off!'

Jonny looked at him, uncomprehending. The man pushed his shoulder roughly. 'I said, finish her off!'

Like a man in a dream, Jonny lifted the bloody baton and hit the deer a second time. She was dead.

He knelt beside the warm body. Had he done this? Why? He stroked the soft pelt. What had he done? He was shaking. His hands were red with dark, drying blood. He couldn't move for some minutes. 'I'm sorry,' he said.

He looked up. The man was gone.

Jonny lifted the deer over the rail, then up onto his shoulders, a warm, dead weight. His mind was blank. He walked back to the Dower House, carrying what he had killed across his shoulders. He dropped it, heavily, onto the kitchen table. Its eyes were glassy. He was still shaking. He washed his hands in the stone sink, pulled off his soaking sweatshirt, running the water against the blood that filled the sink with a red pool. While the water was running, he washed the deer's battered head, then put a paper bag over it. He didn't want Max to see this. He would have to butcher it.

How?

He leaned against the sink, breathing in and out, trying to regain himself.

Where was Max? Wandering about the house somewhere, snooping. He needed her to hold him. He needed her to forgive him. He made the fires roar with fresh wood, lit the candles to support and soften the grim electric light bulb that swung overhead. The kitchen was built for servants to scurry about in. The huge table, the cooking range, the water heater, dented iron pans hanging on hooks. There was a whole rack of hooks. Should

he hang the deer on a hook to drain the blood? He pulled
out his phone. He could look it up. How To Butcher A
Deer.

But there was no signal. He was trapped in the past
with a useless phone and a dead deer. Everything about
the kitchen belonged in the past. He stared, mesmerised,
at the drip drip drip of blood onto the stone floor.

Max came into the kitchen. His heart flooded with
relief.

Then she saw the deer, the blood, the red mess in the
sink. She started shouting at him – it was supposed to be
a pheasant, a bird, but this was an animal. He'd killed an
animal. Was he crazy or what?

And as her voice rose and fell, up and down, in and
out, he stopped hearing the words. Her face had changed.
It was narrow and cold. She was berating him like a little
boy. And what was that in her arms?

She was holding what looked like a pelt. A huge, dead,
skinned animal. Was it moving? It's alive, he thought, it's
a dead thing that's alive. He grabbed it from her – he was
much taller than her. He held it up above his head.

'What is this? Fucking *Game of Thrones*?'

'I found it,' she said in a small voice. 'Upstairs.'

'You stole it, you mean.'

'Jonny?' This wasn't like him. He had always laughed
at what he called her escapades.

His face was hard. 'I'm trying to get us warm and fed,
and you, what are you doing?'

'What do you want me to do?'

Jonny didn't answer. He pulled a couple of S hooks from the pan rack and hitched them over the inch-thick iron bar that ran the length of the kitchen, wall to wall and above the sink. He manhandled the deer off the table, then, standing on a low stool, skewered it on the hooks through its flanks.

'Give me that knife.' He was ordering her not asking her.

He took the knife, sawing clumsily at the head of the animal until he had severed it. Blood poured into the sink.

'Leave it to drain,' he said. 'Overnight.'

Max looked in disgust at the bleeding carcass.

'What are you doing?'

'Living the simple life. Your idea.'

She went outside. There was a bench by the door. Wrapping her arms round her body, she sat waiting for him to come to find her.

He didn't come. She felt the same tight anger and despair that had choked her throat when her mother had died. Max had waited, and waited, a day and a night, but her mother didn't come home.

After a while, Max went to find Jonny. He was sitting at the kitchen table, motionless, his eyes on the deer.

Later, in their pushed-together beds, watching the fire flicker, Jonny seemed more like himself.

He stroked her hair. They started to make love. It felt good, right, until she was under him. He was sweating. What she could smell was animal blood.

In the morning, before it was light, he got up, went

outside. Max went to the window and saw him walking towards the woods.

A few weeks later, in the short afternoon when the light was set to fade, Max and Jonny were in the vegetable garden. Max was picking late spinach. Jonny was chopping his wood. He stood up, straightening his back, the axe held at chest-height.

'Stop staring at her, will you?'

The gardener's boy was only seventeen, soft-haired and soft-eyed. He thought Max was the most beautiful thing he had ever seen. He tried not to look, but he couldn't help himself. The boy had taken her a cabbage and some carrots so that he could stand near her, so that she would look at him.

'You like it, don't you?' said Jonny. 'Your little slave.'

Jonny had never cared about other men. He was so good-looking it didn't occur to him that any woman would be interested in anyone else.

'Stop it, Jonny.'

He slammed his axe into the chopping block. 'I'm going for a walk.'

'Shall I come with you?'

'You don't like the woods when it's going dark.'

'You seem to like the woods when it's dark.'

He didn't answer. He strode off. It was in the woods where he met Edwin.

About a week after the deer incident, Jonny had been out in the woods, bagging pheasants. He had managed to shoot one but now the others had flown away.

Edwin appeared beside him. Jonny hadn't seen him, or heard him, suddenly he was there, just as he had been the first time. He was wearing the same clothes.

Edwin told Jonny to drive the birds into the clearing, and only then to shoot. Two shots, one after the other. Bang! Bang! 'It's a beater's job, to harry the birds out of cover, drive them towards the gun. You'll have to do it yourself. And pick them up yourself, as you've no dog.'

'How do I cook them?'

'That's her job, isn't it?'

'She won't know how to do it either.'

'What kind of a woman is she?'

Jonny was silent.

'Hang them upside down for three days to let the blood drain and the flesh settle, then pluck them, wash them, and roast them. Bacon on top if you have any. Pheasants aren't fatty.'

Edwin sat down on a tree stump, took a pipe out of his pocket, and lit it. 'You want to keep an eye on that woman of yours.'

Jonny felt himself going cold. The autumn day was pleasant enough, yet Jonny shivered. 'I don't know what you mean.'

'You do, though, don't you? With women it's the three Ts. Trust. Temptation. Treachery. Trust is simple when there's no temptation. Once there's temptation, there's treachery. What would you say to a seventeen-year-old girl throwing herself at you?'

'Are you spying on us?'

'I see what I see.'

142

'I'm not some old man in the corner,' said Jonny. 'She gets what she needs from me.'

'You don't know much about women, do you? The man is to blame, so we're told, but men know better than that. Men know who is to blame. It's the women, every time. Silky, soft, big eyes, so gentle, and underneath, they're vipers. Watch your step in this wood, won't you? There are vipers here, always have been. You should be wearing boots.'

'I don't have any boots,' said Jonny.

'Meet me here tomorrow at dusk – I'll find you a pair.'

Edwin got up, walking deeper into the wood. He seemed to evaporate. Jonny waited, then followed him softly. There was no sign of him.

The next morning Jonny was up early. He liked to leave Max still asleep. She bothered him with her chatter. He had learned how to move stealthily, and his aim had improved. He drove the pheasants into the clearing and shot a brace. One, two, clean out of the air.

He carried them home, blue necks limp, their tawny and golden feathers damp from where they had fallen onto the grass. He tied their necks together and hung them by the door. Then he went in and cut a slice of bread from the loaf without washing his hands.

Max had been out early too. She returned from the village with flour, milk, and butter. She saw the pheasants hanging by the door.

Timidly she touched them, still warm and floppy as

they swung. The gardener's boy – Alex – came up to her: he would pluck them for her, if she wanted him to.

'You're so sweet,' she said, watching him blush. She wanted to put out her hand to stroke his cheek, soft with down. She remembered what it felt like to be seventeen. To feel awkward. 'Come in and have pancakes,' she said, and he followed her like a puppy.

Jonny was sitting at the table eating his bread and cheese. He looked up, his face darkening.

'Pancakes!' said Max. 'I'm going to make pancakes for all of us – even Mr Grumpy, if he fancies some.'

'I'm sure Alex fancies some,' said Jonny.

Max glanced at him. 'Alex, go and ask Mr Grumpy if he wants pancakes.'

Alex retreated up the stone stairs. Max put down her purchases, deciding to ignore Jonny's jibes. Let him calm down.

'That bike is so heavy and slow. I'm starving. I must have a slice of bread before I start cooking.' She lifted the loaf out of the metal bread bin. The crusty sides were daubed with blood. She dropped it.

'Jonny!'

He didn't answer. She turned to him, picking up the loaf. 'There's blood on the bread.'

'I forgot to wash my hands, that's all. Wipe it, woman!'

'What did you call me?'

Confusion clouded his face. He snatched the loaf from her and held it under the cold tap, drying it in a cloth.

'I'm not eating that!' said Max. 'Take it with you into your precious woods!'

Jonny looked down at his feet, seemed to want to say

something, but couldn't. He went out, carrying the loaf, as Alex hurried down the stone steps. Jonny deliberately shoved into him.

'Enjoy your pancake. It doesn't need sugar.'

In the kitchen, Alex said, 'Is he all right?'

Max shook her head. 'I don't know. He's usually happy and easy.'

'It's solitary out here,' said Alex. 'You have to like your own company.'

'He used to like my company. Have some coffee. Tell me about yourself.'

And Jonny, hearing them chatting and laughing, stood at the top of the stairs, pulling the tail feathers out of the pheasants, one by one.

That evening, Max had done her best to make the kitchen lovely. She had cut flowers and branches, and the evening gloom was lifted by greenery and colour. They were eating venison again tonight. She'd found a recipe for a stew and put it to cook in the unfathomable oven of the range. Jonny could smell it, a rich red smell. Warm odours of good food. She had brought back a bottle of wine from the village. It stood open on the table.

'Are you going to wash my back?' she asked Jonny.

Max was sitting in the tin tub filled with hot water, she had music playing on her phone, and she seemed to have forgotten about the bloodstained bread.

Her glass of wine was resting on an old wooden stool by the tub, and she was singing. Her voice was melodic and low.

Jonny stood behind her, looking at her. So beautiful. He wanted to touch her, kiss her, laugh with her, the way they were. All he had to do was go to the tin tub, wash her back, kneel beside her. The image in his head, as he thought that thought, was not of her, but of himself, kneeling by the fallen deer.

He remembered his appointment with Edwin.

She heard him go out. She topped up the hot water in the tub from the jug.

She had wanted their life here to be fun, as they learned how to do things together. They had always been enough for each other, and now he was elsewhere, she was sure of that, but she didn't know where that elsewhere was.

When Jonny reached the margin of the wood, he heard a whistle. Edwin was waiting for him. Jonny hadn't noticed the evening mist, but there was a mist around Edwin that Jonny entered into. He could barely see the darkening trees.

The mist was cold.

'Try these,' said Edwin. He held out a pair of worn leather boots, with full laces up the front of the leg, and brass buckles at the top. The soles were hobnailed. 'These were my trench boots. The last ones I was issued. The Americans had improved them.'

Jonny turned them over in his hands. 'Never heard of trench boots.' Edwin said nothing.

Jonny took off his trainers. Tried to get his foot into the first boot.

'Ease it!' said Edwin. 'Here ...' He stood behind Jonny to help him pull on the boot. His hands were so cold that Jonny flinched.

'If I need boots, you need gloves.'

Edwin's breath was cold against Jonny's neck. 'My blood doesn't circulate.'

Once in the boots, Jonny walked around. His feet were protesting at the confinement.

'You need to wear them in,' said Edwin. 'Let's have a walk.'

They set off, not into the forest, but towards the Dower House. 'Who leaves a house empty?' said Jonny.

'That depends on who was living in the house when they left it empty.'

Jonny looked sideways at Edwin, who was walking straight ahead, and staring straight ahead. 'That was her bedroom up there. The big one with the bay window.'

Where Max found the fur coat, thought Jonny. But he didn't say that to Edwin. He said, 'The old lady. The widow. What's she called? A dowager?'

Edwin sneered. 'She was an old lady when she died. A young woman to begin with. She went in there at seventeen and never came out till she came out in her coffin.'

'How do you know this story?' said Jonny.

'I used to work here. Gamekeeper. A while back.'

They were pushing through an overgrown path high with brambles. 'Come round this way,' said Edwin.

They arrived at a set of stone steps, mounted with a broken handrail, that led to a mildewed, weather-battered door. Time had sealed it long since. The handle was rusty and green with lichen.

'This was the discreet way into the nursery,' said Edwin, 'and the nursery led straight to her bedroom. That's the way he used to go in. After the baby was born.'

'Who?' asked Jonny.

'The father of the child. She wasn't married. Shall I take you in?'

'No . . . thanks, it's getting late, it's past dinner time . . . Max will be wondering . . .'

Edwin looked at Jonny with contempt. 'That kind of a man, are you? A fanny man? She's in charge, is she?'

Before Jonny could answer, Edwin gripped his wrist. He took a key from his pocket and slotted it into the keyhole. 'It's the same wherever you go,' said Edwin. 'A key needs a slot. A slot needs a key.' The lock turned. Without wanting it, Jonny found himself on the other side of the door, in blackness.

Edwin lit a match. 'Get up those stairs, quickly!'

Jonny reached the top of the flight of stairs as the match went out.

Standing there, so cold he couldn't think, a second match flared, and Edwin was beside him. How had he done that, so fast and so silent?

The small door ahead of them was open. The two men went inside.

Edwin lit a candle that sat in a sconce on the wall. The room was small and empty – except for a wooden crib.

'Now see this,' said Edwin, striding across the room, and tapping and clicking at the far wall.

A panel door sprang open. 'Neat. Clever. This is the bedroom. Her bedroom.'

'Why are you showing me this?' said Jonny. 'It's horrible.'

'You asked me about this house – and now I'm telling you. She was in here, and he used to visit her – oh, for a year it went on, after the baby was born, yes, a year.'

'Why didn't they just get married – was he poor or something?'

'Oh, no, he wasn't poor. He was her father.'

Jonny felt sick. His mouth was full of saliva.

Edwin was still talking. Something about the fur coat. About the fur coat her father had bought her. 'He liked her to undress. To put it on over her nakedness. He liked to take it off.'

'For God's sake, Edwin. Shut up!'

'It's still in the wardrobe. The fur coat.'

Edwin went to the wardrobe. In the shadows, Jonny could see him, his short, hard body, and the cold mist that hung about him. Edwin let out a sound, like a snake hissing. 'It's gone! Where is it? The coat has gone!'

Edwin threw a rancid garment bag onto the floor. Jonny had to get out of the room. He remembered that Max had unlocked the main door when she stole the coat. All he had to do was to reach the door and open it. Edwin seemed to be in another world, swaying slightly, half vanished, his boots stamping on the torn, stained bag on the floor. Jonny made a bolt for it, opened the door, was gone.

Edwin didn't follow. Jonny was soon down the stairs,

into their quarters, and below, into the kitchen, where Max was chopping vegetables.

She looked up, stopped what she was doing, shocked at his appearance. 'Where have you been? I thought you were hunting in the woods?'

'Yes . . .'

'You're shivering, and your hair is wet, like you've been standing in a mist.' She went to him and touched his hair. He flinched. He pulled away from her. He wanted to speak but he couldn't speak. Max threw him a tea towel to dry himself. It fell to the floor, and as she bent down to pick it up, she saw his boots.

'Where did you get those? They look about a hundred years old.'

'Edwin gave them to me,' Jonny said, but that's not what Jonny said. Jonny said nothing.

Max went upstairs. She wanted some air. Jonny felt like a suffocation. She couldn't breathe with him in the room.

Outside the evening was clear, not damp, or wet. Where had he been that his clothes and hair were dripping? Why did he not talk to her?

She saw the light on in the gardeners' bothy. Alex's head was bent over in the window. She went across. He was sharpening tools.

'Still here?' she said.

'My mum's picking me up tonight. Moped's gone for repair.'

'You work hard.'

'I enjoy it. Would you like a piece of chocolate?' He took a bar out of his jacket, breaking off a square.

She shook her head. 'Dinner time for us.' There was a pause. 'Alex, does anyone else work in the gardens here, apart from you and Mr Grumpy?'

Alex smiled. 'He's all right. No. We manage everything between us.'

'There isn't a gamekeeper?'

'We don't offer a shoot these days. That's why there's so many pheasants. They breed by themselves now. Not many people go out to shoot them.'

'And you haven't seen Jonny with anyone?'

'He doesn't like me.'

'No . . . he doesn't. But that's because you do like me.' And she moved forward and kissed Alex quickly on the cheek. He put his arms around her, and for a moment they stood together, like lost children.

She didn't see Jonny standing outside in the dark. She didn't hear Edwin's low whistle.

A few days later, Jonny went back into that bedroom. He couldn't say why. He crept up the stairs. He stood, looking at the faded drapes, the moth-eaten bedspread. He tried to find the door in the panelling, but the light was too dim.

Going to the window to open the drape, he became aware of someone else in the room. Edwin was standing by the panel door.

'Where've you been?' he asked Jonny. 'I looked for you in the woods.'

Jonny didn't answer.

'She's taken it, hasn't she? Taken the coat? Your little thief.'

'She's borrowed it, that's all. It's winter. Who wants it, anyway?'

'The coat belongs here,' said Edwin.

He came and sat on the bed, facing Jonny. The same clothes, the same look. 'Her father bought her that coat.'

'I don't want to talk about this.'

'She ran away. It was wintertime. She put the coat on to keep warm, and she went into the woods, leaving the baby behind, crying and crying. Her father came looking for her, but she had gone. You can't fathom how angry he was that she had escaped him. He set the gamekeepers out to look for her, with the dogs, told them to bring her back. They were as ashamed of her as the rest of the household, not because of him, no one knew a thing about that, but because she had given birth to that baby, that bastard.

'The family were trying to protect her – that's all the gamekeepers knew. And out they went. We had two keepers and four beaters in those days. She was terrified, what with the dogs and the flares, and not wearing proper clothes. She kept going but they caught her. Brought her back to this room, the coat soaking wet, and her trembling inside it like a drowned animal. He was her father. He had to punish her. He couldn't bring himself to do it with his own hands, so he fetched the head keeper. Told him to strangle the baby in front of her.'

Jonny had bile in his throat. He pushed his nails into his palms to stop himself retching. There was a smell in the room. Something rotting.

'That's what the keeper did, it was his orders and he had to do it, and they left the baby there, on the bed, and locked her in with it for weeks. Decomposing, it was.'

'Stop,' said Jonny.

Edwin didn't pause. 'Then her father came back, through the nursery, up the steps. She heard him coming. She was waiting for him. As he walked through the door, in the dark, with only a candle, she pushed him, pushed him back down those stone steps, with a strength a woman doesn't possess. He broke his neck.'

'Dead?' said Jonny.

'Dead.'

They sat quiet for a moment, then Edwin said, 'After that, she should have gone to a lunatic asylum, but the family didn't want the scandal. Got her a companion, and kept her here, and here is where she lived and died.'

'Poor woman,' said Jonny.

'Poor woman? Don't waste your pity on her. She was at the bottom of it all along, with her pretty ways, and heavy hair, sitting on his knee, her arms round his neck. Drove him mad. What could a man do?'

'She was his daughter!'

'If she hadn't made a fuss, it would have run its course. She could have kept her baby. Why must women always make a fuss? To get the man into trouble, that's why. Seductress. Murderess. That's what she was.'

'Why are you telling me this story?' said Jonny.

*

He was in bed that night when he heard Max get up. He pretended to be asleep. She whispered his name, shook his shoulder. He ignored her. He heard her go into the hall, and then further into the house. He got up, saw the fur coat was gone from the hook. So, she's going out, he thought. Meeting Alex. And he hated her.

He wondered whether to follow. Whether to catch them at it. Confront them with it. His heart was cold. He could wait. Why let a woman break his sleep?

But his sleep was broken. Strange dreams assailed him. He dreamed he was in the woods with Edwin. They were hunting her like a deer.

She was ahead of them, she was always ahead of them, and then she fell.

Jonny woke, sweating, looked across to her bed. He had separated the beds after he had seen her kiss that boy. He didn't want her near him. And she wasn't near him; her bed was empty.

He got up, sitting in the cold on the edge of his bed, his head in his hands. Better go out. Better anything than this. He dressed, without washing, and pulled on the boots. They fitted him better now. He'd polished them too.

In the wet dawn of a bleak day Jonny took his axe and went into the woods.

'Out early,' said Edwin.

Edwin had a way of appearing.

'Don't you have any other clothes?' asked Jonny.

'These are all I need.'

154

He sat down, took out the pipe, lit it. 'She's up in the bedroom if you want to know where she is.'

'I don't want to know.'

'Go up the back stairs and you'll catch her.'

'With him?'

'Her own father.'

'What are you talking about?'

'You'll see. I was the one that did it. Strangled the baby with my bare hands.'

'This is madness.'

'You'll find out for yourself what madness is.'

Jonny felt the mist wrap round him. He couldn't see. He couldn't think. He dropped his axe, and ran towards the house, and up the stone stairs. He slipped as he reached the top, cutting his head. He ran through the nursery into the bedroom. 'MAX! MAX!'

There was no one there.

Out onto the corridor, down the main stairs, shouting her name.

He found her in the kitchen, in her pyjamas. Her face was frightened. 'There's something upstairs. There's something outside.'

He knew that, but he didn't want to know it. All he could see was the mark on her neck. He came and twisted her neck in his hands. 'That's a love bite.'

She tried to tell him it's a bruise. That something up there hurt her. A mouth on her neck. Not alive. Dead and cold. Cold and hard. 'Stop it, Jonny! Stop it!'

His hand is squashing her mouth. She can't speak. Suddenly he lets her loose. She falls onto a chair.

'I didn't hurt you,' he said. 'Don't make a fuss.' Then he's gone.

How much time passes? An hour? A day? A week?

Jonny watches her leave the house. He's hidden her jacket but she's wearing the coat. She's shameless. She's a thief. She's a whore. Edwin's right. Edwin's with him, whistling softly. Edwin will see it through. They agree a plan.

In the heavy rain Jonny waits near the house. She's in the woods. He can hear the gamekeepers and the beaters. The dogs' fierce barking. He can see flares far away lighting the darkness.

She's running. The men are on her. Dogs and flares. She trips over a root.

She falls. She tries to get up. The coat weighs her down. His coat. His arms putting it round her shoulders. His breath on her neck as he undresses her. She doesn't want to be undressed. Get up. Keep running. She knows who betrayed her. It's Edwin. She begged him to unlock the door. He said there would be a price, looking at her breasts. His moustache against her ear. His broken teeth. He had laughed at the horror in her face. 'What will you do, miss? Tell your father?'

Max scrambles to her feet. The coat is filthy, a wounded animal on the forest floor. She can get away. All she has to do is run. She runs. This is what it means to run for your life. She reaches the house, soaked through, panting like a deer, but alive. The moment she walks in the doorway, she senses something's wrong. What is it? She turns, as Jonny's axe falls to kill her.

He misses, his own weight crashing him to the floor. He's hit his head and lies unconscious. She can see a man bending over him. Breeches, tweed jacket, heavy moustache. He looks round at her, his eyes triumphant with malice.

'Who are you?' she asks.

'Edwin, miss, don't you remember me?' He is insolent, cocky. He takes a step towards her. She holds up her hand.

'It's over,' she says. 'I love him.'

Edwin's outline is wavering. The mist of him hovers over Jonny's body.

Max unlaces the boots, pulls them free of Jonny's legs and throws them into the corner. She lifts his feet onto her knees, rubbing them to revive the circulation. Her tears are warm.

How long are they there? A day, a week, a month, forever?

When Jonny comes round, it's the early hours of the morning. His body is freezing. He tries to sit up, wincing. By the light of the dismal bulb, he sees Max lying across his legs. What has happened? He can't remember.

His movement stirs her. She sits up. He sees her clothes are filthy, her face bruised and soiled. They crawl towards each other, holding each other, rocking back and forth, and somehow they get to one of the single beds and lie down again, him pulling the blanket over them both.

The next afternoon, one of them wakes, makes coffee,

brings it to the other; neither can speak. He touches her hand, they hold each other's hands, sitting knee to knee, heads bent.

Two days later her sister comes. Alex had found the letter by the abandoned bicycle and posted it. Her sister, opening the letter before work, does not hesitate. She feels the dread she felt when their mother killed herself and never came home. She'll make sure that Max comes home.

Jonny goes to give the keys back to the gardener. The gardener's boy looks at the floor. Jonny pats his shoulder, smiling. 'It's time you got yourself a girlfriend!' Alex smiles back. Max goes to hug him. The sun is shining.

Their bags are in the car. They are moving slowly past the laurels that line the drive. There's a movement in the shrubbery as the car reaches the iron gates. Max's sister lifts her hand in temporary recognition.

'Who was that?' asked Jonny, peering out of the back at nothing.

'Oh, he opened the gates for me on the way in. Said he hoped to see you again soon.'

'Well, it can't have been Mr Grumpy!' said Max, squeezing Jonny's hand on the seat.

Her sister swung the car towards the village. 'He said his name was Edwin.'

The Door

Blackdog Castle overlooks the North Sea. Massy, dark, brooding, part-ruined, part-restored, the stone buildings sit hunched around a courtyard. The inner windows are large and light, like blank eyes that stare at each other without expression. The windows facing the sea are narrow and impassive. Weather has worn away the sharp angles of the stone into a blunt face.

An S-bend road leads from the castle to the village that is now a tourist attraction and was once a fishing port. Built in 1360, it is no longer a fortification. The castle is marketed as an 'experience'.

Cook in the medieval kitchen! Dance in a kilt! Return to the eighteenth century! Man the big guns in the Battle of the Skies! Get married!

Blackdog Castle is a wedding venue. Stevie and Amy are getting married here on Friday.

I'm Stevie.

Most of our guests arrived with us on Wednesday. Our celebration is a three-day affair. The castle is remote. Anyone travelling this far deserves a drink.

All of us went out to the only pub that night. On foot.

Winding down the roaming road or roaming down the winding road, to drink whisky in a little low-roofed coaching inn, had a romance of its own. No one wanted to leave the big, bright fire warming the panelled room set with wooden chairs, tables, and a candle on every table. The barman had promised us a story. There's always a story, isn't there? A story of somebody drowned, somebody murdered, somebody who died for love.

'Oh, mine is a love story,' said the barman, 'indeed it is! Like *Romeo and Juliet*.'

The barman was filling up our whisky glasses from an oak cask. No bottles. No measures. His forearms were the size of ox haunches. He wore an earring that glinted above his beard.

'Aye, but mind you, my story is a sad story. When did love stories start to have happy endings? Can you tell me that?'

He has a point. Lancelot and Guinevere. Tristan and Isolde. Dido and Aeneas. Medea. Anna Karenina. Cathy and Heathcliff. Poor Oscar Wilde . . .

'I prefer the sad ones,' said the barman. 'The tale I have to tell has a haunting in it for you too, unless you fear ghosts?'

As he said this, the wind rattled at the window, and everyone laughed. 'Na fear, then, that's guid,' said the barman.

He turned down the lights. He leaned forward. He raised his hand.

'At Blackdog Castle, in the Keep, you will find an

inscription on the wall. You may see it for yourself with your own eyes. It's from the Bible. It says,' (he paused to be sure of our attention), *'Love is strong as Death*.

'Now, why would someone scrape that into the wall, with a knife, the night after a murder?'

I didn't stay to find out. Unnoticed, I slipped away, a dark shadow on a dark night. Weddings are not solitary occasions, but I am a solitary person. I like to see my friends happy and together. And then I slip away.

Are you afraid of the dark? Not me. It's a relief from electric light. From the relentlessness of our lives. Out here, I can hear the roaring of the sea. The sky above is like a black beach set with shining stones.

What's that?

Two stars. Are they shooting stars? Brighter than the rest, holding my gaze. They should be dropping and disappearing now, but they are not. Perhaps they are satellites.

Of love.

Why not?

I returned to the castle. A single figure in a single space.

Amy and I had separate rooms. An old-fashioned custom and a good one. We would create the space where we longed to be, and then find it, on our wedding night. Our gift to each other.

My room was in the oldest part of Blackdog Castle. The stone walls were hung with long, thick tapestries. A single electric light overhead had little effect on the resolute blackness that occupied the room.

I switched on the bedside lamp, an ugly iron thing, so heavy I could barely shuffle it nearer to my book. I put on my pyjamas and got into bed. Mercifully, the bed was warm, and soon I was reading *A History of Scottish Ghosts*.

Blackdog Castle boasted the expected list of clankers and chain-rattlers, disembodied sporrans and floating bonnets. There was a monk, a priest, a maiden, a warrior, and the story of two lovers who had perished in the sea on their wedding night.

Nothing about a murder.

The barman, it seems, has an eye for business. My eyes are closing. I'm tired and happy.

Then I heard it. What's that?

'Go through and never come back!' A man's voice. Nearby. Outside.

I got out of bed and went into the bathroom that overlooks the road to the village. I pushed open the narrow window and leaned out. Wind. Cold. The sound of the sea. Far down on the track were two wavering lights making their way towards the castle. It must be two of our guests coming home from the pub.

Yes, that's right. I smiled to myself.

It's so quiet here that noises carry far. They must be joshing each other. It's horseplay, tipsy revellers, perhaps retelling the story they just heard. I must find out the gory version in the morning. I wonder if Amy is in her room yet?

I padded back into my bedroom to look across the courtyard towards her low light shining behind the drapes. Yes, she's there. There's nothing to fear.

A terrific crash made me cry out. The room went dark. I heard glass breaking. As I turned around, I saw the bathroom window, open under the moon, like a cut in the night.

The wind had funnelled itself through the sullen gap with enough force to bowl over the iron lamp. I moved slowly forward, banging my body against the wall in an effort to find the single main switch.

That's when I saw it – in a moment of moonlight – the outline of – what's that? A figure? In the bedroom? With me?

Footsteps in the corridor. The footsteps halt at my bedroom door. My bedroom door is opening. An inch. A chink. Wider. My heart is beating like a trapped rabbit. Coming in, slow, unsteady . . . lit-up, a short, bulky shape.

'What the . . . ?'

There's a burst of laughter. It's Tommy. Drunk Tommy, whose room is next to mine. 'Stevie! Why are you standing in the dark in your pyjamas?'

'Oh! You arse!'

'Sorry! Wrong room!'

Tommy is wearing a head torch. He comes in. We close the window. Between us we right the lamp. The bulb is broken – that's all.

'Everything all right?'

'Thanks, Tommy, just the wind. Good time?'

He hugs me, leaning heavily on my shoulder.

'Better get some sleep.'

Next door, I hear him fall on the bed. These bed springs are like accordions. My heart is nearly steady now. My eyes are closing. Only faintly do I imagine the sound of a pistol.

The next morning the first thing I do is go to Amy's room. 'How was your night?' I kiss her.

She's sitting up in bed drinking scalding tea. The weather is squally. The sun is barely risen. It seems that we both woke early.

Amy said, 'Someone came into my room last night.'

'It wasn't me!'

'The rain woke me. I think it was the rain. But then someone was sitting on the edge of my bed, looking at me.'

'How do you know that?'

'We all know when we are being looked at.'

'It was dark.'

'No – it wasn't. It should have been dark, but it wasn't. That's what was strange. In the dark there was an impression.'

'An impression of what?'

'A person.'

'Well, if it's any comfort, Tommy came crashing into my room last night. Frightened the life out of me. He was drunk.'

'I was drunk,' said Amy, 'but not when I woke up.'

'Did you go back to sleep?'

'Yes, but as I turned over, my foot pushed against a solid weight.'

'Your handbag on the bed?'

'What do you imagine I keep in my handbag?'

We hugged each other. I thought she was fine now. But she said, 'There was someone in the room. I am sure.'

I held her as tight as I could. 'We didn't come here to be frightened. Was it the story the barman told you?'

Amy looked at me. 'Let's go and see the inscription. In the Keep.'

'What, now? Don't you want to stay here with me?'

'I want you to come with me. Go and get dressed.'

She kissed me. Her eyes are grey, like the sky over the sea today, and behind them, not always visible, but always there, is the sun.

I went back to my room. No one else is awake. Quick shower. Go in the bathroom. It's fully light now, and I notice what I didn't notice an hour ago: on the floor there's a brass button. A button from a military uniform. It's dirty, pitted, like it's been buried. There's something written in the roundel. I'll clean it up when we get back.

Amy and I walked hand in hand through the courtyard arch and towards the castle Keep. Seabirds dipped overhead, their lonely cries like voices in the air. 'They are guillemots,' said Amy. She likes birds. She can identify them. We are walking in step. I know her so well, yet I don't want to get used to her. I don't want to lose her specialness to habits of thought. She squeezes my hand as if she can read my mind.

Love is strong as Death.

There it is. There's the inscription.

We traced the letters with our fingers as though the

message had been written in Braille. The letters, some deep, some shallow, were not the work of time and leisure, but done quickly, like graffiti, like anger. That's what I felt; anger.

'I'm cold,' said Amy. I wrapped my scarf round her throat.

There was a flight of stone stairs in the Keep that led to a door. I went up, rattled the handle. The door wouldn't open. Returning, it felt oppressive to me, this place. Claustrophobic. Too small for itself. Where was Amy?

'AMY!'

'OUTSIDE!'

I went out, stepping through the tough, high grass to find her. She was looking upwards. There was the door – the other side of the door, that led to nothing. To a sheer drop down the cliff. It was fenced off. But what was it? A door that leads nowhere.

'Go through and never come back!'

'What was that?' Amy was looking at me oddly. 'What did you say?'

'Nothing. I didn't say anything.'

'I heard you. Stop trying to frighten me! You're supposed to love me!'

I was bewildered. 'I do love you.' (What's she talking about?)

'Then fight for me! Fight for me!'

'Amy?'

Amy was the one confused now. 'I don't know why I said that.'

I took her hand. 'What is it?'

She said, 'Perhaps it was the story. Shall I tell you?'

I nodded.

Amy began. 'She was a young girl from a wealthy family. He was a soldier. Poor, young and handsome. She was expected to marry the local landowner. Instead, she and the soldier fell in love when she met him here, by chance, at the garrison. They planned to run away together, but they were caught and killed.'

'It says in my book of Scottish ghost stories that they jumped off the cliff hand in hand – for love.'

'Rory says they were murdered.'

'Who's Rory?'

'The barman! He says it's a gruesome tale of murder. Their spirits will haunt this place till wrong is made right.'

'MUURDAH! That's how he says it, with two "U"s, a rolling "R" and the "DAH" like a stabbing.'

'Are you trying to cheer me up?'

'Yes! He must tell that story every week of the year.'

'I know . . . but it's that door. It's horrible. The door that leads nowhere.'

'Whatever happened, it was a long time ago. Maybe that's what haunting is: time trapped in the wrong place.'

'Are we being haunted?'

'No! We're getting married. Come on! Shall we go and get breakfast?'

The rain came then, suddenly, and heavily, out of nowhere. We had no choice but to return to the Keep for shelter. Coastal weather is unexpected. I could see how fast the clouds were moving. Soon we could go and find toast and kippers and more hot tea. I put my arms round

Amy. She rested her head on my shoulder. I was looking inwards, towards the staircase, towards the door. Does the door open when we are born, to let us into this life? We won't notice it again until we are done, until it's there at the top of the stairs, waiting for us, our entrance then, our exit now.

Amy, you and I are real. We are here now. For this brief time in the world, we exist. But if you go first, I won't be able to find you; I'll run my hands over the wall where the door used to be, as I used to run my hands over your body, the openness of you, the door you opened for me, so unexpected and welcome. The door into the sun.

Stay for me there . . .

What's that?

You said, 'I like your hands on my hip bones.'

I felt a chill run through me when she said that. I had moved my arms from her body down to my sides when I sensed a movement behind me. Then, distinctly, into my shoulder blades, I felt the pressure of a head. Someone was leaning on me from behind. Leaning on me, their arms round my body, and their hands on Amy's hips. I kept still as a hunted animal, my mouth dry with fear.

Then Amy said, 'Look! The rain has stopped.'

She pulled away gently. She seemed not to know what had just happened. What had just happened? As we walked into the weak sunlight, I made myself look back. There was nothing there. Nothing, of course not, and what did I expect to see?

*

After breakfast, Amy had an appointment with the reverend who is marrying us. Amy is not religious in a churchgoing way; she is spiritual. We agreed to meet later in the day.

I went back to my room, hanging up my jacket – it's a tan woollen peacoat, double-breasted with a yoke across the shoulders. I haven't had it for long. As I took it off, I saw that the brown lining inside, where the yoke sits, had faded to beige, patchy beige, like the coat had lain outdoors for too long. The fading was strange. The only way I can describe it is to say, well, I suppose it was head-shaped.

It looked like what happens to a coffin lining as the head releases fluid. That's why crimson linings were popular in the nineteenth century. The custom of the open coffin for three days – sometimes longer – could be problematic unless fluids and blood were drained from the body, and that took time, skill, and money. It was easier to line the coffin in a colour that didn't register the speed of decay.

This makes me sound creepy. I am a medical doctor.

I examined my coat. There were no marks on the outside. As I rubbed at the staining with my fingers, the lining fell away. That's what it did. Crumbled to dust.

There must be an explanation. The dry cleaner? I had it cleaned for the wedding before we left. I didn't check it. I just put it on. There's no other explanation. There is no other explanation that is acceptable to me.

That's my phone ringing. More guests arriving. This is a happy time. Nothing else matters.

*

It was after lunch that I saw Amy walking back towards the castle. At her side was someone I didn't recognise, wearing a red coat and long boots.

'Who was that?'

'I had lunch with Sarah.'

'The young man walking beside you as you came towards the castle.'

'There was no one, Stevie. Stop it! I know this is a game you're playing.'

'No . . . truly . . . I . . .'

'You're making me uneasy.'

'I am?'

She was frowning. 'It's as if I am trying to remember something. Something I never knew. I feel a bit crazy. So don't wind me up.'

'Honestly – look, I was mistaken.'

She smiled her Amy-smile and kissed me. 'Oh, let's have a drink. It's the party tonight!'

We went to my room and I gave her a whisky. 'I found this,' I said.

I showed her the brass button. She looked at it intently. 'Where was it?'

'In the bathroom – no idea how it got there. I meant to clean it.'

Amy went to the tap. I could hear her with the hot water and nail brush. She came back into the bedroom, drying the button on some loo paper. We sat together on the bed, the accordion springs playing a tune. 'I don't think this is the right bed for a wedding night . . .' I said.

Amy wasn't listening to me. '*Semper Amour.* What does that mean?'

'Love Always. Always Love. It's a sign for you and me. For us. It's a wedding present.'

Amy didn't reply. Her fingers played with the button.

'Do you mind if I keep it?'

'Keep it! It's yours.'

'Yes,' she said, 'I think it is mine.'

I found that odd, but I didn't reply.

That night the whole castle was lit up. We had booked a band called The DeLoreans – something about going back to the future. They were a great seven-piecer with a brass section. Everyone was dancing, drinking, laughing, all the things you do before a wedding. Tomorrow I would marry Amy.

Where was she? I felt her absence – and it wasn't quite right.

We had danced, and I had gone to get water, leaving her spinning round with a couple of our girlfriends. Now I was looking for her, not finding her, and I felt nervous. Wedding nerves, that's all.

The ballroom had wide windows that opened into the courtyard – a courtyard lit with lanterns and flares. Lots of the guests had gone out to cool off. She's out there, I guess. As I went into the courtyard, I saw him again. I saw the figure in the red knee-length coat and long boots. He was standing still by the arch that leads outside the castle.

There was Amy. He turned. She set off to follow him. Is this someone she used to know?

There are stories, aren't there, and they don't have happy endings? Stories of a past that only one person in the couple knows anything about.

We'd only been together a year. He was with her this afternoon. She had denied it. Am I a fool? Does she love him?

I began to run to follow them.

Outside the courtyard the land was dark. Behind me were lights, warmth, safety. In front of me ... what? Should I turn away? Forget this?

I could see the two of them clearly. They weren't walking together. He was ahead. He moved so quickly. I kept my pace at a steady jog, near enough to see, not too near for attention.

He went inside the Keep. Amy was standing, hesitating, uncertain. I caught up with her. I was defensive. 'What's going on?'

She shook her head. She didn't speak. Her eyes were glazed over – as if she was in a trance. I snapped my fingers. 'Amy?'

Then I did something I never thought I would do. I shook her by the shoulders. She shrugged me off. She didn't answer. She walked into the Keep.

The Keep was lit with tallow-flares. Fat dripped down the walls. The young man in the red coat was looking wildly around. He didn't seem to see us. He came towards me. I pushed him. It had no effect. He moved his hand as though he felt a rush of air against his face.

We're ghosts, I thought. We're not here at all.

The cold I felt was not the weather or the temperature.

There was a noise behind me. A small, slight woman in a cloak and hood ran into the Keep.

'Kate!' The young man's face changed as he saw her enter. There was no mistaking the love. They embraced.

'It is too dangerous,' he said. 'Leave me.'

Kate kissed him on the mouth. 'I will never leave you! If you love me, fight for me!'

He took out a ring and put it on her finger. They knelt together and began to recite their wedding vows . . .

With this ring, I thee wed. With my body, I thee worship . . .

I glanced at Amy. She was swaying slightly from side to side. Her eyes still had the same glazed look. I was afraid she was in a catatonic trance and that to wake her would injure her.

I moved to be close to her. The two young people went on with their vows, and I felt that we were witnesses.

But before they could conclude, a posse of men burst into the Keep. The men were armed. The boy reached for his pistol, but he was immediately overpowered.

'Run!' he shouted to Kate. She did not run.

The men tied his hands, shoving him ahead of them towards the stairs. One of the thugs undid the boy's hair, mussing it with his big fists. He ripped open his red coat. I saw a button fall to the floor. Then it was his shirt that was torn off him, to reveal a bound chest.

They soon had those bandages off too. The fat one ran his hands over the slender, naked, shivering body.

'Pretty little miss, ain't you, fine sir?'

Hair down, breasts naked, the boy who's a girl aimed a kick at her molester. It landed directly between his legs. He doubled over in pain, then lunged out in anger at the boy's face, cutting their lip with a blow. Kate ran forward, but she was knocked back, one of them pinning her arms behind her as they marched her lover up the stairs. Kate was shouting, 'Death will not part us! Love is strong as . . .'

A single gunshot to the head. They pushed the boy-girl through the door that opens into time. I could smell gunpowder, acrid and smoky. 'Go through and never come back!'

And then it was done. The flares went out. The Keep was plunged into darkness.

I stood still, blinded by the dark. 'You saw them, didn't you?'

A voice. A flashlight. Rory, the barman. 'I knew you would see them.'

At the sound of his voice, Amy seemed to come to herself. She was blinking and shaking her head. I saw beads of sweat on her forehead, despite the cold. Rory took a hip flask from his pocket and passed it amongst us to swig. I have never been so glad of the warming taste of whisky. When we had done, he put it away, his hands in his pockets.

'The stories are not always told,' he said. 'That boy – born a girl – ran away to be a soldier, and nobody knew the truth about him, because he was brave and bold, nobody suspected a thing, not till he fell in love with Kate. Kate didn't care. She loved him. How it was all found out, I don't know. That never came to light. But what did come to light was enough to ruin them both.'

'What happened to Kate?' asked Amy.

'Kate was kept here for the night, all alone, in the cold and the dark, to come to her senses. Oh aye, they imagined she would be ready to behave herself by the next morning. It was during the night that she carved the inscription with her knife.'

'This isn't the story you told in the bar!'

Rory shrugged. 'I tell the official version in the bar. The one the tourists like to hear. Now, d'ye wish to hear the end?'

We nodded.

'The next day, the men went back, and she seemed quiet enough. She asked to look out over the sea – to say goodbye. "Will ye not give me leave to say goodbye?"

'They let her up there, they did, thinking it was a kindness. She stood for a moment, then she flew off the side of the Keep like a black guillemot, her dark hair spread out behind her like the sea. Her heart flew to be with his spirit. Her body broke on the rocks below.'

We were silent, listening to this. Amy said, 'Why us? Why have we seen this?'

Rory shrugged again. 'You two are getting married tomorrow.'

'Lots of people get married here.'

'Aye. They do. Yet you are the first two women to

marry at Blackdog Castle . . . since the first pair who tried their best and were killed for it.'

'I wish we could change the past,' I said, 'but most people wish that.'

'You could invite them to your wedding,' said Rory.

'They're dead!'

'That never stopped anyone,' said Rory.

We walked back towards our party. Amy was quiet. She had no memory of leaving the party to go to the Keep.

'There's a theory about memory,' I said, 'that a memory is cognitive information imprinted on neural tissue. A memory is retrieved when some outside stimulus causes the neuron-set to fire. A memory isn't inside a particular neuron – like a file in a drawer. Memory is interactive. It's a network.'

'Is the memory itself in the Keep? Haunted place working as a memory store?' Amy wondered.

'Maybe, but that would make memory what it isn't – something stored in a drawer. The haunted place being the drawer that holds the memory – static.'

'No, you're wrong,' said Amy. 'Not everyone has a haunted experience even in the most haunted places. It depends on who is there, as well as the place itself – it's not static. There has to be an interaction. Like Rory said, we are the ones who saw this.'

'So, what do we do now?'

'Invite them?'

'Yes.'

'How?'

'Same as anyone else. Ask them. You should do it. You have the connection.'

The following morning Amy and I were married.

Our friends stood in a circle around us. She and I were facing each other. Over her shoulder, standing behind her, I could see the soldier in the red coat. I almost turned my head to look behind me, but Amy nodded, meeting my eyes, telling me what I knew; that behind me stood the woman, with her dark hair spread out like the sea.

We walked that night out to the Keep. Amy stood on the cliff edge and threw the brass button into the waves.

In bed together, later, we knew we were alone.

JW2: Unexplained

I was five years old when my grandmother died.

She slept in a bed in the sitting room downstairs, and I used to get up before anyone else, to go down and be with her, climbed on the bed. Throat cancer meant she couldn't speak, so we looked at Bible story picture books together, and I read to her. I wasn't at school then, but my mother had taught me to read at an early age. Words were my friends.

One morning, Grandma got out of bed and went to the big bay window overlooking the garden. This was my grandfather's house. Our own house was a terraced house – a row house – with just a rear yard. My mother was nursing Grandma through her cancer, and so we all moved into Grandad's house. It was an unhappy, tense time. My mother hated her father, and he hated having us in the house. But he could save money on hiring a nurse, cook, and cleaner. The one thing everyone enjoyed was the roses. Old-fashioned, scented English roses.

Grandma spoke. She couldn't speak but she spoke. 'Look at the Queen of Denmark.'

I scrambled off the bed and went to the window. We stood together. She touched my head. Then, she walked through the window, into the garden, and along the rose hedge. It was so natural. There she was, in the garden, among the flowers she loved.

I heard someone coming downstairs. It was my mother. I ran into the hall and told her that Grandma was in the garden with the Queen of Denmark. At that moment the telephone on the hall table began to ring. This was in the 1960s, but the telephone was from the 1920s. My mother was born in 1922, and she said she remembered when the family motor business got the telephone. The style was called a Sit Up and Beg.

My mother picked up the receiver and the base; speaking and listening were in two parts on those telephones.

'Hello. Woodfield House. Hello?'

There was no one there. We went into the sitting room. Grandma was in bed.

Grandma was dead.

My parents were wartime parents. My father had been in the D-Day Landings. My mother was an air-raid warden. Twenty-five years before the war experiences of my parents, my grandad had fought in the First World War. I lived with two generations of traumatised adults who had been taught to laugh it off and carry on. They all had tales of the Dead. All of them, without sensationalism, told me stories of being visited by a wartime pal, or loved one, only to discover later that the person was already dead.

I accepted these stories as children do accept what grown-ups tell them. At the same time, I had (and have) a vivid imagination. Like most children I didn't fully distinguish between living and non-living objects. My teddy bear was as important to me as my cat. My grandma's behaviour on the day of her death seemed like part of everything else – a world not clearly divided, but entangled. So, what did happen that day? I know I wasn't frightened, and I can still see the scene clearly.

It may be that as we pass from one state to another – even if that subsequent state is oblivion – we have a rare period of non-body presence. We are not yet dead, but we are not body-dependent.

Perhaps my grandma was thinking of the rose garden as she sensed that she was leaving her body behind – and perhaps her thought was powerful enough to transmit to me. Children are wonderfully receptive to thought-visions. It may be that what they 'see' are powerful mental projections.

Or it may be that the imprint of a person can escape from their mortal self for a time. Shamans certainly believe that. I don't say 'soul' or 'spirit' because those words imply immortality, or at least an onward destination. 'Imprint' measures only the moment of appearing, with no conjecture as to what might happen next.

If the Dead are present, contact with the living seems to happen at times of heightened stress – either for an individual, or for a whole country. The number of ghost-sightings during any war, anywhere, is extraordinary – and whether or not you believe any of it, the phenomenon itself is worth some thought. My parents were religious and believed in an afterlife. For them, ghost-sightings were to be expected, and perhaps sent by God to help the living with their loss.

My mother told me she had talked with Grandma on two occasions in the following week. This comforted her. The obvious explanation is that her longing made the experience seem real. Humans are pattern-makers. We make patterns with other people in our lives. We are enmeshed. Break-ups mess with the pattern. Death is a break-up of a relationship, and with it, a part of the self.

What do I think? What do I believe? I don't know – and that's the best answer I can give. I do know that scrubbing away all traces of the supernatural hasn't worked too well for the human psyche. There is a valve, a pressure release, that comes with being able to say, 'I can't explain this.' It's not anti-science, it's not superstitious.

Many of us have experienced telepathy – even the simple kind, when we think of a friend a second before she calls. We can't explain it, any more than we can explain the felt presence of the recently dead. Perhaps what we sense is not the ghost of the person but the ghost of the pattern.

The Queen of Denmark is the name of a beautiful English rose with a powerful scent. After Grandma died, my mother cut bunches of our abundant roses to fill the room. When I was in a position to have a garden of my own, I bought that shrub rose, and planted it. I too love old-fashioned English roses, but more than that, it is a living connection to an event I can't forget and I can't explain. What comforts me about my story is not the belief in life after death, but the fact that a bed-bound and exhausted woman was on her feet, and happy.

If death frees us from the prison of the self, even for a second, before we meet with oblivion, then death is more than a biological event. It might not be a bridge to else-where, but perhaps it can be a blessing.

PEOPLE

No Ghost Ghost Story

What kind of a ghost story has no ghost?

Towards the end of your life, you promised me that if it were possible, you would send a sign, a sign to let me know that somewhere out there is the person I love. A person recognisable as you.

I am sitting at my garden table watching the night. As I type this, I hope the keyboard starts to type by itself – a Ouija board with Wi-Fi.

Every night I want to be Heathcliff with Cathy tapping at the window. I want to be Hamlet on the windy battlements. I want the *Flying Dutchman* to dock. I want what everyone who has lost someone wants: a visitation.

Every second, someone dying is promising to come back from the dead. Every hour, waiting for it to happen, someone living notches up another hour lost.

For the Dead, time stops. For the living, time slows. I am in slow-motion now. It takes me twice as long to clean my teeth, half the morning to make coffee and wash the cup. When I go shopping, I don't remember what I need.

That's because it's you I need. I stare at the bag of potatoes, the packet of bacon. Absurd. Go home.

How could I not go on talking to you? How could I not expect to see you when it's the end of the day? Our life together was many things, concrete, tangible things, that included bacon, potatoes, coffee and toothpaste, but it was also a pattern. We had flow, colour, texture. We were the originators and makers of the shared life that we worked on every day. Now, I have to work on it alone. What I have are memories. The past. The present is no longer a work in progress.

Soon after you died, I went to visit a medium. Madam Sheila. She asked me to bring a personal item of yours, so I brought your favourite cashmere scarf, the one with moth holes.

'Yes,' said Madam Sheila, holding the scarf. 'I can see your partner clearly.' (She was looking at a photograph of the two of us.) 'Your partner is laughing. You both laughed a lot together, didn't you?'

The session went on like this for nearly an hour. Trite, predictable, everything you would have hated. I didn't feel comforted, only disappointed and upset.

'I hope this has been some help,' said Madam Sheila, as she placed the cash in a drawer.

'I don't believe in the Afterlife,' I said.

'Then why did you come here?'

I didn't answer. I turned to go, hating the low light overhead, and the shiny testimonials on the wall.

'Don't forget your scarf!' she called, standing up, handing it to me. She squeezed my hand. She means well, I suppose.

I took the scarf, went slowly down the stairs. There was the next customer, sitting on the single upright chair in the hallway, by the communal front door, staring at his shoes on the carpet tiles. He looked up. 'Did she help you? She's highly recommended. I can't afford her, but she is recommended.'

'Yes,' I smiled at him, 'she did help me.'

The man's face lit up. 'I only want to talk to Ann again,' he said. I touched his arm and left.

Out on the street, the day in full busyness, the city indifferent to the micro-lives of its citizens, I was too trapped in thought to notice the bus as I stepped out in front of it. The bus driver started shouting at me, and I stood, looking at him, his mouth open, his eyes close together, a face full of anger. I couldn't say what I wanted to say: It doesn't matter. Alive or dead, it doesn't matter.

I sat down on the steps of some municipal building, twisting the scarf round and round my hands. Madam Sheila has helped me – helped me to realise my own foolishness. There is nothing when we are gone – at least nothing that means anything to those left behind. Dead is gone. But still we hope.

The minister who conducted your funeral came to see me. We knew her, a little, and I don't doubt her sincerity. She's edgy too, not tea and biscuits clergy.

Nevertheless, she wants me to believe that God will take care of both of us – you up there and me down here, I suppose – but as God has not been taking care of us so far, why start now? She looks patient, in the patient way that impatient people do, and she says that people are unaware of how many times an invisible hand guides them or protects them. She wonders, perhaps, am I a little too crude in wanting a sign?

This offends me, but my spirits are so low, I can't rally to my own defence. 'Life is not a movie,' she says, 'and God is not a special effect.'

I still have enough about me to remind her that the Old Testament is stacked with stories starring God as a Special Effect. It's his USP. Appearing as a Burning Bush. Parting the Red Sea. Flooding the World. The God I read about is extravagant, a show-off, and not on a budget. The New Testament isn't much more toned down. What are miracles, if not special effects?

That's not what she means. She looks pained. The clergy have a particularly pained look when they look pained. So, what does she mean?

'We trust our senses and we trust our intellect. If religion has any value, it lies in its intuition that there is a supra-sensory, meta-minded way of knowing – and what is known in that way cannot be known in any other way.'

'Do you believe in ghosts?'

'I have never seen a ghost.'

'That must be disappointing, in your line of work.'

'But I have felt the presence of others, many times.'

'Wishful thinking.'

'As I said, go beyond the senses, go beyond the mind.'

'Too mystical for me.'

'Why should the Dead be there for us?'

'You're right. They are gone.'

'That's not what I said,' she said.

She left me, the sound of her car engine dwindling away. Am I too crude? Must you rattle the window or walk the battlements to be here? For me to believe you are here? I am dimensional. You are not. Is that the real problem? Then, as I was sitting there, guilty and full of self-doubt, I thought about the Resurrection. The keystone of the Christian Church. The vicar's got a nerve.

Why go to all the trouble of physically coming back from the dead, if ordinary, half-hearted, inadequate human beings don't need living proof that death isn't the end of the story?

Death is the end of the story. You are dead and I am not. My mind is turning round and round like a cornered dog. There's no way out of this.

Soup for one tonight. Again.

I want you to come back to me in your strong, safe body. I want to lie down with you without the fear of waking alone. I want to fall asleep with my back turned towards you. I want to feel your hand against my shoulder blades in the ambient warmth of our bed.

Our bed. My friend says I should get a new mattress.

I know that the universe is a closed system and that energy cannot be created or destroyed. That's the first law of thermodynamics – and people misuse it to tell themselves that the Dead have only changed their form. To be alive is to live in a state of low-level entropy – fending off the ultimate disorder of death. Death is disorderly, and your energy, even if I could reach it, will be like listening to a badly tuned radio caught in between stations.

(Shall I have a tin of tomato soup or a tin of mushroom soup?)

I shall not hear your voice again. I shall not see your face. Yet, when I wake, it is your face I see when I open my eyes, and it is you who seems to say to me, 'Come on, get up.' And I do, in the gentleness of the soft sun that feels like hope at first, before the sick sense of loss that thickens in my throat. Sit on the edge of the bed. Breathe. Another day. The sun is gone. Morning hardens on the wall.

Mushroom soup. Bowl. Spoon. Sip. Cold. Oh!

The second law of thermodynamics introduces the concept of heat. Roughly – you can't transfer heat from what is colder to what is hotter. There is heat – even an iceberg generates some heat energy, but it's not a place to warm your hands.

Your body is cold now and will not warm me.

I must heat up the soup.

Do you remember when we met? When we were introduced by a friend who thought we would like each other? When we arranged to take a walk a few days later because we were both too shy to speak to each other at the meal with the friend? I kept glancing at you; eyebrows, eyelashes, hoisted cheekbones, a full, rich, tentative mouth. Tentative because you get nervous in company and don't say much. Long, strong arms rested on the table. Fingers that play the piano. I could see by the way you tore the bread that your fingers would be useful for other things.

I don't know if you looked at me.

On the walk together, we experienced the phenomenon that lovers who are not yet lovers recognise; they are not touching, yet they feel the charge. The space in between is filled with energy. The spark. The dance. The movement. The wave and particle that is everywhere and nowhere, because nothing else is. The strangeness of that early time is common and rare. There is no use seeking it again and again. It happens, perhaps, because we are not solid. The body frees us from the body.

If I hold my hand up to your face, I feel its radiance. I can feel your field. You are more than your dimensional self. I am thinking about this now because I want what came afterwards – even though it was an illusion – the long sensation of your skin.

Touching you. Let me touch you. The strange thing is that I never did – not because we were celibate or germphobic, but because solidity is an illusion. We are made of atoms, and atoms are not cheery little balls that crash into each other like life on a badly built billiard table; they are not 'units' at all. It's better to describe them as probability-spheres – a rowdy collective of electrons, neutrons and protons. Electrons are simultaneously particles (here I am!) and waves (catch me if you can). My electron-cloud can't touch your electron-cloud because there are no hard edges.

Atoms that don't have space between their cloudy

edges-that-aren't-really-edges have become part of one molecule. They are still not touching because they have become the same thing. Is this what happens when couples merge? Is this what happened to us?

And later, oh, much later, when homeliness and daily-ness had become part of our pattern, there was no loss, only a change. The pattern changed because we changed it. Usable energy stayed constant.

This time the pattern changed because you changed it. You had no choice. Death puts an end to choice. And yet, you were ready to die (so tired and thin), whereas I was not ready for your death. For the first time in a long time, we were out of step. That was a jolt. I got backache.

It's not that I dislike being alone. I like being alone. I dislike not being with you. I cannot bear the days that must pass before we reach – before I reach – the first anniversary of your death.

I ask myself why it was easy to say goodbye to you for two years when you took a job abroad, knowing that we would write letters and speak on the phone, but rarely see each other – this was long before Zoom, and when email was webmail, and looked like text cut out and sent by a stalker who hated punctuation. We found that the phone calls made us sad, and we never knew what to say, because each was living a life that the other couldn't share, so we stopped the calls, agreeing to write letters only.

It was common, before air travel, for loved ones to separate for months and years on end. Overseas postings, military service, missionary work, adventure, the merchant navy, emigration. A bad debt could send a man fleeing for the boat-train. A broken heart was the quickest way to go abroad. People said goodbye, never knowing when, or if, they would see their loved one again.

I am not talking about war, or the fear war brings, only about ordinary life. The earlier back in time we travel, the further the distances become. In the 1700s the fastest journey time from Plymouth, England to Sydney, Australia was a hundred days. With the weather against you, that could stretch to four months. Arrive. Write a letter. Months later the letter reaches home. How long since you heard a word? Maybe the best part of a year.

When the *Mayflower* set off down the Thames, in 1620, to find a new life in the New World, the voyagers endured ten weeks of daily sermons, seasickness and salt-biscuits before Cape Cod came into sight.

People who didn't live as long as we do – people who were often dead in their fifties – understood both distance and apartness in a way that we don't. All travel is time travel.

So, I try to think of this absence from you as a long separation. I must take care of the house and garden, and I am trying my best. You liked things neat and elegant. Taking care of myself is harder. Laundry, showers, cooking. Why bother? I have nearly run through my cache of clothes.

A separation. Yet I don't imagine we will be reunited – and it would be awkward if we were, don't you think? I am not the one and only person you have loved. Don't laugh at my jealousy. It's all right, I don't mind your colourful past. In fact, it's proper. Life is for living, that's what you always said when I sulked. But tell me this: Who gets to be reunited? Is the Afterlife polyamorous?

And if there were such a thing as an afterlife, or a continuation of some kind, or even a new beginning, do the Dead not forge any further connections? If not, then why not? Is affection entirely to do with biology? That can't be true. It can't be true, because sentient machines are not far off, and they will not be biological entities. But we will forge relationships with them. There will be connections between circuits – my circuit board, because I too am electrical, and the machine's circuit board. The longed-for 'spark' will mean something much more specific.

Oh, but listen, and why would it not be true – if there is such a thing as life after death, perhaps you will meet someone else?

At first that thought is unpleasant. Yet, I want you to be happy.

We didn't split up. You left because the only thing as powerful as love came for you: the Angel of Death. Death is final.

No. Not final. I love you past your death.

I would like a cup of tea. No milk. Go to the store. I wander the aisles – why must they always move things? Life is hard enough without searching for milk. Absurd that the shelves are restocked every day, but you will never come back.

'Don't go!'

'What's that?'

'I'm sorry. I was talking to myself.'

'You OK?'

'Yes. I'm grieving.'

'Oh! Accept my sympathy.'

The Caribbean woman at the checkout isn't embarrassed by me. She's kind and that helps me. The man in his office suit, standing in the queue behind me, stares anxiously into his shopping basket, as though crisps, cornflakes, a microwave curry, and a beer will save him from a tricky human encounter.

He needn't worry. I don't want any human encounters. My mind had slipped back in time, that's all, because the mind has only a slight hold on the present, or perhaps I mean only a slight interest in the present. We're always roaming around in the past or the future. The present is a hard place to live.

I leave the store. I have enough food for one. Your passport has been cancelled. Your bank accounts are closed. Other people are wearing (most) of your clothes. I sold your car – I hate automatics. I had to write DECEASED on a letter the other day. Just posted it back in the box. What's the point? You don't need to apply for a new credit card.

And yet my mind is full of you. If you had never lived, and my mind was full of you – a fantasy figure with whom I am having an intense personal relationship – they'd give me treatment. They'd lock me up for being delusional. As it is, yes, it's an embarrassment.

The black-armband days were easier. It was a sign to say – I am a bit odd. Give me space. Give me time. Grief takes time.

I am grieving. I discover that grieving means living with someone who is no longer there.

Engine roar of a motorcycle. Cars with their windows down, radio blasting. Kids on bikes yelling. Dog barking at a squirrel. Delivery truck's reverse beeping. Tired woman talking too loudly to her child. Child crying. Everyone on their smartphones, earbuds in, living in their alternative world. As I walk back home, another store on the street is closing down. EVERYTHING MUST GO.

That's fine by me. Take it all away. The cars, the people, the goods for sale. Strip it back to the dirt under my feet and the sky over my head. Turn off the soundtrack. Blank the picture. Nothing in between us now. Will I see you walking towards me at the end of the day? The way you did, the way we both did, coming home from work? Hey! I went to get milk! Look up, and we see each other, first far away, and then near. Your gait. The slope of your shoulders. The way you carry your bag so carefully like it's full of water. The energy of you in human form. The atomic shape of your love.

CLOSING DOWN SALE. EVERYTHING MUST GO.

It's gone already.

At home, it's evening. The moon, full and strong. I am walking through mercury, a silver path moving as I move, a liquid that acts like a solid. A soft metal.

We bought this old house together. You were digging, and unearthed a big, industrial cast-iron pump that housed a valve floating on mercury. We drained the mercury and kept it in a glass jar. Sometimes we played with it, which is not health-and-safety conscious, I know, but it was beautiful and fascinating, and we took care not to breathe in the vapour.

Mercury amalgamates with other metals – like gold and silver, tin and copper, one thing becomes another. It's a slippery customer. Called quicksilver. Prized by alchemists and dentists. Mercury can be used to extract gold from iron ore and to bond with silver to fill teeth. Toxic and seductive.

Also, the Messenger of the Gods. And the fastest little planet whizzing round the sun at 107,000 miles an hour.

For those whose life together is not one shiny, sunny thing, and often a mixed blessing, Mercury is the natural ruler. We were not easy, you and I. You were trouble and I am difficult. You were faithless and I am fixed. You said you had struck gold when you met me – but you loved bonds that could be broken – gold dissolves in mercury just as salt dissolves in water – but, in reality, nothing is lost.

Death, though, is a different reality. You are dissolved. Into what? Into time, into space, into the leaky container that is me, who will also dissolve into time, into space. No. 80 on the Periodic Table, you are gone. But before I take up my role as the long-suffering one – the gold-band-wearing survivor who was always there and is still – I am aware that mercury makes possible the extraction of gold from poorer-quality ores. You brought out the best in me.

Tonight, as I came in through the door, I had a mental image of you standing in the kitchen, making toast. You loved toast. You turned and offered me a slice, spread with butter and goat's cheese.

'Yes, please, William. I am so hungry.'

'You aren't eating enough. Put some pasta on the stove.'

I filled the big pan with water. I made pesto last week because it's something we always did, towards the end of the summer, when the basil plants were getting floppy under their own weight and trying to make furry little flower spikes. You used to twist them off with your long fingers, separating the leaves into neat piles, while I pounded the pine nuts. I smiled at you across the kitchen. You were wearing that heavy collarless linen shirt I still keep in the wardrobe. You look well, not thin and tired, not at the end. Yes, I could have a glass of wine. I haven't had anything to drink since you died. Don't want to turn into an alcoholic.

'Oh, for Heaven's sake, Simon!'

'Is that where you are? In Heaven?'

'Just open a bottle of red and grate the Parmesan.'

I know you aren't in the kitchen. I know that this conversation isn't taking place, but something is taking place. The moon is shining in through the skylights, like she's watching what happens, and I am going to put some music on. All I hear these silent days is the clock ticking.

Keep the house and garden going. But I can't be both

of us. I have to let you go. I'm begging you to be with me, to be real, to be present, begging you in a way I never would have done if you had left me for another person. I'm the one who is living like I'm dead – not eating, not drinking, not sleeping, not working. When they lifted your body off the catafalque I went with you – burying my heart with yours.

I put my hand on my heart. It's still beating. 'You know,' I said, 'I have thought about killing myself. I kept enough morphine. Told the hospital it was all gone. To be dead feels cleaner, kinder, the best way to stop living in this haunted house.'

'There is no haunted house,' you said. 'I am not here. Don't step out towards death like it's a speeding car.'

How neat you are. How perfect. Entropy is a measurement of disorder – but of the two of us, I am the one who is disordered. My shirt has soup down the front.

Dear love, you would hate to see me like this.

I put the spaghetti into the pan – it's a fancy pan with a perforated inner sleeve that lifts out to drain off the water. You were a serious cook. You said that part of being serious about something was to have the best you could afford. When you were young you saved up for a knife. It's still sharp.

There's time for a shower while the pasta is cooking. Hot water. Clean shirt. There's one left, and it's yours. It's the one you are wearing, or would be wearing if you were a ghost, though why do ghosts wear clothes when they have no body? Is it so that we can see them?

'Simon! There's no ghost. I'm not here!'

'That's all right, William, don't worry. I'm not going to set the table for two – but I am going to set it for one. Do you see? Not soup in a bowl on my knee.'

I won't get over you. I don't want to get over you. You're not a high spiked fence in the way of the rest of my life, but that's just it – there is the rest of my life, and it's the most valuable thing I have. I would gladly have given it in place of yours, but that was not the bargain offered. To honour you is to live. To love you is to live.

There's the pasta steaming in the bowl. My first proper hot meal in weeks I don't want to count.

You promised to send a sign, if you could, and every day I have thought about what you promised, looking for the sign, and forgotten what I promised you, your eyes on mine, the light in them fading as stars fade at daybreak.

I promised you I would live. Not a half-life, not a haunted life, not a shadowlife.

I'm saying all this out loud – as if you are here and in the kitchen with me, just as before. The music – I'll put some music on, what would you like?

I'm about to find some Rickie Lee Jones when my radio starts to glow. It's a valve-amp I restored. I know the electrical circuits can be dodgy, but I haven't switched it on. It's warming up. Buzzing. What time is it? After midnight. Have I been talking to you all this time?

I feel like both of us are in the same body.

The thing about those useful laws of thermodynamics is that love is left out of the calculation. You cannot transfer energy to me – I am warm and you are cold – but the valves are lit up and my hands are spread out in front of them like a blaze.

I can't explain this. I say your name, again and again, and it merges with the shipping forecast on the radio, as though you are some far-away place with your own weather. An imaginary island. A coordinate for me.

And later, lying down, watching the street lamp like a lighthouse outside the window, I feel my eyes closing in sleep. Is that your hand on my forehead? It can't be so, but it is so.

The Undiscovered Country

'*Atlantic low expected 200 miles west of southern Rockall 972 by midnight.*'

Simon and I were listening to the shipping forecast. I could not speak but I could still hear words. '*Sole. Lundy. Fastnet. Irish Sea.*'

You were holding my hand. The warmth of you was strong against my skin. As I listened to what I knew so well, the radio chanting our night-after-night ritual, the words began to falter. They were no longer words but sounds. Then, your hand strong in mine, as though you were trying to pull me out of the water, the sounds themselves ebbed, and what was left was the deep whoosh of the sea, as it is when you hold a shell to your ear. I was lying at the bottom of the sea, underneath the shipping forecast.

'William? William?'

No lights, no angels, no trumpets, no tunnels, no relatives, or friends floating forward to greet me. My name. The last human thing left to me.

I felt you closing my eyes.

*

I am a cadaver. A special zone. A protected habitat for necrophagous insects. As Carl Linnaeus put it in 1776, 'Three flies could consume a horse cadaver as rapidly as a lion.'

I am glad it is winter.

We agreed that I am to be buried. So long as there is no coffin, burial benefits the soil. Every dry kilo of my body mass will return 32g of nitrogen, 10g of phosphorus, 4g of potassium, and 1g of magnesium to Mother Earth. It's the least I can do. She has been good to me. I shall be laid in wicker that will decompose faster than I will.

The undertakers lowered the coffin down on the straps. Simon threw in the last rose of winter.

Do you see me, my clothes with mould on them, my body busy with life that isn't mine?

It doesn't matter. I am gone. End of the show. As an actor you would expect me to be fine with that. Let me tell you, death takes some getting used to – for the Dead as well as for the living.

Still, I was surprised to find Simon visiting a medium. He looked her up on the internet. Trustpilot. Five stars. Madam Sheila.

She told him I am now a being of light.

Simon is an electrical engineer. His hobby is pre-transistor radios – the things with glass valves that light up and glow. He knows that the human body is an electrical circuit – and he knows what happens when the power shuts down.

We all do. At rest, the average human runs on 100 watts of electricity – in theory, you are your own light bulb.

I have gone dark.

Simon sits in the dark so many nights, looking out of the window as the sun goes down. In winter, the sun goes down too soon, and still he sits there, holding between his knees a bowl of soup he barely eats. I wish I could tell him that life is all we have. Turn on the light! Eat the soup!

That said, I never liked soup. But Madam Sheila?

She's not exactly a fraud. She believes she's taking messages from the other side, and that she is in touch with a spirit guide called Colonel Boot.

None of this is the case; she's a good storyteller, that's all. Then again, we're all in the same business, this business of telling stories about our lives. Our genuine inventions.

It's the liars who are the problem.

Madam Sheila is not a liar. She is not perpetrating a fraud for personal gain. So, I can't judge Madam Sheila for telling a story about a story about a story, back and back, as far as you like. Colonel Boot was in the American Civil War, apparently. Unionist side. She doesn't say why he would want to lodge in a carpeted flat over the railway line with Madam Sheila.

Oh, Simon, don't be sad. I can see you sitting on the stone steps of that municipal building, twisting my scarf round and round in your hands. The scarf is as much its moth holes as it is the wool. So much of what is true is in the gaps – is that what the story allows? Gives us a way to see through it?

I used to love those Barbara Hepworth sculptures

made of stone with a hole pierced through. In fact, it is stone shaped round a hole. It is the hole that matters. Surrounded by stone, the hole becomes visible. We can see what God sees. The astonishingness of nothing.

Nothing is made of nothing. Emptiness is full.

What is happening to me now?

Can I put it like that? Happenings happen in time, and I am out of time.

As far as I can tell, I am coming apart. I am an assemblage. A portmanteau. A jigsaw tipped up, pieces all over the floor. Not my body – we are aware of what is taking place down there in the ground. No, not my body. I am not talking about my character or my plot either. I am condensing to paragraphs, sentences, letters. Single letters.

Every alphabet humans use finds its way back to the Phoenician alphabet. The thing about alphabets is that they are adaptable. Twenty-two letters, as it was back then, and look what we did with twenty-two letters.

I am returning to my alphabet state.

Does this mean I am being recycled? Not reincarnated, but maybe the good stuff that I am/was can go to a new home. Not all of me belongs down there in landfill.

'I was born in the year 1632, of a good family, in the city of York, though not of that country, my father being a foreigner of Bremen who settled first at Hull.'

No, that's not me – that's Robinson Crusoe. A fictional character. I am not a character, fictional or not, because I'm no longer a story I can go on telling. If consciousness is an emergent property of mind, then consciousness must fade as mind fades. I can't remember when I was born, or the names of my parents, who, according to the myth, should be standing side by side to greet me, both returned to their prime.

My mother was a drunk and my father was a brute. I remember that. A small child forms simple words from wooden letters.

ME is a simple word but it takes a lifetime to find the words that go with it. I had a library version of myself – a sound hardback copy of ME that the public could borrow and read. And then they were sure that they knew me, and then I felt safe.

Elsewhere, in a drawer, was the ME I was writing, quietly, and alone. It wasn't much of an adventure, though it was a mystery, because what is more mysterious to us than ourselves?

Later, with luck I didn't deserve, I met Simon. I told him some good stories, entertained him, created a character I thought he would like, but one day he said, 'I do like you, but I can't love you until I discover who you really are.'

'The undiscovered country,' I said, embarrassed, playing for time.

He made me sound like a man in disguise. An impostor. It's difficult to come out of hiding.

'I have startled you,' he said. 'Let's start here.'

Taking a pen, he wrote the word START. STARTLED. Then he asked me what should be the next word?

I took the pen. I wrote SHY.

And then, holding the pen, NERVOUS. Other words were less obvious: GOLDFISH.

But perhaps I had been swimming round and round in my bowl for long enough. Or perhaps I felt under scrutiny. Or perhaps I was breaking through the lid of water to your hands above me.

'Or perhaps you would like me to feed you?' said Simon. We laughed. Began again. TRUST.

Letting go of coherence was uncomfortable. Any story is better than no story. For a while I had no story. The one I had told Simon was theatrical but unserviceable. We began something better; better because it felt true.

And now, it seems, I am in that confused place again. Forgetting, unravelling, letting go. A man without a story to tell.

A story without a man to tell it?

In the *Epic of Gilgamesh*, Gilgamesh goes looking for his beloved friend, Enkidu, after Enkidu is dead. When they were both alive, the friends could not be parted. Every night, in the Forest of Cedar, Enkidu built a little house for Gilgamesh to sleep in, while he, Enkidu, *'Like a net, lay himself in the doorway.'*

A net is mostly holes. Look at the state of my body. I am starting to look like my scarf.

But my solid-state was an illusion. Simon, ever the scientist, preferring facts over magical thinking, told me that the average human body contains around 6.5 octillion atoms. (That's twenty-seven zeros – thank you, Simon.)

And atoms are mostly empty space. It's energetically empty space, but it's still empty. I never was a solid man.

But I was alive. That is, I had biological certainty.

As I come apart, remember less, know less, am less, my life isn't flashing before me, it's fading. I am a light out at sea. I am a star disappearing at dawn. I am trying to follow myself and I can't. One thing is clear – whatever death is, it isn't a continuation of self – myself – in the way I imagined my lived-life to be.

Self seems like it's a suit to wear to meetings. I don't need it now.

Maybe, after all, consciousness isn't an emergent property of mind/brain.

Maybe consciousness exists, just as the light spectrum exists. Think of consciousness as part of the reality-spectrum – not unique or separate. I appear to be still conscious – though what it is I am conscious of is changing.

What hasn't changed is my love for you, Simon. But what use is it to you now?

Simon is broken-hearted, in the dark, with a bowl of soup, because I am not a permanent object. Everyone knows this truth. No one can accept it.

Love requires an object. We all need somebody to love. And then, sooner or later, along comes death.

I am an icon now deleted. But not in the trash.

I haven't joined the infinite either. Where the hell am I?

No sign of Hell yet. Fingers crossed, if I had any left.

In so much as I am anywhere, I am with Simon. I've

trailed him all over town, stopping him getting run over by a bus, taken him to the shops to buy food. The lady on the checkout was kind to him. It helps.

Now we're in the kitchen, and I want to get his attention, but nothing I do makes any difference. How is it that all those people posting on the internet see ghosts, yet Simon can't see me?

He doesn't believe in ghosts, is that it?

I sit with him until it's midnight – his time. We're in different time zones now, but I am aware that midnight is supposed to be 'my' hour.

This is when ghosts appear.

I stand at the bottom of the stairs. He walks right through me – as he does so, he runs his hand through his hair, as if he feels something. I touch his face. It's wet. He's crying.

In the bedroom he gets undressed in the same way. Trousers first, then pulls his still-buttoned shirt over his head, like a little boy. I loved his smooth, slight body the first time I saw it, and I still do.

Simon, lie down, don't be afraid. Here I am.

He doesn't lie down. He paces. He goes to the spare bedroom. That's where I died. We agreed it would be too upsetting, at the end, for me to stay in the bed we had shared for so long. He deserves better memories than that. Remember when I first came here? Remember when I moved in? Remember how you swapped sides for me because I need to sleep on my left? Remember my arm over you?

He opens the door to the death-room. He calls my name. I answer him. He doesn't hear.

There's no bedding on the bed. The drapes are closed. The bedside chair is pushed against the wall. The books we had scattered about, reading them together, are in a neat pile. The radiator is turned off. He shivers. Gently, I push him back out of the room. I take his hand. He looks up. 'Is that you, William?'

'Yes.'

He can't hear me. He says, 'Every night I believe you will come.'

'I'm here.'

'I wish I could talk to you.'

'You are talking to me.'

'I know we have reached the last page. Why do I turn it over?'

He gets into his own bed, his knees drawn up, his arms on his knees, his head on his arms. He sobs.

I am so near. I am so far away.

The night-hours collect like rain in a bucket. Time drips so slow. He sleeps fitfully, checks his watch each time he wakes. Sometimes, he turns over towards me – and I wonder, am I closer to him in sleep than I can be in waking? The sleeping body mimics death. The strange unconscious stillness of the night. I will watch over you. I can't protect you, but I am here.

The next day he says to a friend, 'I dreamed of William last night. I dreamed he was with me.'

The friend is a good friend. Yet she's embarrassed. She tells him he's grieving, and that letting me go is part of grieving. She's right, but the fact is, Simon dreamed of me because I was with him.

Undeterred, he writes it down. He writes, 'I would sleep all day if I thought I could be with him.' And then, 'Nothing happened in the dream except that we were together.'

I try to meet him in daylight, but the forces of life are too strong. Day is bright, busy, rushed, and rushing. I find that our best chance together comes when he is lightly sleeping – in the early hours, the REM sleep where dreams happen. I can enter him then, like a room with an open window – a window open onto the night where the traffic between the living and the Dead passes without hindrance. It's not the night that ghosts need, only the lowering of consciousness that night allows. The mind is undefended.

The doctor prescribes sleeping pills. Really, they are anaesthetic in pill form. The Ambien cudgels him into oblivion. He does not dream. He wakes distressed for lack of dreaming – for lack of the dreaming of me.

Friends are concerned. Is he losing his mind? I am dead – rot has made a meal of my body. Meanwhile, Simon barely eats.

One day, out walking, he sees a young man with a cat scooped on his shoulder. For the first time, he's curious. For a few moments, he forgets me. They sit down together on a bench and Simon strokes the cat. The cat is kind to Simon, rubbing its face against his hand, and he looks surprised that his hand has touched a place that is not made of grief.

The young man explains that the cat is a support-animal. Before the cat, he was on antidepressants. Off they go, and Simon watches them, unconsciously stroking his own hand. I try to touch him but he feels only the breeze against his neck. I wonder if there is such a thing as a support-ghost?

That night, he doesn't take the sleeping pill. It's hard for him to fall asleep, but eventually he does, and later, in the small hours, so-called because the world rolls up to a ball, Simon's mind opens, and I slip through the gap.

In the morning he starts eating breakfast again.

This becomes our routine. The dream is the same. I lie with my arm over him. I am the strong body he remembers. Which is strange because I don't remember it at all. I remember Simon remembering me. He is the clear channel. I remember myself less and less. I have the sense that I am disappearing. I am here because I love him. I stay here because he loves me. But it can't last.

What's that you say, Simon?

In this night-soaked bed with you it is courage for the day I seek. That when the light comes, I will turn towards it. Nothing could be simpler. Nothing could be harder. And in the morning, we will get dressed together, and go.

It is our last night. I am faint. I am the bottom-most row of letters on the optician's chart. I can barely see myself.

Simon is in the kitchen, and at least he's having bread with his soup today. I am an amalgam of electric shocks. A short-circuit. This understanding provides me with the last idea I will ever have – and my last words to

Simon. The valve-amp radio he built stands on the kitchen counter. I'm going to make it crackle. I am going to wrap my entirety around it – like jump-starting an old car.

There's a slow glow – and the set is coming to life. It's beginning to hum. If love requires an object, here it is. Simon! Turn around from the soup pan.

The set is tuned to BBC Radio 4. It's 12:48am. *'And now the shipping forecast issued by the Met Office on behalf of the Maritime and Coastguard Agency at 00.48.'*

Simon stares at the radio.

When we were home together, we always listened to the shipping forecast before bed. The lullaby of language.

'Viking. North Utsire. South Utsire. Forties. Cromarty. Forth. Tyne. Dogger. Fisher. German Bight . . .'

Thirty-one sea areas. A strict limit of 380 words.

Simon comes over to the set – stretches his hands towards the valves, now warm and lit up. They hum like a cello string.

'Rockall. Malin. Hebrides. Southwest gale 8 to storm 10 veering west, severe gale 9 to storm 11. Rain then stormy showers. Poor becoming moderate.'

The intonation is steady and modulated. The language, runic. *'Atlantic low 988 expected Faroes 975 by midnight tonight.'*

It's a modernist poem for everyday use. It's a changeful chant. Lying down at night, with the lights low, the world feels steady and ordered, its changefulness part of its predictability. The world feels like it will go on forever. We will be here, tonight, tomorrow night, the lights low, listening to the shipping forecast.

Simon stands as though he hears his name from far away. His head is at an angle, like a dog who catches the sound of a voice he knows.

Simon holds out his hands, warming them at the valves, now fully lighted, as if the light and the heat and sound are flowing into his body. In the dark kitchen his hands are shining.

I am standing near him – that is, I am near him, in a shape I don't recognise. Is it a shape? That would assume dimensionality and I have none. What felt like memory loss, a kind of astral dementia, has passed. There's something coming, but I don't know what it will be – oh, listen to me, still using that handy grammar of past, present, future, when it is only a rule of thumb (I have no thumbs either, BTW), only a way of managing the nonsense of time.

But Simon, time is real for you, and you are travelling through it without me now. I won't be waiting for you on the other side, because I find that there is no side, and there is no self, and in this *undiscovered country from whose bourn no traveller returns*, there are no borders; it is world without end – and it may be that something that was you and something that was me will occur – that is the best word I can think of – yes, perhaps we will occur again, together again, in the strangeness of ... The strangeness of what? I don't know the word. Shall we call it the strangeness and leave it at that?

In the Strangeness, nothing is how we expected it to be – what we were told to expect – not oblivion and not glory. No home and no hell. The Strangeness has some sort of electromagnetic force – it's as strong as gravity used to be, and it's pulling me towards. Towards what, I don't know. Away from what is clear.

Away from you.

I am here because I love you and that is not forgotten not lost not diminished not weakened not faded. It needs no punctuation. No explanation.

Love doesn't leave me, but I am leaving me, and I am leaving you. I am sorry.

In the after-light glow of the switched-off set, I stand so close to Simon that I am inside him, his pulse, his heart-beat, his blood, his sweat. I can pass through him because he is not solid. In his quirks and his quarks, he is what you are too; empty space and points of light. It's not so different where I am. Not so different to be dead. To be dead is to become aware of the oddity of solidity – that is, the counterfeit of solidity. The story changes but it doesn't end.

I have no memories now. My achievements are gone. My history is done. Happiness and loss are gone. The last earthbound part of me is dissolving into a crystal reflection. The clearest image I can give you is of a constellation. Not one thing. Not one star. A moving cluster of light.

Simon is talking to me. I can't understand what he is saying because I have lost language. I can see him

218

gesturing – he's replying to himself, he's excited, he's making food. The kitchen is steamy. He's going to open some wine. I can see how thin he is, how hungry he is. He goes on talking to the radio – the back of the radio – the valves glowing and buzzing. It's the first night he's been himself.

Later, when it's time for bed, Simon goes upstairs wearing me like a safety net. I am fastened around him. I won't let him fall. When he lies down, his eyes are open, staring at the street lamp outside. I close his eyes gently, as gently as he closed mine. I cover him with the last of me, and I love him, and he sleeps.

Canterville and Cock

As a child, my favourite fairground ride was the ghost train.

Remember those? The older ones? The black façade painted with ghosts and spiders. The man in a funeral cloak and top hat tearing tickets, the cars to ride in shaped like coffins. And straight away, the peal of manic laughter as the doors flew open, bats around your head. Scream now!

The ride I loved set off with a bone-shaking lurch round a blank corner where a luminous skeleton raised his ossified arm.

Mist filled the chamber. There was a hideous plunge, down and down, into the dark water, lit up from underneath with grinning faces. On went our coffin boat, past witches and spooks, haunted castles, where lightning flashed over the tower, tombstones, jagged and dripping, a hand rising out of the burial yard to grasp the prow.

Worst of all were the cobweb sheets suddenly draped over the boat. The cold breath on your face, and the unexpected gear-switch backwards, for a silent second, just as you hoped you would burst through the rickety wooden doors and back into the blessed daylight.

Has anybody ever wanted daylight so much?

As I child, I carved Halloween pumpkin lanterns. Trick or treat, where the most frightened person was me.

As a teenager I went total Goth, sleeping in black bed-sheets, and mooching around in candlelight. My nightly reading was ghost stories.

As a student, I realised there was good money to be made by walking people round eerie places and telling them chilling tales of murders, and beyond-the-grave revenge. Nobody believes it but everyone wants to believe it.

That's how I started Canterville and Cock, Illusionists. A haunting is an illusion, but it's a powerful illusion. Back then, it was easier to find old buildings waiting to be renovated, and I learned how to devise pop-up shows, making the most of the dereliction and cold of the sur-roundings. It's amazing what you can do with bedsheets, mannequins, an actor in a wig with a candle, and a soundtrack.

Now, I mostly stage live-action immersive weekends. A promoter rents a castle, or some grand house, that's supposed to have a ghost, and the guests pay to eat, drink, not sleep a lot, and do a version of the ghost train round the castle, at night, on foot. Scare everybody crazy and have a good time. We supply a Ouija board with a magnet underneath so that I can move the glass with a wire as I sit at the table. After dinner, my partner with the deep voice reads M. R. James stories by the fire.

A key part of the experience is that the guests wear period clothes. No jeans and trainers. It's dresses for the ladies and suits for the men, the style depending on the theme of the weekend.

This weekend, we're in a fancy seventeenth-century pile that hosts summer-long parties for punters who want to live the high life. Downton Abbey for accountants. In winter, the posh-but-no-cash family wants to arrange ghost weekends.

The only problem is they don't have a ghost.

Now, of course, we provide the ghosts, that's our job, but it's better to have a bona-fide ghost story to run alongside what we do. We're looking for walled-up ancestors, wronged wives, pale-faced children trailing a teddy, a drunk uncle who fell to his doom.

In this family, they all seem to have died in their sleep.

I am a professional, and lack of a real ghost is an opportunity to invent one – after all, ghosts themselves are an invention, aren't they? One of my favourite ghost dramas is the story of the Cock Lane Ghost. In 1762, the public lined up night after night to stand spooked inside a seedy lodging house near Smithfield Meat Market, in London. A haunted room, and a possessed little girl, had become infamous for their rapping and tapping. It all turned out to be an elaborate hoax, but it thrilled the crowds, dukes and plumbers alike, and made the perfect template for hoaxers like me.

As the family rambled on about their meek and mild dead ancestors, it turned out there was a scandalette in the family – an American woman, called Pamela, had swished off with one of the sons, back in 1962. The son had returned home a year or so later, married a nice English girl, and that was the end of it.

Still, I thought, a Sixties-themed weekend could be fun. Hot dogs and cocktails, narrow ties and loafers. An episode of *Mad Men*.

Plus ghost.

'Who is the ghost?' asked the family.

'She is! Pamela.'

I decided on a Miss Havisham-style story; a woman jilted by her lover, a woman who could never get over it. She killed herself by jumping off the Brooklyn Bridge. Now, her ghost haunts the East Wing.

'But why would Pamela bother travelling all the way from Brooklyn back to Berkshire?'

I had to explain that distance is irrelevant to a ghost.

I don't know that for sure, of course, and it's true that ghost stories tend to locate the ghost near its home. But why not expand the brand?

'Did Pamela have a room in the house here?'

'She stayed in a guest room, from time to time, but mostly she sat out on the terrace, scheming and smoking.'

'We'll use the terrace then, and the smoke.'

'The ghost may smoke but the visitors may not.'

I agreed with all this, and we set about recreating

Pamela's bedroom. It didn't have to be authentic – only effective. Heavy leather luggage with straps and labels, a few little suits in the closet, a martini glass, filled, on the nightstand. In the end, we chose a room right over the dining room, so that we could bang on the floor during the dinner, before the night tour started.

I called one of our regular actors to come and impersonate Pamela as she would have been back in the 1960s. We went the whole Jackie Kennedy, pillbox hat, white gloves, pink suit. She looked fantastic. Pamela was blonde, but our girl didn't want to dye her hair. No matter. Ghosts can be brunette.

Our first evening couldn't have gone better. Ten couples, enthusiastically dressed, some trying out bad American accents. They'd all read the doomed love story on the website.

We dressed the waiters to look like they were straight out of an American diner and set the guests off with tuna-stuffed cherry tomatoes, shrimp cocktail and martinis, followed by Chicken à la King, and Waldorf salad. The chocolate fudge cake was saved for after the tour. It's important to get everyone more than halfway drunk before the fun starts, so there was plenty of wine.

Towards the end of dinner my accomplice made some impressive thumps from Pamela's bedroom.

'It's time,' I announced, 'to Summon the Dead.'

(I always dress in black tails and white tie whatever the theme. I am the Master of Ceremonies.)

Downing their drinks, the company took their seats at the Ouija-board table. The table is a favourite prop of mine. The board itself is a circle of black letters with a picture of a horse-drawn hearse in the centre. It sets the right tone.

The lights were dimmed. The greenish lights I use give a ghastly hue to the healthiest complexion. Already the guests were glancing at each other, a little nervous.

I instructed the table to hold hands and to close their eyes. One of the women started giggling.

In a solemn voice, I asked: 'IS ANYBODY THERE?'

'I'm here,' said one of the guys. Another breakout of giggles.

I tried again: 'Rap once for Yes. Twice for No.'

Immediately there came a rap. (I do it with a foot pedal, like on a bass drum.)

Sharp intakes of breath. Now I had them. 'Will you tell us your name?'

RAP!

The table sat in silence. I instructed two of the women to place their forefingers on the top of the upturned glass. I positioned my magnetic wire. The glass began to spell P.A.M.E.L.A.

'OMG! OMG! OMG! Can I go and get a drink?'

I was stern. 'No one may leave the table during the séance.

'Pamela!' I said. 'Are you speaking from the other side?'

RAP!

'Can you send us a sign that you are speaking from the other side?'

The radio on the drinks trolley roared into life. The Supremes singing 'Where Did Our Love Go?' (1964).

'This is awesome,' said one of the women, the one dressed like Elisabeth Moss.

I pushed my advantage. 'Have you anything to tell us, Pamela?'

This time I indicated that two of the men should put their hands on the glass. Men are harder to impress when it comes to visitations. Jaggedly and swiftly, the glass moved around the letters, spelling B.R.O.K.E.N.H.E.A.R.T.

'Oh, this is so sad!' said another of the women, the one dressed like Cher when she was with Sonny. 'How can we cheer you up, Pamela?'

D.R.I.N.K. spelled the board – which was strange because I wasn't using the magnet. I guessed the guys were having a joke and that things might get silly. I decided to Take Back Control.

'Everyone hold hands and let the glass move by itself,' I commanded. Using the magnet, I spelled out B.E.D.R.O.O.M.

'Foxy lady!' said the guy who had come as Don Draper.

I pointed out that this was not an invitation but an instruction.

'Ladies and gentlemen! Guided by our spirit visitor, I suggest we begin the Pamela Tour.'

At that second, the dim lights over the Ouija table were extinguished completely, leaving us all in the dark. No one dared to move. One of my assistants, silent and unseen, released the perfume vial. Chanel No. 5.

With a white-lead face, in came another of the team, dressed as an undertaker, carrying a tray full of lighted candles. These were distributed to the group. With myself at the head, we left the ground floor, and made our way in the shadows, up the oak staircase.

I had placed a stooge in a large suit of armour. On cue, the visor flew up, red smoke issuing from within.

The ladies screamed. 'I admit that is for your entertainment,' I said. 'But can you tell what is an illusion and what is real?'

'Can you?' asked the man who had come as Dr Strangelove.

The group took the long way round to Pamela's bedroom, past a loudly ticking clock that only added to the silence. Outside the room, I paused. 'This was Pamela's bedroom. You may go inside.'

The room looked as though Pamela had just left it – the turned-back bedspread, the novel on the bed, the fresh martini in the cocktail glass, and a Sobranie Black Russian, half smoked, in an ashtray. A pair of stockings hung over a chair. Once again, we were assailed by the scent of Chanel. A perfume atomiser stood on the dressing table.

We had placed a boxy duck-egg-blue Dansette record player on top of the chest of drawers, its needle aimlessly scraping back and forth at the end of the record Pamela, presumably, had just been playing.

As the group crowded in, the drapes in the window began to move on their own, billowing a little into the room. This is one of our favourite tricks, and managed by a small wind machine behind each drape.

'Will you look at that? JEEZ.' I had impressed the woman who thought she was dressed as Marilyn Monroe.

'Pamela is asking us to look out of the window,' I said. I pulled back the drapes theatrically, but this allowed me to conceal the little wind-makers.

A few of the guests went to the window and looked down over the garden terrace. 'Can you see anything?'

'Nope.'

A clock chimed the hour.

On cue, there's a sizeable scream. 'I can see her! It's Pamela.'

Everyone crowds to the window. Nobody is looking for a wind machine. My actor is walking up and down, smoking a cigarette. A haze of mist (dry ice) surrounds her.

'This is awesome.'

'Can she hear us? Hey, Pamela!'

There is, of course, no response from below, and still she walks, up and down. It's a pity her head can't be tucked underarm – it's more impressive, but we only offer that for Tudor shows.

Before anyone can get too inquisitive, the undertaker knocks at the door to announce that pudding is served.

Happy and drunk, my crowd follows behind him, back to the fireside for ghost stories and chocolate cake. I bring up the rear as far as the staircase (can't have people wandering off) and bid them goodnight. I have tidying up to do.

Humming, I reach Pamela's room.

Sitting cross-legged on the bed, there's a blonde woman wearing Capri pants and a white blouse. Her feet are bare.

'Who are you?'

'I could ask you the same question.'

'I'm Paul, from Canterville and Cock, Illusionists.'

'Are you responsible for all this?' She gestures around the room. 'And THAT, out there?' She gets up and looks out of the window.

'If you mean the Pamela Tour . . .'

'I am Pamela.'

'That's impossible, she's dead.'

'Certainly she's dead. He killed her.'

'Who killed her?'

'The chinless wonder I ran off with. Hugo. The youngest son, the family darling. Can you believe he's still alive, in a bungalow, in Bournemouth? I've been to visit him, made a few things happen – ectoplasm, electrical failures, horrible noises in the night. He's so stupid he doesn't notice. He'll be dead soon and then I'll make his life hell.'

I had no idea what to say so I said nothing.

Pamela put the record on the Dansette. That is, I saw the needle lift and fall, and I could see Pamela, but her hand didn't grasp the arm, because as she appeared to touch it, her hand wavered into thin air. (Have you noticed that it is only in ghost stories that air becomes thin air?)

'If you are dead, then what are you doing here?' I asked her, as she began dancing to the music.

'You called me back.'

'I most certainly did not!'

'That idea of yours, about Pamela, that was me right beside you making you think about me. I was following you around for days.'

(This thought was not appealing.)

'When you landed on my story, it was great! I was able to visible-ise myself.'

'Visible-ise?'

'What would you call it?'

'I would call it an illusion. Illusions are my business.'

'Believe it or not, Paul, I am Pamela. In return for my invitation this weekend, I'll play Pamela for you, that is, be myself, for the rest of the tour.'

'Oh, this is silly,' I said. 'Are you a member of the family?'

'I should have been, and would have been, if he hadn't pushed me off a balcony in Miami, the deadbeat little misfit.'

'They told me you had run off with a car dealer from New Jersey.'

'I had a fling – that's all. I wanted a Corvette. But it needn't have bothered Hugo. I had no idea he was the jealous type. It wasn't enough to warrant me dead. In any case, he had already met the English girl. She was as lively as a double dose of Valium.'

'Is she in Bournemouth too?'

'Oh, no. She's somewhere out at sea. What's left of her. I saw to that.'

'You murdered her?'

'I pointed her in the right direction. The edge of a cliff.'

I thought it was time to go and get a drink.

'I'm dying for a drink,' said Pamela, and then, reading my mind, 'I spelled out DRINK on your silly Ouija board, you know I did.'

For the first time in the conversation, I felt uneasy.

I left Pamela dancing to 'Strangers in the Night' (1966). When I had bought the vinyl 45s, on eBay, for the Dansette, I had assumed Pamela would still be alive back then, presumably driving round New Jersey in her Corvette. Now, it appears she was dead by 1964. What am I talking about? That woman isn't Pamela. That woman isn't a ghost.

I hurried downstairs. I could hear Joe reading spooky stories in his sonorous voice. I had time for a piece of cake and a brandy.

As I was comfort-eating, Melvin, the house owner, came in to congratulate me on a splendid evening. I thanked him and asked him how he knew that Pamela had run off with a car dealer. 'Oh, it's all in Hugo's letters to his mother. Fast and loose, Pamela turned out to be.'

I was about to caution that it is ill-advised to speak of a woman in those terms, when a large serving dish crashed from the sideboard behind him. He jumped up, catching his foot in the chair. 'What the devil? Is that you, Paul?'

It was not me. Pamela had thrown it at him. She was

balanced on the dresser in her Capri pants and bare feet. She was, though, quite a bit smaller than in the bedroom. Is size approximate for ghosts? I mean, why should she be forever 5'2", after death?

Caught in my ruminations, I didn't answer Melvin, leaving him glaring at me, and hopping from foot to foot. I had to pull myself together.

'Melvin, I do apologise, but I can assure you that the tureen was not one of my special effects.'

'I should bloody well hope not,' grumbled Melvin, downing a large brandy. 'Well, I'll see you in the morning. If I can walk.' He hobbled off.

Pamela came to sit by me. 'He's a creep. I can tell you for sure that he's having an affair. They're all the same, this family.'

'How do you know?'

'I saw him riding out to meet some woman on a horse. They did it standing up.'

'I really don't want to know.'

'It's no fun for a woman, doing it standing up. No friction.'

'Pamela!'

She laughed. 'At least you used my name. Now do you believe in me?'

I didn't answer. 'I see you are your usual size again.'

'Oh, yes. Gravity. It's not a problem these days. I can stretch –' and she stretched, so that her blonde curls bobbed under the ceiling light '– and I can shrink.' She shrank. 'If you were in space, Paul, your body would stretch and stretch.'

'Yes, but it wouldn't shrink. It would just come apart.'

'Maybe I don't mean gravity. But as I can float' – she floated – 'I do mean gravity.'

'Ghosts are not subject to the laws of gravity?'

'Sure. That's right. We have no mass.'

'You've taken the trouble to research this,' I said.

'I've been doing fieldwork for seventy years. Plus, you meet a lot of interesting people when you're dead. Physicists, and so on. I've met Robert Oppenheimer.'

'The atomic-bomb man?'

'That's him.'

'What about Einstein?'

'No, no! Don't you know? This is supposed to be your job and you don't know anything? Ghosts are those who died violently. Murder, suicide, war casualties, executions, a terrible accident, sometimes a disease. Robert Oppenheimer had throat cancer. Cigarettes. Bomb. We're the ones who stay around.'

'For how long?'

'Until we are able to leave.'

I longed to leave. I could hear the evening by the fire drawing to its close. 'Pamela, I must go to bed.'

'See you tomorrow, Paul.' And she was gone.

I put my hand into the space she had occupied. Is that the right word? For the disembodied? Whatever the word, the newly empty, empty space was as cold as ice.

I lay in bed staring at the ceiling. Why do we keep our eyes open when we know we can't see anything?

Only two paths were open to me. A) I had lost my wits. B) Pamela is a ghost.

The next day I was up early, long before my guests, rigging the walkway for the evening's spectacular levitation. The narrow stainless-steel platform is built in sections, and tonight it will run the length of the balcony. Pamela – that is, my actor Pamela – will appear to be walking in the air. Dry ice will conceal the simple prop behind the illusion. The balcony itself will be closed off today and not visible from either the house or the grounds.

It's barbecue night tonight. Hot dogs, hamburgers, and corn on the cob. Pitchers of negroni, beer on ice, and later, Baked Alaska. Then, when the guests have drunk enough not to be too sharp-eyed, the séance will commence. Tonight, 'Pamela' will direct the guests to the lawn. Immediately after her levitation, fireworks will allow us swiftly to remove all traces of the walkway.

By story time, and brandy time, Pamela will be done. One Pamela will be on the train back to London, and the other Pamela, I hope, dematerialised.

Yes, that's the right word. Ghosts materialise and de-materialise. They don't visible-ise. She must have picked up this habit of turning adjectives and nouns into verbs from a young person. A young dead person.

As long as Pamela de-visible-ises, I can forgive the grammar.

The day passed and I saw nothing of Pamela. I was beginning to think that she had been dragged back through the time-portal like some blonde, trans, Don Giovanni at the end of the opera.

Are the Dead in control of their comings and goings?

Pamela had said that she couldn't materialise until, somehow, I had made it possible – but if I had made it possible, could I de-possible-ise it?

This optimistic thought kept me going until it was time to light the barbecues. We'd hired a fantastic Rock-Ola jukebox. American, with two hundred hit records from the Sixties. I had my back to it, heating the rolls in the mini-oven, when music burst across the terrace. The Beatles, 'Can't Buy Me Love' (1964).

I turned round – the Rock-Ola was flashing its neon lights and Pamela – slightly levitated – was poring over the jukebox menu.

'Hi, Pamela! Weren't you already dead when *A Hard Day's Night* came out?' She faced me, smiling sweetly. Today, I could see right through her to the jukebox on the other side.

'Pamela, you seem a little more transparent today . . .'

'I know, darling. My energy is low.'

She seemed to have one arm missing. 'Do ghosts suffer from low energy?'

'Oh, yes. And it takes a lot of energy to visible-ise.'

'The word is "materialise".'

'Don't be a bore, Paul. Not when I'm making such an effort.'

I saw my chance. 'If it's such an effort, why not disappear? You don't need to be here, do you?'

'I have a plan,' said Pamela. 'And since I am here, I might as well make the most of it. You have no idea how dreary it is to be dead.'

Melvin came hobbling across the courtyard. 'Morning, Paul. Talking to yourself again, are you?'

'How is your foot?'

'Swollen. I was supposed to be going riding this morning. With a friend.'

'I told you he's having an affair,' Pamela said.

'Will you shut up?'

'I beg your pardon?' said Melvin, his red face reddening.

'I wasn't talking to you, Melvin. Sorry.'

'Are you quite right in the head, Paul? All this illusionism might be taking its toll.'

(Illusionism?)

Pamela had floated up behind Melvin, her head above his. She started pulling silly faces. I began to laugh. Melvin didn't find this funny. 'I'll tell you what,' he said, 'you might need to see a doctor.'

'Possibly,' I said, and then (why did I do this?), 'Are you having an affair, Melvin?'

His face told me the answer. His expression moved as fast as island weather; incredulity, shock, horror, then outrage.

'Who's been gossiping? The housemaid? I'll sack her!'

'Pamela told me.'

'Pamela! Don't be a cretin, Paul. I don't believe in ghosts, but I do believe that you are a snoop. A sly snoop,' said Melvin. 'And if you say a word to my wife . . .'

'She knows . . .' said Pamela.

'She knows . . .' I said.

Saved by the negroni. At that moment, some of the

237

guests came over, cocktails in one hand, waving at me with the other. Everybody loves a magician. Melvin had to smile. They were paying, after all. As he hobbled away, he wagged a stained, stumpy finger at me. 'You'll be sorry!'

'Horrid man!' said Pamela. 'Horrid family. Don't worry, darling. Don't forget I have a plan.'

'Have you thought of visiting Bournemouth?' I asked.

'There's plenty of time,' said Pamela.

And I guess she's right about that.

The barbecue was a success. Food, drink, and no other-worldly materialisations. Well, one. As I was sitting exhausted, on a bench, having eaten nothing since lunch, a hot dog hovered, torpedo direction, in front of my mouth. There was no sign of Pamela. Then I heard her voice: 'I'm conserving energy, Paul. Now come on, eat up!'

I took a big bite. Chewed it. The remainder of the hot dog moved closer. 'And again.'

I haven't been fed by hand since I was about four years old. When I had finally finished, Pamela wiped my mouth with a paper napkin.

Darkness was falling. 'It's time for the Ouija board,' she said. 'I'm looking forward to this.'

The guests sat around the table. The green lamps were lit. The mood was expectant. I had positioned the magnetic wire, but I had a feeling I wouldn't be needing it.

'Pamela!' I said. 'Have you anything to tell us?'

RAP!

'Could two of the company, any two, place their

forefingers on the glass please, so that the spirit of Pamela may speak to us?'

Immediately, the glass began to whirr round the letters. I thought she was going to set the board on fire.

M.E.R.D.E.

'Is Pamela French?'

'What's MERDE mean?' asked the woman dressed as Brigitte Bardot.

'Shit.'

'Oh!'

'Wait! It's moving again! It's pulling my arm off!'

M.U.R.D.E.

M.U.R.D.E.R.

Silence.

I don't know what possessed me. (I do.) 'Pamela! Who has been murdered?'

M.E.

There was a ripple round the board. A full orchestra and chorus of OMG OMG OMG OMG OMG.

'Who did it, Pamela?'

H.U.G.O.

Horror among the guests.

'It says in the brochure that Pamela left Hugo!'

'Every family has a secret,' I said. 'Pamela! Where is Hugo now?'

I heard her voice whispering in my ear. 'How do you spell Bournemouth?'

Before we could go any further, Melvin had stormed in. He switched on the strip lighting. 'That's enough!

Quite enough. More than enough! I didn't hire you bunch of charlatans to slander my family name! Pamela was a gold-digging whore. My great-uncle Hugo is a saint. A saint living peacefully by the sea in an assisted-living bungalow. How dare you?'

The guests sat shocked and silent.

'I think it's time to go out onto the lawn,' I said. 'Pamela may be walking on the terrace again tonight.'

As the guests got up, gratefully, to make their way outside, I said to Melvin, 'If you want them to ask for their money back just carry on as you are.'

He looked surprised. There are men in this world who imagine they can say and do whatever they like without consequences. Melvin was one of those men.

'I'll see to you afterwards,' he said.

I went outside. My assistants had filled the terrace with dry ice and actor 'Pamela' was 'levitating' beautifully. One of the guests came to console me. 'This is a great show. A great weekend. I thought the murder theme tonight was a masterstroke!'

'Thank you,' I said. 'Melvin is a literal sort of person. No imagination.'

There was a whoop of awe from the onlookers. Actor Pamela was walking the walk, but her hat had been lifted off her head and was levitating all on its own about a yard above her. It wasn't on its own; it was the other Pamela, but she was invisible, even to me. My actor was taking it well. As she reached the end of the platform, the dry ice was cued to envelop her while she climbed down the ladder to disappear indoors. Then, to the rear, so that the guests had to turn round, we would set off the fireworks. In fact, as my 'Pamela' turned, for a last, blood-curdling stare, she let out a blood-curdling scream. The other Pamela had lit her up like a personal electrocution. A bolt of lightning shot out of her head.

I raced across the lawn, leapt the low wall, and coughed my way through the dry ice. Actor Pamela was sitting up looking ashen, which is how you would look after being electrocuted. Her face was sooty. Her body was steaming. Without thinking, I turned the garden hose on her. She sizzled.

Slowly, I helped her to her feet, and got her indoors. The fireworks were booming outside.

'I'll pay you double-time,' I said.

She put her hand up to her hair. 'Something's happened.'

It had. Her straight brunette bob was now a poodle perm.

'I'll pay for the hairdresser,' I said.

'This is the last time, Paul. I told you when you sewed me into that mermaid's tail, and we had to go to hospital to get it off. Now I mean it.'

'I'm so sorry.'

Black puddles were forming at her feet.

Unfortunately, I had to leave her to my assistant because Melvin had reappeared. He gestured me towards him with an ugly look. 'I want a word with you, Cock.'

'My name's Canterville . . .'

'Cock! Canterville! You're for it!'

Melvin led me through a deserted passage – that is, a

passage that should have been deserted. In fact, an eerie light filled it with Presence of Pamela. I knew it was her.

The passage led to a small internal courtyard. High stone walls surrounded me. Small, barred windows looked down on us. Melvin unhooked a pair of comedy boxing gloves from the wall. They were bright red and padded. He pulled them on and started punching his right fist into his left palm. 'Going to teach you a lesson, Cock.'

'Canterville.'

He stepped forward and hit me. Smack! Just like that. I stumbled. He came again with a left hook. Bam! I thought he had broken my jaw.

'Paul!' said Pamela. 'Pull yourself together! Step with me! Follow my feet!'

Two luminous bare feet appeared. Melvin was swinging towards me, uttering oaths. He swung, he missed, he swung again, he missed. Lurching, he caught my shoulder.

'Paul! Pay attention! Quicker! Left! Left! Left! Left!'

I followed the feet. Had Pamela been a boxing coach in a previous life? Frustrated at missing and missing, Melvin roared straight at me for a headbutt. I closed my eyes. Next thing, an awful shout, long, far too long, but fainter and fainter, as though Melvin were moving far away. Which he was.

Splash. Like a pebble down a well.

I opened my eyes. It was a well. I was looking down at a narrow chute. A black hole.

'Put the cover back on, will you, Paul?' said Pamela.

'That's why I haven't been visible all day. It took all my energy to move that cover. It's cast iron.'

'Shouldn't we call for help?'

'Why? He's dead.'

'Are you sure?'

'I should know!'

Can't argue with that. I dragged the cover across the well.

'But why did you kill Melvin and not Hugo?'

'Oh, Hugo will be dead soon anyway. I popped down to Bournemouth while you were all enjoying the barbecue, and I hid Hugo's panic alarm – the thing he wears round his neck. Then, I tripped him up as he was shuffling out to feed the birds. He's lying helpless behind the frosted-glass door to the garden.'

'Can we get a drink?'

Pamela and I went back inside to the kitchen. I fixed two martinis and placed them side by side.

'I could have left Melvin to kill you, you know. I thought I might.'

'Kill me?'

'Yes, then I could have you all to myself.'

Pamela was sitting cross-legged on the kitchen table.

'Instead, Paul, I decided to give his poor wife a break. She doesn't deserve Melvin. And also . . .'

'Also?'

'Now the house really does have a ghost story. A haunted well.'

'Is Melvin coming back?'

'Oh, for sure. He's furious.'

'I hope he won't give you a hard time.'

'I know how to deal with men like Melvin.'

I nodded, drinking my martini.

'You know, Paul, I'm not a girl who lives with regrets. Not even about the balcony in Miami. But I wish we had met sooner. When I was alive.'

'I wasn't born.'

'Yeah. That's the trouble with time. Never happens when it should. What a mess. That's the only good thing about being dead. No more time management.'

She smiled at me. A beautiful, radiant smile. And then she started to disappear, beginning with her feet.

'Where are you going, Pamela?'

'I do seem to be going, don't I?'

Now she was invisible from the waist down.

'Will I see you again?'

'I don't think so, Paul, but I'll be around.'

Now there was just her head and neck.

'Pamela, I wish we had met sooner too.'

That radiant smile. 'I'll come back for you. When it's your time.'

'What if I die quietly in my bed?'

I could hear the guests coming towards the kitchen for cookies. All that was left of Pamela was her smile.

'I'll make sure that doesn't happen. Bye for now, Paul!'

I leaned to kiss her. I felt an electrical tingle on my lips. Already the guests were in the kitchen.

Pamela was gone.

JW3: All the Ghosts We Cannot See

I wrote earlier in the book about seeing the departing spirit of my grandmother when I was a little girl.

Soon after she was decently buried, but before she had been decently mourned, my grandad installed his mistress in the house.

They planned to get married. This was no consolation to my mother, and as we were all living under the same roof, things were tense. I understand now that the trauma of my life with the Wintersons was not the trauma of sudden shocks, but the daily trauma of our madness.

Mistress Alice worked in a pub in the evenings – she was a 1960s blonde barmaid with a beehive and boots. Bizarrely, she also wore thick-framed 1950s-style glasses, which gave her a misfit look – a cross between the bargain hunter's Brigitte Bardot and Austin Powers.

The pub was bad enough for teetotal Mrs Winterson, but the side-hustle was worse. Alice advertised her services as a medium. She was a channel to the Dead.

My mother believed in spirits but she did not believe in contacting the Dead. If ghosts appeared, well, what could you do? Summoning spirits was forbidden – and when it happened, it never went according to plan – see the Witch of Endor story in the Bible, First Book of Samuel.

Alice didn't care about Mrs Winterson's feelings. She spent her free time summoning a quiz team of dead relatives, available to answer any question on any topic, but chiefly chipping in on how great Alice was for Grandad, and how they all wished them well in their new life together.

While this was predictable stuff, other things were strange.

Windows opened and closed on their own. Bangs and crashes happened at odd moments and with no obvious human agency. Scents of flowers filled the rooms – not the scent of roses, but of mimosa, Mrs Winterson's Most Hated Plant.

The oddest manifestation was a scrubbing noise, like someone on their hands and knees, washing a floor with a bucket and brush. I used to hear it when I went in the kitchen in the mornings. I had a habit of climbing out of my railed high bed to explore the house alone. I still prefer to be alone early in the mornings.

Mrs Winterson soon had enough of scents, bangs, scrubbings, and exhortations to happiness – especially those. Happiness was not an emotion she trusted. She decided that Alice could take over the running of Grandad – his cooking, cleaning, washing, and so on – and so we left behind the detached house, with three gardens, that backed onto a clough, and went back to our own cramped terraced house, on a long, stretchy street, with a town at the bottom and a hill at the top.

This was probably what Alice wanted to happen. She wouldn't be the first to use a ghostly invasion – real or invented – to rearrange a household.

Back home, we had no inside bathroom. The toilet was in the yard next to the coal-shed. Both were full of black spiders, which wasn't the spiders' natural colour. Everything in the 1960s was coal-washed.

Our kitchen had a stone sink with a water heater above it, a gas oven that left meat raw or burned it black, and a roomy larder. No fridge. We couldn't afford a fridge, but in truth the kitchen was so cold that we never needed one.

As well as spiders, there were mice. Plenty of mice. Mrs Winterson thought mice belonged in low-class homes (like ours) but she was not low-class, so she refused to admit that we had mice. Whenever I saw a grey flash vanishing behind the larder, Mrs Winterson said, 'Ectoplasm.'

The whole endeavour of our family life was to call things by other names. As long as it wasn't rightly named, it wasn't real. We all know those fairy stories where naming is power. Know the name of the other-worldly little fella, and his power is yours. Rumpelstiltskin. All that straw. All that gold.

Often, in life, we seek not to know, not to name, or to re-name, and de-name. It's not mice (we're cold, poor, dirty). It's ectoplasm. We're special.

Ectoplasm, in cell biology, is the outer wall of the cytoplasm, but that's not what was running around our kitchen. In the late nineteenth century, the word started being used by mediums to describe the physical manifestation of ghostly energy. Often mediums just

247

spewed it up – which is unpleasant – but it could appear pretty much anywhere.

Mrs Winterson blamed all kinds of domestic malfunctions on ectoplasm – whether it was blocking up our drains or jamming the pictures on the telly.

Living like this, in degrading poverty and towering pride, wrapped in a faith that depended on the supernatural as the cornerstone of truth, what could we do but expect other-worldly encounters?

My dad told me that as a young soldier in the Second World War, he had returned on leave, in 1941, to visit his mother in Liverpool. Arriving too late for the last bus, too exhausted to walk any further, he looked for shelter in a row of evacuated houses. A soldier he didn't know came up to him and showed him an empty house. They both went inside. Dad pulled down a dusty curtain, wrapped himself in it, and went to sleep on a broken couch. He remembers the man nodding at him, smiling. He said his name was Stephen.

The next morning, Dad was woken by a policeman. Every house in the row had been bombed except his. Dad was so tired he had registered nothing. He was used to sleeping under the sound of bombs and bullets. Dad went looking for Stephen, but there was no sign of him.

In the pub later, Dad asked around. Stephen? Yes, that's the house where he lived, where Dad slept the night, but Stephen had been killed in 1940.

What to make of any of this? My childhood was lived so vividly on more than one plane that I can't unthread the lines of reality and imagination. I am not sure they are separate – not if reality and consciousness really are part of the same stuff. Our ancestors accepted reality as layered, both visible and invisible. Those who believe in a god continue to experience reality on different levels – or believe that they do.

Humans can see less than 1 per cent of the electromagnetic spectrum. We call this visible light. We can't see radio waves, gamma rays, X-rays, ultraviolet light. We manage just fine; our mistake is to rename visible light – what we can see – as reality.

There's more out there than meets the eye.

VISITATIONS

Thin Air

In the Bernese Oberland of Switzerland is the famous ski resort of Mürren. Mürren cannot be reached by road. You must arrive by train at Lauterbrunnen and from there take the cable car to the village.

Three peaks stare you down: the Eiger, the Mönch and the Jungfrau. The British started going to Mürren in 1912.

That was the year Captain Scott died at the South Pole. There was much talk of him that year, talk of his heroism and his sacrifice, talk of how the British must bear their burden of Empire, half the world coloured pink like a tin of salmon.

Then the war came.

When the British returned to Mürren in any numbers the year was 1924. Arnold Lunn pitched up with his father, Sir Henry, a minister who had failed to convert the Indians in Calcutta to Methodism, and decided, instead, to evangelise the British to the glory of the Alps.

It was young Arnold who fell in love with skiing and who established downhill skiing as a competitive sport – rather than just the fastest way to get to the bottom of the hill.

In 1928, Arnold and some friends climbed to the top of
the Schilthorn, above Mürren, and skied the fourteen hair-
raising, eyebrow-stripping, gut-churning, knee-wrecking,
leg-breaking, mind-numbing, heart-soaring kilometres
down to Lauterbrunnen. They enjoyed it so much they
did it again. And again. They called the race the Inferno.

And every year the world comes here to do it again
too.

My friends and I are not Inferno material. Rather we
rag-bag along at the start of each New Year, putting aside
our lives around the world and meeting to share old times.
We've worked together, or been at college together, or
been neighbours, until one or the other moved away.
Wives and husbands are not allowed on the trip. This is a
friendship club. It's not Meta or TikTok. We don't Insta or
upload. We don't keep in touch that much over the year.

But if we're alive we'll be here, in Mürren, every New
Year. We stay at the Palace Hotel and organise the first
dinner for ourselves on January 3rd.

It was after a good dinner of trout and potatoes, sitting
in front of a blazing log fire, drinking coffee or brandy or
both, that one of our number proposed that we tell ghost
stories, real ones – supernatural happenings that had happened to us.

Mike was like that – a larger-than-life type with an
appetite for anything new. Since last year, he said, he'd
been researching the paranormal.

When we asked him why, he claimed it had started
here, in Mürren. OK, so why hadn't he told us about it
before?

'I wasn't sure. And I thought you'd laugh at me.'

We were laughing at him. Who believes in ghosts except kids and old ladies? Mike leaned forward, holding up his hand to stop the flow of quips and comments about ghostbusters and too many drinks.

'I wasn't drunk,' said Mike. 'It was daytime. You were all on the chairlifts for the slalom. I decided to go cross-country, clear my head – you know I was having difficulty with my marriage last year.'

Suddenly he was serious. We listened.

Mike said, 'I was alone, skiing pretty fast, but on the pass above me, I saw someone else, frighteningly high up, like he was skiing a tightrope. I stopped my skis, waved and hollered, but the figure went on. It was like he was airborne. I got myself going again, thinking that later, in the bar, I'd try to find this guy who skis in thin air. Then, about an hour afterwards, not too far from here, I saw the same man. He seemed to be looking for something.

'I skied across to help him out. I called out: "You lost something, buddy?"

'He looked right at me – I'll never forget that look; eyes milk-blue like the blue of the sun on the snow in the morning. He asked me the time. I told him. He said he was missing his ice axe. I thought maybe he was a geologist, you know? He had a knapsack that looked specialist.

'He was dressed real strange. Like he'd just gone out in his clothes and fastened his skis on. Thick seaman sweater – those cable-knits, y'know? No hi-vis microfibre. He wore ski boots – but they were old leather things with those long wrap-around laces they used to have. And his skis – I'm not kidding you here, his skis were wooden; can you believe that?

'But it wasn't just those things. I had the sensation that I was looking right through him. That he was made of glass or ice. He didn't seem to be feeling the cold but he made me feel cold. I was shivering. He didn't seem to want company, so I skied off a little way, and then I turned back. There was no one there.'

We had listened in silence. Then we all butted in at once. We each had our own explanation to offer: they do historic skiing demonstrations here sometimes – the old skis, the heavy clothes, that kind of thing. And Mike admitted he had been tired and more than a little strung-out. The air does that to you.

None of it equalled ghost. Mike shook his head. 'I'm telling you, I saw something. I've been trying to under-stand it all year. There's no explanation. A man comes out of nowhere and goes back into nowhere.'

While we were arguing, one of the managers here, Fabrice, came over, offered us drinks on the house and asked if he could join us. 'It's ghost night, Fabrice,' said Mike. 'You ever heard anything like this here?'

Mike started to repeat the whole thing, like a drunk in a bar grizzling about his girl. Yes, he was drunk but I could see he was agitated too. I needed a quieter night, so I got up and excused myself. I wanted a little air. When you first arrive here it takes time to adjust. The fire and the brandy had made me sleepy but I didn't want to go to bed. I went outside, intending to walk around the hotel.

I like looking back into rooms filled with people. I like the silent-movie feel of it. I used to do it when I was a girl, watching my parents and sisters, knowing they couldn't see me. Now, in the crisp, starry air, I looked in and saw my party, my friends, laughing, animated. I smiled to myself. This is what it means to have friends; this ease, this contentedness.

Then, as I was watching, another guest came through the library. Not one I recognised. You get to know the usual faces. This one was young and strong. He carried his body well. Judging from his clothes, he was British. He wore wool trousers, khaki shirt, and short tie tucked inside a fitted tweed jacket. The timeless look the Brits do well. He didn't even glance at our group; took a book from one of the shelves, and disappeared through a door set in the panelling of the wall. The library here is modelled on a gentlemen's club of about a hundred years ago when the hotel opened. It's leather, wood, warmth, books, animal paintings, old photos in frames, newspapers.

I went back inside – the others were having a good time, but I still wasn't in the mood. On impulse I followed the man the way he had gone. The hotel had done some building recently. This must be the new part.

But when I went through the door, following the unknown man, I realised I was in the oldest part of the hotel. It must be the service side because I had never come across it before.

I could see the man's legs disappearing up a narrow staircase. Why did I go after him? I wasn't trying to pick him up or anything. But I experience a freedom here – actually a recklessness. It's the air. Yes. The air is radiant here; like breathing in light.

At the top of the stairs a low glow came from a room with a small door under the eaves. The room looked like it had been tucked in as an afterthought. I hesitated. Through the half-open door, I could see the man, sitting with his back to me, turning over the pages of a book. I knocked. He looked round. I pushed the door open.

'Did you bring the hot water?' he said. Then he realised his mistake.

'Don't apologise,' I said. 'I'm the one who's disturbing you. I'm with that noisy group downstairs.'

The young man looked puzzled. He was broad-shouldered, rangy, built like a rower or a climber. He had taken off his tweed jacket. His trousers were held up with braces. He stood in his shirt and tie, touchingly formal and vulnerable in that formal and vulnerable way that Englishmen can be.

'I was about to settle down with this book about Everest,' he said. 'I shall be going there later in the year. Come in. Please. Won't you come in?'

I went in. The room was not at all like a hotel room here. There was a low fire burning in the grate and a single divan pushed against one wall. There was a wash-jug and bowl on a nightstand. A heavy leather case lay half-unpacked in the middle of the room, a pair of striped pyjamas rumpled on the top. Two candles dripped on the mantelpiece. There was an oil lamp on a desk by the window. An upright chair matched the desk, and a pink velvet armchair was drawn close to the fire. There didn't appear to be any electricity.

He followed my gaze. 'I'm not rich. The other rooms are better. Well, I'm sure you know that. But this is cosy. Would you like to sit down? The armchair is quite comfortable. Please . . . Miss . . . ?'

'Hi, I'm Molly,' I said, holding out my hand.

'Sandy,' he said. 'You must be American.'

'Why?'

'You don't sound American, but you seem very sure of yourself.'

I laughed. 'I knew I was intruding . . . I'll go.'

'No! I mean it, please . . . my terrible manners. Sit by the fire. Go on. Do. Please.'

He rummaged in a knapsack that seemed to be made of canvas and leather with pockets all over it, and pulled out a hip flask. 'Will you have a brandy?' He poured us two generous amounts in the only glasses to hand – a pair of tumblers holding his toothbrush and toothpaste.

'I've never seen this part of the hotel. It's so quaint. I guess they never restored it. Is it part of their historic?'

Sandy looked puzzled again. 'Historic what?'

'You know, the demos they do – skiing the Arnold Lunn way, all of that.'

'Do you know Arnold Lunn?'

'I know of him – if you stay here, who doesn't?'

'Yes, he's quite a character, isn't he? Do you know the Sherlock Holmes connection?'

I didn't know it, and I could see he wanted to tell me.

He was so eager and enthusiastic. He leaned forward, pushing up his sleeves. His skin was bone-white.

'The old man, Sir Henry, Arnold's father, loved those Sherlock Holmes adventures, read them aloud round the fire at night – he always said they were made to be read aloud, and I agree. At any rate, Conan Doyle was in the Bernese Oberland with Sir Henry, on one of his Alps tours, and Conan Doyle was mooching around in a pretty mournful state, because he wanted to kill off Sherlock Holmes, so that he could devote his life to paranormal research. Can you believe it? Paranormal research! And stop writing bloody detective stories.'

Sandy was nodding, laughing at this. He took a big gulp of his brandy and poured us both an extra shot. His hands were big, strong, and the whitest hands I have ever seen on a man.

'It's pleasant to have company,' he said. I smiled at him. He was really good-looking.

'I didn't know Arthur Conan Doyle believed in the supernatural.'

'Oh, yes – he converted to Spiritualism. Absolutely believed in it. So, Sir Henry, though he didn't like to see the back of Sherlock Holmes, wanted to help his friend out, and he said, "Push Holmes over the Reichenbach Falls." Conan Doyle had never heard of the Reichenbach Falls, had no idea where they were. Sir Henry, a great expert in the Alps, took Conan Doyle to the falls, and Conan Doyle knew he had found his answer. And that's how Holmes and Moriarty died. I so enjoyed that story: "The Final Problem".'

I said, 'If you have to go, you might as well do it sensationally. And you might even stage a comeback.'

His face changed. Pain and fear. He stood up abruptly. He seemed to be talking to someone. 'Hold on to the rope! Can you hear me? Hold on!'

I was confused. 'Sorry, Sandy? What are you talking about?'

Sandy passed his hand across his head. 'Forgive me. I'm rambling. That is, I mean to say, the English prefer to live well rather than live long.'

'Really?'

'There were so many chaps, just too young to fight in the war, who never forgave themselves for not making the ultimate sacrifice. Those chaps would take on anything, go anywhere, do anything.'

'Why would anyone needlessly risk their own life?'

'For something glorious! Why would you not risk your life? That is the very best a man can do.' Then he paused, thinking for a moment. 'Certainly it's different for women.'

'Because we bear children?'

'Someone must take care of the children. Though now women have the vote I wonder how it will be?'

'Exercising your democratic rights doesn't interfere with taking care of the children!'

'I suppose not. I haven't thought of things from a woman's point of view.'

Normally I would be offended by now – but there was something about him, real and sincere, that had no offence in it.

He looked into the fire. 'Would you like to come skiing with me tomorrow? I know some interesting routes. You seem strong enough.'

I smiled. 'I'll take that as a compliment. Yes, why not? That would be a pleasure. Just clear up a question for me, would you, Sandy? When you talk about the war, you mean . . .'

'The Great War.'

'That was a brutal war. But it was a long time ago.'

He frowned. He nodded slowly. He fixed me with his eyes like blue lasers. 'Do you believe in the Afterlife?'

'Not at all. Do you?'

He was silent. I liked his earnestness. He hadn't checked his smartphone once. And he read books. Old ones. I could see the one he had borrowed, open on the little desk where he had put it down.

'It's not a question of belief,' he said, finally. 'What we do or don't believe makes no difference. In the end it is what it is.'

I didn't want to get into a debate about what happens when we're dead, so I changed the subject.

'Did you say you are going to climb Everest?'

His face glowed from the fire. He nodded eagerly.

'Yes. It's an official British expedition. I'm in charge of the oxygen cylinders, nothing glamorous. I don't expect I'll get to the summit, but it's an honour to be chosen. Everyone else is much more experienced than me. I've always been fascinated by mountains and wilderness. Cold mountains. Cold wilderness.

'When I was a boy, I devoured all I could get my hands

on about Captain Scott and the Antarctic – and that cheater Amundsen.'

I held up my hand. 'Whoa! Amundsen used dogs, not ponies. That's why he arrived first. He wasn't cheating.'

Sandy downed his brandy. 'Amundsen should never have run against Scott to start with. Ours was a scientific expedition. Amundsen wanted glory.'

I shrugged. 'Welcome to the modern world.'

'It was a cheap stunt. I don't want to be cheap.'

'Why do you want to climb Everest?'

'Mallory said it better than I can: "Because it's there." Don't you know ... ? I hope you do ... I hope you understand – when the call comes, you must never refuse the call.'

Sandy was looking out of the window. He seemed as white and remote and monumental as a marble statue.

I shivered. Perhaps it was the fire dying down, or that my face had flushed and cooled with the brandy, or perhaps it was the moon shining in through the bare, bright window. I looked at him, those long, thin fingers, his axe-head jaw. He might have been carved from moonrock, this boy.

'How old are you, Sandy?'

'Twenty-one. I can't ask you the same question because it's not done to ask a lady her age.'

'I'm forty.'

Sandy shook his head. 'You're far too handsome to be forty. I hope you don't mind my calling you handsome. I prefer handsome to beautiful.'

I didn't mind at all.

'I'm leaving for the Himalayas in April. By way of Darjeeling. Then, to a monastery right at the foot of the mountain. Rongbuk. We'll stay there. The monks believe that the mountain – Everest – sings. That the music is too high-pitched for us to hear, but certain of the Buddhist masters can hear it.'

'That's a bit too mystical for me.'

'Is it? When you're here at Mürren, don't you feel light-headed?'

I nodded. 'Well, yes, I do, but that's because of the thinness of the air. It's physiological. It's –'

Sandy interrupted me. 'People feel light-headed on mountains because the solid world dematerialises. We are not the dimensional objects we believe ourselves to be.'

'Are you a Buddhist?'

Sandy shook his head impatiently. I was failing him, I could tell. He tried again, looking directly at me. Those eyes ... He squatted on his heels so that his face was underneath mine. 'When I am climbing, I understand that gravity exists to protect us from our own lightness of being, just in the same way that time is what shields us from eternity.'

As he spoke, my shiver turned to a chill. A cold thing entered me. The temperature was dropping. My hands were numb. Then I saw that there was ice on the inside of the windowpane.

Sandy was looking past me now. As though he had forgotten I was there. And I noticed something odd about those eyes: he doesn't blink.

When he spoke again it was with a wild despair in his

voice. 'I never sought to avoid the overwhelming fires of existence. It's not death that's to be feared. It's eternity. Do you understand?'

'I don't think I do, Sandy.'

'Death – it's a way out, isn't it? No matter how deeply we fear it, isn't there relief that there will be a way out?'

'I've never thought about dying.'

He got up, suddenly, and went to the window. 'What if I told you that dying isn't a way out?'

I got up. I needed to move to keep warm. I said, 'I'm not religious.'

'You'll find out. When it comes to it, you'll find out for yourself.'

It seemed to me that the night was late. How many hours had passed? There was no clock in the room. I checked my watch. The glass had broken. 'Broken, is it?' said Sandy. His voice was far-off, as if he was talking to someone else. 'You should put it in your pocket.'

'I must have banged it.'

'This bloody shale! The mountain is rotten.'

'What mountain? The Eiger?'

'Not the Eiger! Everest. Isn't that name a bad joke? No rest. Ever. Not on that pitiless, relentless rock. No pause, no sleep, wind speeds of 150 miles an hour if you're unlucky, and you are always unlucky – and the British called it Ever Rest. Do you suppose he was thinking of the Dead?'

'Who, Sandy, who was thinking of the Dead?'

'Sir George Everest. You don't think a mountain in the Himalayas was named Everest by the Tibetans or the

Nepalese, do you? Royal Geographical Society 1865 – named after the Surveyor General of India, Sir George Everest. To his credit he objected – said it couldn't be written or pronounced in Hindi. To them Everest will always be the Holy Mother.'

'Strange kind of a mother who kills so many of her children,' I said.

'There are sacred places,' said Sandy. 'Places we should not go. I didn't know that until we stayed at the monastery in Rongbuk.'

I said, 'You've already been there? I thought you were going.'

He pushed his hands through his hair. 'Yes. Yes. That's right. What time is it? The sun has gone down.'

He seemed confused. I decided to carry on the British way, as though nothing had happened. 'The Chinese destroyed the original Rongbuk Monastery in the Cultural Revolution back in '74, didn't they?'

Sandy wasn't listening to me. He was searching in his knapsack, his big body curled over it like a child's. His voice was tired, hopeless. 'I have lost my ice axe.'

I knew I had to get out of the room. I moved to put on my coat. My feet barely shifted. I was colder than I realised. The room was slowly petrifying.

Whitening. The warm tones of polished wood had bleached, like a bone in the sun, like a body left on a mountainside. The fire had gone out, its ash a mountain of its own, grey and useless. The drapes looked like sheets of ice framing the frosted window.

What's this? I reached behind my head. The back of

my neck was wet. Cold and wet. The pink velvet chair was dampening and spotting. As Sandy continued to kneel, half-prayer, half-despair, I saw his khaki shirt had snowflakes on it. Frightening. Beautiful. Can that be the same thing?

It had begun to snow inside the room.

'Sandy! Get your jacket. Come on! Come with me!' His eyes were such a pale blue.

The wind started up. Like the snow, the wind was inside the room.

The wind was raising and dropping the lid of the leather suitcase on the floor. The room was rattling. The wind blew out the candles on the mantelshelf. The oil lamp was still alight, but the clear flame was faltering now, and the inside of the glass canopy was fogging with carbon dioxide. The air in this room is too thin. The wind is blowing but there is no air. Sandy was standing motionless by the window.

'Sandy! Come on!'

'May I kiss you?'

Absurd. We're about to die and he wants to kiss me. I don't know why, but I went towards him. I put my hand on his chest, stood on tiptoe, as he bent his head. I will never forget that feeling of his lips, the burning cold of his lips. As I opened my mouth, just a little, he breathed in through his mouth, like I was an oxygen cylinder – that was the picture in my mind.

He breathed in. I felt my lungs contract with the force of the air rushing out of me. His hand was on my hip, gently resting there, so cold, so cold. And now my lips were burning too.

I pulled away, gasping for air, my lungs ballooning with the effort. He was less pale now, his cheeks stung with colour. He shouted, wildly, 'Hold on to the rope!'

I was at the door. I had to use both hands to get it open against the drift of snow piled against it. I half-ran, half-fell down the steep stairs, stumbling in the dark. I found my way, somehow, back to the main part of the hotel. I had to get help.

The bar was closed. The library where we had been sitting after dinner was deserted. The fire had long since gone out. I ran through into the lobby. The nightman was on the desk. He seemed surprised to see me. I said, 'Where is everyone?'

He raised his eyebrows and spread his hands. 'It is 04:40 in the morning, madam. The hotel is in bed.'

I can't have been gone so long. But this was not the time to argue. 'The young man who's staying in the old part of the hotel – the snow's coming in. He's going to freeze to death.'

'There is no one in the old part of the hotel, madam.'

'Yes! Through the door at the end of the library – I'll show you!'

The nightman picked up his keys and his torch and came with me. We went back through the library to the door in the panelling. I turned the handle. The door didn't open. I was pumping the handle up and down, shaking it. 'Open it! Open it!'

The nightman gently put a hand on my arm.

'That is not a door, madam; it is for the decoration only.'

'But there is a staircase on the other side. A room – I'm telling you the truth! I was there!'

The nightman shook his head, smiling. 'We can look again in the morning, perhaps. May I escort you to your own room?'

He thinks I'm drunk. He thinks I'm crazy.

I went to my bedroom. 5am. I lay down wide-awake, sleeping fitfully until broad daylight. When I woke, the sun was full on my face through the open blinds. Outside, I could hear the noise and bustle of ski parties. And I was in agony. I put my fingers to my mouth. Got up. Went to the bathroom. Stared at myself. Purple and torn.

My lips were frostbitten.

It was another hour before I was ready to go downstairs. I sat, writing down the events of the previous night, so clear to me, without any doubt. I needed to get into that room. I needed to know the truth.

I showered, changed, coated my lips in Vaseline, and went to Reception. Some of our party were standing in the lobby with their skis. 'Hey! What happened to you last night? You just disappeared! We sent you messages! Did you meet someone?' (Laughter.)

Mike was there. 'Did you see a ghost?'

More laughter. 'I spent the evening with a man ...'

'We guessed it! Is he rich? Good-looking?'

'Mike – will you come with me? I went through that door. Over there.'

We went together to the door in the panelling. Again, I tried to open it. The handle turned. It must be locked.

Mike put his hand on my arm. 'Steady! This isn't a door. It's faux. For the olde-worlde library look.'

I knew he was right, so I made him come outside with me, around the back, where the window to the room should be, if there was a window.

But there was no window. No room. Only a wall. I was babbling like a fool. The kiss. The rope. Everest. The boy was going to climb Everest. That's when Mike's face changed. He said, 'Come and talk to Fabrice.'

Fabrice was in his office, surrounded by paperwork and coffee cups. He finished his phone call and listened carefully to my story. He did not seem surprised by anything I said. When I had finished, my fingers at my chapped lips, he nodded, glancing at Mike, and then looking directly at me.

'It is not the first time this young man has been seen on the mountain, but it is the first time he has been seen in the hotel. The room you describe – yes, it used to exist, more than a hundred years ago; I accept that you cannot know this – but see, I show you the photographs.'

Fabrice lifted a leather-bound volume from the shelves behind his desk. Each page had a photograph carefully tipped in under the cardboard corners.

'As you can see, here is the Palace Hotel in the early days of the Alps tours.' A party of men holding wooden skis stood in a row, outside the snow-covered eaves. Fabrice pointed them out, one by one, with his pen. 'Sir Henry Lunn. His son, Arnold Lunn . . .'

I interrupted. 'That's him! That's Sandy.'

'*Voilà,*' said Fabrice. 'That is Mr Andrew Irvine. You know the name perhaps?' I shook my head.

Mike's voice was low and not steady. 'Andrew Irvine? The guy who climbed Everest with George Mallory?'

Fabrice nodded. 'That is the one. He was young. Just a boy. Irvine and Mallory made a last attempt to reach the summit and failed to return on June 8th 1924. Unlike Mallory, Irvine's body has never been found.'

'Irvine stayed here,' I said.

'As you can see. Staying in a third-class room in the hotel. He was a remarkable young man. Born in 1902. A gifted mechanic and engineer. The story goes that Mallory chose him as his partner for the final fatal climb because only Irvine could fix the oxygen cylinders.'

'How did he die?'

'No one knows. Mallory's body was not found until 1999. The rope was still round his waist.'

Suddenly, I can see Sandy, in the white-out. I can hear myself saying, 'Hold on to the rope!'

'Excuse me?' says Fabrice.

We were silent. All three. Staring at the photograph.

Eventually Fabrice spoke. 'Irvine's ice axe was found on the mountain in 1933. There have been no clues since. But, if they do find his body some day, and perhaps, you know, with global warming, they will find him, then there will be a camera slung around his neck, and the people at Kodak say it is likely that the film can be developed. We may discover that Mallory and Irvine reached the summit of Everest.'

What did Sandy say? 'Never refuse the call.'

To answer it would be to live in thin air. To step off the mountain, to go and not come back.

I put my hands in my pockets. I felt the rough surface of the cracked glass of my watch. I took it out and put it on the desk. 'That's strange,' said Fabrice. 'Mallory's watch was found on his body, broken in his pocket. Broken, perhaps, at the moment when time stopped for him.'

'I came across this,' said Mike. 'Read it.' He handed me his iPad.

And joy is, after all, the end of life. We do not live to eat and make money. We eat and make money to be able to enjoy life. That is what life means and what life is for.

George Mallory, New York City, 1923

The snow is falling round them. The sky is a sheet drawn over their faces. In their eyes, the old stars lighting cold and bleak, in different skies.

Fountain with Lions

It was a winter of steam-like fog.

Endless rain. Warming cold and cooling warm delivered the city over to a strange and spectral vision of itself. Buildings loomed out of the mist. On the streets, people materialised from nothing, too close, too sudden, their bulky bodies in winter wrappings like travelling mummies, then, just as suddenly, they disappeared, unravelling, so it seemed, in grey bandages of fog. Look behind and there's no trace.

Sounds were muffled and unexpected – without visual clues, a siren, a barking dog, a screaming child, came from nowhere and returned to nowhere.

If you knew your route, still you missed the turning. Thoroughfares became cloud-roads. Side-streets were sealed with mist, as though guarded by wraiths. The swirling fog carried all with it, a choreography of the moving and the solid.

Through the café window, the air-conditioning grille under the street frothed up the fog like grey milk. There were patterns in the fog, spirals of intent on the point of leaving a message, then swept away. This ghostly calligraphy had a forlornness to it, as though the Dead were trying to tell us something they could not tell, as though language had floated away from meaning, leaving behind only signs, whispers, gestures.

Judith wrote her name on the window glass, paid for her coffee, and left to walk home. Looking at the window from the outside, she saw her name in reverse, like letters in a magic mirror. But life had been reversed, she felt, in the sense that the fog made it impossible to sense any forward motion. The city was a vast white sea and everything in it was treading water.

She had gone to work by bike as usual. Her lights and sensible fluorescent waterproof jacket hardly made her visible, but perhaps less invisible. She kept time with the other cyclists until it was her turn to exit left to her destination.

This afternoon she was leaving early to walk home. Her bike had a puncture. She would go through the park. Cycling was not allowed in the park.

The fog had returned the park to the monumental formality of its nineteenth-century origins. Statues of great men, long forgotten, assumed a new importance as navigational aids. Turn right at Lord Palmerston. A bandstand, now disused, was notable for its weathervane – a foundry-cast cockerel that seemed to hover in mid-air, roosting on an invisible perch. The sundial of the Twelve Apostles indicated the eastern exit.

Laid out with paths and shrubberies, the park's atmosphere of wholesome exercise for the deserving poor had been relaxed in recent years to include a children's playground, a dog area, skateboard run, bright benches and a coffee bar. All of that was lost in low-level mist, and today, what could be seen were close-ups of specimen spruce trees, and the stern iron railings around the rose garden, designed to deter anyone from even thinking of picking a rose. Judith looked in at the remaining blooms of winter – all white, and in this mist luminous, or so it seemed. Judith had visited this park with her mother since she was a child. They always stopped to look at the roses, and then they went on to the fountain.

The triumphant heart of the park was an ornamental fountain built of cut stone and lead, whose splashy noise rang out through the fog, metallic, and far-off.

Judith walked along the central path, an avenue of spruce trees, like soldiers either side. As the noise of tumbling water grew louder, the fog lifted a little, and Judith could see the fountain clearly, its Empire lions spouting plumes of water into the wide, deep pool beneath.

There was no one in the square where the fountain stood, except for a woman in a long grey coat, that matched the colour of the leadwork. The woman was tall. She was standing with her back to Judith. She was quite still and watching the water.

That's my mother, thought Judith, her heart quickening like her pace, her face smiling. She called out, 'Hello! Hello!'

The woman did not turn around.

Judith stood, a few yards away, the cold sweat of her confusion trickling under her layers of clothes. She remembered, how could she not, that her mother was dead.

The fog returned in a swirl, and by the time Judith had

reached the spot where the woman had been, there was no one there. She looked ahead – but she could barely see to the other side of the lion-torrents of water. She pulled down her hood, letting the wet mist envelop her head. It was no good straining her eyes to see what she could not see.

She walked on, long legs, hood down, hair getting damp in lank strings round her ears and mouth. She wondered if she would overtake the woman who was not her mother?

Blank paths radiated to the sides, but the only person ahead was a man coming towards her with an invisible terrier yapping at his invisible heels. Traffic noise told her she would soon reach the main road beyond the imposing wrought-iron gates of the park.

Now she was back in the real world, with its fast food and retail, and dogged buses nose-to-tail at the traffic lights. She hopped on the 36 and was soon near her door.

Front door. Relief? Dread? Pleasure? Rarely is a door only a door.

Judith's own front door to her basement flat comforted her. Her space. Her way. For the first time in her life, she wasn't sharing with friends she didn't like or a lover she didn't love. Her mother had left her some money. It was like living inside her again – those distant nine months when life is safe and the door to the beginning of time is still closed. There's no time in the womb.

There's no time in the tomb either, thought Judith, letting herself in. Her mother had been dead for nine months. She would take some flowers to the grave at the weekend.

It must have been an hallucination. It's easy to see what's not there. What had she seen? A tall woman in a grey coat. Her mother wasn't the only tall woman who wore grey. How like her, though, just to stand and stare at the jets hitting the water. She loved to notice things. Had taught Judith how to be still in a world that moved too quick. 'We're not mice,' she used to say. 'There's no need to scurry.'

And now she was gone.

Judith had entered straight down the hall and into the kitchen at the back. It was just as she had left it, her breakfast things not cleared up, the post unopened. Special offers for things that weren't special and weren't offers.

Cruises, electric blankets, a trolley jack attached to a smiling man in a hard hat. A letter from the insurance company. Leave it till later.

In the sitting room she looked surprised. Piled on the coffee table was her hi-vis jacket and her work bag. She had left those things at work when she realised she couldn't fix her bike. The wheel was buckled from the pothole.

What were her things doing here? How had they got here?

Judith sat on the sofa looking at the pile. Was she losing her mind? Had she brought them home in a bundle, and forgotten what she was doing, because of the mirage of her mother?

The cold sweat on her body – she had wanted it to be, so badly wanted it to be – and believed it to be her mother.

A shock, and just when she thought she was getting over the death. Her friends at work had been patient and kind, but it wasn't their mother, and after a month or two, life must go on, and Judith behaved as normally as she could, keeping her grief like a secret.

She was popular at work, diligent, a team-player, but she didn't have close friends. In a different age she would have been unremarkable – a single woman, what did they call them? Spinsters? A single woman. Miss Dot Dot Dot. Anonymous. Left alone. Respected. A teacher perhaps, or a missionary. Now, everyone had to have a friendship group for their mental health, and a partner for their self-esteem. She was a loner.

There was someone she could call – her friend from work, Emma, who kept a key for her and lived nearby. What was she going to say? *I thought I saw my dead mother?*

Her phone wasn't in her coat. She went through the usual stations of panic – cartoon hands moving manically, returning to pockets already triple-checked, then she thought to look in the bag she didn't remember bringing home. The phone was there. Switched off. Its screen badly cracked.

It must have happened when she went over the pot-hole. Yes, she remembered now. That was a bad swerve and her bag had swung smack into the nearside wall. The relief at finding her phone was clouded by the realisation that she must have brought back her things from the office without any recollection of doing so.

For a moment she was afraid. She called Emma. 'Hello? Hello?'

There was no reply. The second time the phone went to voicemail.

She decided to get a takeaway. She wasn't hungry, but she was restless. As she came out of the front door, she saw there was a bunch of flowers on the step. They hadn't been there when she came in – she was sure of that much. She picked them up – a loose bunch of white roses. She thought of the roses in the park. These were English roses, not blooms from Africa from the supermarket. No name or card.

She took them inside and put them in the cafetière filled with water in the sink. She would arrange them later.

What was that strange beeping? Low-level, monotonous. Probably a smoke alarm with its battery failing. That could wait too.

There was a mirror in the kitchen – the last-minute check before the dash to work – no boiled-egg bits or coffee dribbles. In the mirror, Judith caught sight of her face, her hair wet through from the walk. It was the gash on her forehead that was a shock. Deep. Wide. She put her fingers to her head, tentatively. It didn't hurt. There was dried blood on either side of the cut. The fall? Yes, the fall, but why hadn't they given her a plaster at work? Why couldn't she remember what had happened after the accident? Did she have concussion? She should get this checked out. She felt more confident – this explained the image of her mother, the things in the sitting room – clearly, she had done some temporary damage. A bit of concussion. Check it out to be on the safe side. She would go to the hospital.

*

She had always walked quickly – at first, as a child, to keep up with her striding-ahead mother, and then, as her legs grew longer, she found her natural gait. In another life, as Miss Dot Dot Dot, she could have been an explorer. Like Isabella Bird, the only female to be found in the park, and not as a statue, but on a plaque commemorating missionary work in India.

Her mother had told her all about Isabella Bird. But tonight, Judith couldn't go back through the park – it was locked at this hour, so she went straight ahead, faster than usual, or so it seemed to her, until she arrived at the entrance to the hospital.

She hadn't been here since her mother's death. That night, after she had left the body, a sheet drawn over the worn-out face, she had remained standing in the porch at the main door. A porch that offered shelter without comfort.

Modern, impersonal, a draughty lid above the automatic glass doors. How many hours did she wait there? She didn't know. An ambulance man had given her a cup of tea. She hadn't drunk it, held on to it for the warmth, warmth that gradually ebbed away, as she had felt the warmth in her mother's hand ebb away, colder to cold, until, at last, the nurse gently asked her to leave. The body must be removed.

Removed. What matters is gone. The body becomes an effigy. How hard it is to let it go. She wished her mother had died at home. The farm cottage at the top of the track. Too risky. Too remote. Her brother had made the decision. The doctors had listened to him. He had authority, like one of the statues in the park. He wasn't at the hospital when their mother died.

The cottage was sold. Half each.

Judith went into the hospital. Reception desk. A queue of people waiting to register. She hesitated. No one seemed to notice her. She put her hand to her head. It felt fine now. She wasn't in a daze. Her mind was bright and white, like sun on snow.

She slipped into the toilets. In the mirror, she pulled her hair back from her forehead. There was no cut. No sign of blood. She was herself. Her hair had dried too. It must have been the bad light in her kitchen, some smears of blood, no need for a drama, and yes, she had been in shock, but things were steady now. She would go home, and in the morning, get to work and retrieve her bike.

She came out briskly. Straight to the automatic doors and out into the night. As she walked on, away from the blank glare of the hospital, down the main road, she was about to skirt the park, when she noticed the gate was open.

Why not cut through? It was probably dangerous, but she felt invincible. And happy, yes, that was the word. Happy.

The park was empty. She sped along the central path, past the rose garden, towards the fountain, its lions now silent and sullen, their torrent turned off for the night.

She stood for a second, looking into the deep, still water, a dark mirror in which no stars were reflected. She couldn't even see her own face. Only water. She put out her hand to break the surface. Instead, she rested her hand on the top of the water, wondering if she could walk on it. Humans need gravity to walk. Every step is an act of resistance that propels us forward.

Judith looked up. The outer gate to the park was closing. So slowly. So steadily. It must be on a timer. She had to hurry.

She was soon home.

As she came through the front door, she had a sense that she wasn't alone. That someone was in the flat. She should have been afraid, but she had no fear.

Hesitating a little, she called out. 'Hello? Hello?'

There was no answer. No sound. She left the front door open and went into the sitting room.

Her mother was sitting on the sofa.

They looked at each other. Her mother in her long grey coat. Judith had buried her in that coat. It was her favourite – expensive, years ago, worn every day, worn-out, as she had worn out, but elegant, with a swing in the cut. Now, the coat was still worn-out, but her mother was not. She looked well. She smiled at Judith. Then she got up and drifted out of the room. It was like a single sound on a keyboard – not steps – a short, continuous movement. The front door closed with a soft click.

Judith ran to the door. Ran onto the street. There was no one there. It was late. What time was it? She didn't seem to be wearing her watch.

The kitchen clock said nearly midnight.

Already? Where does the time go? Where does time go when we are done with it?

Did she sleep? She didn't know. She didn't dream. She

was conscious of an insistent, but intermittent, sound, a beeping, regular and low. Bloody smoke alarm.

She came to, rather than awakened, terrified that she could not breathe. Her mouth was open, sucking in air, then the panic left her. She was calm.

In the morning, wearing the same clothes, she set out for work. The fog had cleared. Completely cleared. The day was alpine in its clarity. That must be why she felt so cold. Numb with cold. Her fingers were white.

In the park, people greeted one another cheerfully. The fountain was filled with birds bathing. Judith went on, and, leaning through the railings of the rose garden, broke off a white rose. She took it to the missionary-work memorial tablet and left it for Isabella Bird. Her mother would like that. Her mother. Where was she now?

Yesterday, Judith had been anxious and confused by the sight of her mother – now it seemed natural. Despite the coldness in her body, she was so much better than yesterday. Today is a good day.

Judith arrived at the offices where she worked. Her bike wasn't locked up in the bike rack where she always left it.

Had it been stolen? She walked around. Nothing.

Round the back of the building was a dumpster. Judith saw the wheel of her bike sticking over the top at an awkward angle. Who had rubbished her bike? A vintage Peugeot. She was tall enough to reach in and haul it out. The beauty of a lightweight bike.

She propped it up against the wall. Both wheels were twisted, and the frame was broken in two. Only the pedals and the saddle were intact. All this for a pothole? No wonder they had thrown it away. Who had thrown it away? And where was she at the time?

Involuntarily, her hand went to her forehead. She could feel the bumpiness under the skin. She began to explore the geography of her head. At the rear of her skull there seemed to be a dent, a crack. She hadn't noticed this before.

There was blood on her hands, stickiness, and a jelly-like substance. She could hear voices, but not what was being said.

Then she remembered what had happened.

Dutifully cycling in line, not overtaking, not going too fast, Judith had waited at the stop-light where she turned left. There was an articulated lorry rumbling next to her, its wheels as high as her handlebars. Didn't matter. Vehicles had to drive straight on. Left turn was for cyclists only.

The lights had changed, only visible in the fog because she was directly underneath them. As she turned left, the lorry turned left too, its cabin first, followed by its towage.

She looked up at the cabin as it came around the corner. She pressed harder on the pedals to outgun it. There was no room. He couldn't see her, didn't see her, didn't register the slight bump under the double wheels as the whole length of the lorry made the illegal left turn.

Crushing Judith into the wall.

There was nowhere for her to fall. She didn't fall. The

lorry inched forward, so many people shouting, because the road was narrow, and the lorry was stuck.

Judith felt someone unclip her cycle helmet. Split in half. Then she felt nothing.

Now she was walking away from the dumpster round to the entrance to her offices. She saw Emma coming out, speaking on her cell phone. Judith was pleased to see her and went over to Emma. 'Hello! Hello!'

Emma took no notice. She was intent on the phone conversation. Abruptly, she sat down on a step. All Judith could understand was something about *when*. She thought to herself: *When what?*

She saw that Emma was crying.

As she was about to comfort her, Judith felt a hand on her shoulder. She turned round. It was her mother. What was she doing here?

'I should be asking you the same question,' said her mother. She was smiling. Emma stood up. Ended the call. Went back inside.

'What has happened?' said Judith to her mother.

'A brain haemorrhage.'

'Whose?'

'Yours.'

'I went to the hospital last night,' said Judith. 'I was fine.'

'You were taken to the hospital yesterday morning by ambulance after the accident,' her mother said. 'You are in a coma. They are trying to save you.'

'But I was walking home last night! And I was at home.'

'Your spirit was out of your body,' said her mother,

'you were visiting your own life. That is why you can see me. You are moving in between life and death.'

'Death?' Judith was confused. 'What about my stuff? My bag? Phone? I took them home with me, didn't I?'

'Emma brought your things back to the flat.'

'I should talk to her! Explain.'

'She won't hear you,' said her mother. 'She can't hear you.'

'Why didn't you tell me about this when I saw you?' said Judith.

'Nothing is certain until it is – not even death.'

'Can anyone see me?' asked Judith.

'They cannot.'

'But at the hospital last night . . .'

'When you arrived at the hospital last night, you understood that you would not be able to get back into your body. But you were still alive – your heart was beating. Your heart is beating now.'

Judith put her hand to her chest. She felt nothing. 'Beeping. I keep hearing beeping.'

'That is the heart monitor.'

Judith was silent. 'I was so cold this morning.'

'That's normal – when death begins.'

'What happens next?'

'The usual things will happen to your body.'

'What about me?'

'That's why I'm here.'

Her mother held out her hand – as she used to do when Judith was a little girl. Her hand felt warm and firm.

They travelled together out of the city, away from the roads, across into open countryside. They moved quickly. Or was everything else moving slowly?

Soon they were in sight of a high moor that stood above the city like a watcher. They went side by side, hand in hand, up the rough track, as they had done so often.

At the bend in the track, Judith knows what she will see: the compact stone cottage built on the edge of a sheer drop to the river, where the river narrows, its force tumbling over shiny black stones. Who built it here? So precarious? It's as if a bird dropped the seed of a cottage that took root and grew.

From beyond the gate Judith can see it all. The grass not cut too short. The rose bushes neatly pruned to make a hedge on the margin of the track. There's a water barrel by the front door, and a tin cup on a chain. In the little garden stand two apple trees, either side of the path to the door. The stone slates are mossy and green.

'Do we still live here?' asked Judith. She looked in through the window. A fire was burning in the kitchen. Her cat, Tibbles, was sitting on the table.

'Until we are ready to go,' said her mother.

'Didn't we have to sell it?'

'What we sold was like a limited-edition print. Anyone can buy one of those – but it doesn't mean they own the real thing. This will always be our home.'

'Until we are ready to go,' said Judith.

'Yes,' said her mother, 'until then.'

Judith put her hand on the low wooden gate. It didn't budge. Her mother said, 'When you come through you can't go back.'

Judith nodded. 'I don't want to go back.'

She could hear the birds singing, as they do first thing in the morning, even though the daylight was low and filmy. She realised the beeping sound had stopped.

She pushed the gate. It opened easily. They went through together.

Judith turned round, just for a second, she didn't know why. The gate was a mile or more away – and receding, like a dock when the ship is out at sea. But where had they sailed?

The sky was absolute and everywhere, rolls of black cloth pinned together with stars. The rushing noise must be the force of the water behind the house.

Or was it time itself she could hear, ceaselessly falling away towards its source?

No, that was too grand. Death was smaller than she had thought. Or was it life that was smaller? A city on lend-lease. A park with statues. A fountain with lions.

Night Side of the River

My story begins on an autumn night in London. The River Thames. Westminster Pier. Waiting for a boat.

On the eastern reaches of the Thames stands London's oldest remaining riverside pub: The Prospect of Whitby. A collier-boat of that name, bringing sea-coal from Newcastle to London, used to anchor there. On the return journey, Whitby coming into view, on the wild and rocky English coast, was assurance to the sailors that home was not so far away. Home is inside us as well as outside us. An image we hold in our minds. Some people like to say that when we die we are going home. But it's a strange home. We never visit it, until we do, and when we do, we never return.

I am not the most sociable person. I'd rather spend the night in with my cat than go out to a party.

Attendance at this party was mandatory. Our company had been taken over by an American tycoon, and those of us still with a job were promised a bonding experience with our new colleagues. That felt like all the fun of Christmas lunch with your in-laws.

I need a job, so I queued up, smiling a false smile, getting my ID checked, as we boarded the boat.

We'd been put into pairs, like animals herded onto a Wi-Fi-enabled Noah's Ark. Our pairs were randomised, the only criterion being that we didn't know the person we were paired with. Speed dating for the desperate. I'm useless at small talk. Before we'd crossed the gangplank the handsome, ambitious man from Sales had realised I was nothing he wanted to pitch to. We were the last to board, and while we waited, one of the sailors came running past us from the quayside, and as he did, he slapped my back. I felt his hand flat between my shoulder blades. It didn't hurt but it was an intrusion. I looked behind me, and for a second, planned to slip away. But it was too late. We were at the red rope. Time to get onboard.

My paired mate immediately excused himself to talk to his boss. Fine by me. He had talked about himself for eighteen minutes, not even asking me my name – in fact he had told me my name, reading my badge. 'You're Linda!' He said it like it was a discovery I needed to know.

I live alone. I prefer it.

I took a drink from the bar and went to stand on a step, slightly above the fray, with a good view of my new colleagues. It was a relief to let the micro-conversations and bad jokes swirl under my ears like water washing away. I feel submerged at parties. I wade out of my depth and I can't swim. I will stay here, holding on to the handrail. Safe.

I had a feeling I was being watched. Don't be silly. Nobody wants to look at me. The American women were dressed like supermodels in killer heels. It's a crowd of people, that's all. Eyes everywhere, calculating the competition. I scanned the room, anxiously. I know a few people. It's OK. Deep breath. I shouldn't drink cocktails. But I can't stand here without a drink and no one to talk to. I don't want to talk to anyone.

Another deep breath but the air got trapped before it reached my lungs. Am I having a panic attack? I sway, the room tilts, there's a smell of salty water. A ship at sea. It's dark.

In this darkness, only visible to me, I can see him loom up out of the crowd. A young man. Motionless. Staring at me the way an animal stares. He's pale and thin. His dark hair hangs loose and long, falling onto the shoulders of a seaman-style coat with brass buttons. He must be one of the crew. I am sure he is the man who pressed my back as he jumped onto the boat.

He's not smiling. He stares. He beckons towards the prow of the boat.

Not knowing why, I followed him.

I passed invisibly, it seemed, through the crowd, no one stopping to talk to me. I reached a set of metal steps, ten in all, as I count, leading from the covered lower deck to the open top deck. A few people were up there, leaning on the rails, laughing, enjoying themselves, watching the river float by.

What's the matter with me? What is this cold fear that fills me? I want to leave but I can't get off the boat.

Rain. Dark drops. Dark night. Shivering. I should go back inside. To the lights. To the warmth.

Light and warmth are behind me. Ahead there is only darkness and cold.

The figure of the man stood in front of me, his back to me. As I turned to go, he said, without looking round, 'My name is Jonathan. They told me you would be here.'

'We're all here,' I said. 'It's a party.'

He turned to face me now. He looked at me, or through me, so it felt. His watery-blue eyes had a glance of malevolence in them. I saw that he was soaking wet. As though he had fallen overboard.

He said, 'Who is here? There is no one here.'

I looked behind me, my breath tight in my chest.

No stars. No sound. No movement. The boat was empty, rocking from side to side in darkness.

'Quickly,' he said, 'time is short.'

'Who are you?'

He did not answer. He took a step towards me and grasped my arm. He was wearing black leather gloves, grotesquely swollen. I realised they were bloated with water. Where he held on to me, stinking salty water poured down my arm as though this man was wringing out his body.

I resisted him. He was strong. I pushed harder. He gripped me, dragging me with him.

'What are you doing?'

'I have come for you,' he said.

A clatter on the metal stairs behind me broke the spell.

I heard a deafening noise like gunfire. I put my hands over my ears. Then, like a miracle, people I knew were swarming onto the top deck.

'Hey, Linda! Amazing fireworks!'

The boat was full again, bright again, and my colleagues were pressed around me, happy and half-drunk as the boat sailed under Tower Bridge, lit up like a toy fort.

A friend from Accounts came up to me. She looked perplexed. 'What happened to your jacket? It's soaked!'

Like someone in a daze I squeezed my dripping arm. There was no sign of the pale young man.

I read somewhere that when we are frightened, our ears can only hear distant and loud noises; we can't hear close-up conversation. So I have no idea what anyone said to me, as our boat sailed smoothly towards The Prospect of Whitby.

The inn sits right on the river, with steps at the waterside for landing craft. In the past, this inn had other names: The Pelican, and before that The Devil's Tavern.

There was a gallows here in the old days.

But tonight the pub was cheerfully lit, with food on the tables, and before long I was eating fish and chips with people I knew, drying my jacket on a radiator, and deciding not to say anything about what had happened. What had happened? A drunken man. A crazy guy.

Annoying. Normal.

I got up to go to the bar for another drink. I was feeling warmer and calmer. As I stood waiting, people ahead of me and behind me, I felt someone pressing the full length of their body against my back. Their wet-through body.

GET AWAY FROM ME!

'Linda! What's the matter?'

It's my friend Lisa. She puts her hand on my back and steers me away. Then she says, 'What have you been doing? Your back's wet. Did that stupid bloke spill his drink down you?'

'Yes, must have,' I said. 'I think I'll go home.'

I went to get my jacket from the radiator. The sleeve was still wet, but where it had begun to dry, I could see a rim of salt-stain. Crystals. Salt? The Thames is a fresh-water river. I turned the jacket over. It's nothing special, cheap red leather with a warm lining. On the back, between the shoulders, was a handprint. Like a scorch mark.

'That's where he touched me,' I said to Lisa.

She looked at me. 'Who did? Nobody did this, Linda – look, it's part of the leather.'

'It is now.'

Lisa thinks I'm drunk, or worse. 'Come outside for a minute. Get some fresh air.'

We went to the back door. I can feel his eyes on me.

'Who is that?' I asked Lisa. 'Him, over there, the pale young man in the long blue coat.'

And I turn to look at him. And there's no one in the room but the two of us. The pub is weather-beaten. Shadowy. The wooden panelling is scuffed.

Distemper falls in patches from the ceiling. A small round windowpane gives onto a dank courtyard. A long table fills the room. Benches either side. A candle sits in a tin candlestick. There's a rope coiled on the table. More than a rope. A noose.

The door opens. The door opens into nothingness. Black. Beyond. Empty. It's Lisa joggling my arm. 'You're not well, Linda. Come outside. Come on.'

Outside, under the street lamp, a couple of people are smoking. Everything feels all right again.

'Who is he? He's so pale.'

Lisa shook her head. 'Search me. They're all pale. Too many hours sitting in front of a screen.'

'Can you get me my bag?' I asked her. 'The brown canvas briefcase. I don't want to go back in.'

Lisa went through the swinging door into the noise and brightness of the pub. I want to get away. I'm thinking to myself, What time did they say the boat is leaving?

'The boat is leaving now.'

I hear the voice. I have heard that voice already tonight.

The yard behind The Prospect of Whitby is deserted. I turn and turn, round and round, like a figure on a musical box. There is no one here.

'There is no one here.' Jonathan's voice.

Am I going mad? Who is answering my thoughts?

I don't know why I didn't go straight back into the pub. My hand was on the door. Instead, in my panic, I tried to get away.

There's an alley to the side of the pub leading down to the Thames.

I made my way, dim-lit, alone.

It must be getting colder tonight. River-fog. Fog hovering on the top of the water. I can see our boat bobbing gently up and down. I felt such relief. I could go and sit inside and wait for the others. No one will miss me.

In my ear, so close this time that my skin twitches, I hear him: 'That is true. No one will miss you.'

The pale man called Jonathan is behind me. He puts his arms round me. I fight back, but he is taller and heavier than me. When he pushes his weight against me, it isn't ordinary weight, not muscle, not strength. What is it?

Sickened, I suddenly know what it is: he is water-logged.

He wrestles me, pushes, kicks me, half-carries me, onto a deserted boat. 'This isn't our boat!'

But he is untying the anchor rope and pushing away from the jetty with an oar. While he busies himself, I get up from the deck where I fell. I stare around me, frantic for any way out.

The boat is dark, tarred, an open, dirty, battered vessel from another time. There is a shape at the helm swinging a big capstan wheel. As my eyes adjust, I see a double line of figures seated at row. Dully, their arms pull the oars.

Most of them wear clothes that don't belong in my world; jerkins, heavy boots, shawls, torn jackets that cover collarless shirts, caps on their knees.

'Who are you?'

No one answers me. There's a girl at the top of the

rowing silent figures. She's wearing flared denim jeans, a headband, love-beads, a sheepskin coat, filthy, but recognisable.

'What's happening here?' I ask her.

'We're trapped,' she said.

'Trapped? How? By what?'

'This boat is a trawler. We are the trawled.'

'Where are we going?'

'Where we are always going.'

'I don't understand.'

'To the night side of the river.'

By now, the boat was in the centre of the Thames and heading east, away from the lights of London and towards the darkness that has no end.

'How long have you been on this boat?' I asked her.

'Since my birthday. June 3rd, 1972.'

'1972?'

'Yes. What year is it now?'

I did not answer. I looked at the others, older and stranger. I went over to one of the women, bundled in a shawl. 'What are you doing on this boat?'

She did not answer. I am a mild person. Yet I leaned forward and shook her shoulder. Still, she did not answer me, or raise her head. I shook her again. 'ANSWER ME!'

Her shape – I cannot call it a body – crumpled under my hand. She fell forward; nothing but a heap of rotting clothes.

I stepped back, away from the mound at my feet, and I felt myself caught by the wet force of the pale young man.

'You will take her place,' he said. 'Sit down! Row!'

I hit him so hard I landed on my face on the deck.

My blow had met no resistance. And yet he bent down and hauled me to my feet. What was he who could be so saturated and solid at one moment, and the next, as vanishing as air?

'Where are you taking us?'

He smiled his empty smile. 'There is no destination. There is no arrival. There is no journey's end.'

I pushed past him, and, hardly knowing what I did, hurled myself at the impassive shape at the wheel. I was trying to turn the vessel back towards the bank. Yet, however I pushed this figure away, he returned instantly to his position.

'Are you dead or alive? Show your face!'

The shape was shrouded in a deep hood. It continued to look straight ahead. The pale young man shoved me off. 'Go to your place! Row.'

'Why does he not speak to me? Why does he not show his face?'

Jonathan's eyes fixed on mine. 'What if he has no face to show?'

Jonathan jerked back the mariner's hood. There was nothing there. The shape, headless, continued to steer. Jonathan returned the hood, and it assumed the contours of a man's head.

Senseless, stone-like, I stumbled to my place at the oars, and began to row. My hands were soon slippy and sore. I felt myself – whatever myself is – dissolving. I felt myself becoming my watery equivalent. I was drowning. I was disappearing. My mind was spongy. I could not think. I could not be.

This is death, then.

This is the sleep from which there is no waking. Yet, I must stay awake. I must not let go. I must remember my name. Say your name. Again. Again. Again.

I looked up. The moon had pierced the clouds. The moon. The river. These were real things in the real world. This ship of death was still in the real world. But soon we would pass into the shadow-space from which there can be no return. I understood that the boat had a limited licence to drift into time, to gather others like me, and to return to the empty seas of dark eternity.

Jonathan was standing at the prow with the motionless mariner. Around me, next to me, there was only the rise and fall of the oars. The scoop of the vessel made it difficult to see over the side, but what my eyes could not see, my body could sense. The cold. The deathly quiet, the moon beginning to fade now. We were crossing the bar.

Now or never.

I laid down the oar in the oarlock. I stood up. To my horror I saw water oozing like blood from my legs. Dark water. I was paddling in my dissolving self. Silently, I moved from my seat to the side of the boat. I jumped.

There was a shriek of rage and fury. Jonathan was at the side of the boat with a billhook. The hook caught my shirt. He was fishing me out. I felt myself being dragged back. I kicked with all my might, twisting my body as I tried to swim.

Surely my shirt would rip? I half-turned onto my back, the billhook in my ribs, as the fabric tore. I will never forget his look of hatred.

I was free.

The water was deep and cold. I swam, not looking behind me, fearful of what I might see; the boat returning for me. Silent and deadly.

I don't know how much time passed. I swam in darkness. Eventually, above me, I saw the moon again, and that distant globe seemed like a friend to me. I don't know how I got to the muddy bank of the river, the tide out, me half-stripped, and shivering. I don't know how I got help, but I was saved that night.

The story goes that I fell overboard, drunk, got swept out into the Thames. I was lucky to be alive.

I am lucky to be alive.

I researched the site of The Prospect of Whitby, and there are many dark stories, but none that answers mine. What violence and fear, what evil end, urged Jonathan to ruin others as he had been ruined?

I learned that a man named Jonathan Strong had been hanged for smuggling in 1838. His corpse was thrown into the Thames.

Still, I wake up, thinking my body is wringing wet. Still, I fall asleep unsure of where I begin and end.

I used to believe that the world is dry land with firm

edges. I used to believe that life and death were separate states.

Now I know that things are liquid, porous; not solid at all.

I go out of my way to avoid the River Thames. Somewhere, in the dark and rain, moonless, motionless, Jonathan is there.

JW4: The Future of Ghosts

There's a theory I like that suggests why the nineteenth century is so rich in ghost stories and hauntings. Carbon-monoxide poisoning from gas lamps.

Street lighting and indoor lighting burned coal gas, which is sooty and noxious. It gives off methane, and carbon monoxide. Outdoors, the flickering flames of the gas lamps pumped carbon monoxide into the air – air that was often trapped low down in the narrow streets and cramped courtyards of industrial cities and towns. Indoors, windows closed against the chilly weather prevented fresh oxygen from reaching those sitting up late by lamplight.

Low-level carbon-monoxide poisoning produces symptoms of choking, dizziness, paranoia, including feelings of dread, and hallucinations. Where better to hallucinate than in the already dark and shadowy streets of Victorian London? Or in the muffled and stifling interiors of New England?

Ghosts abounded – but were they real?

Real is a tricky word. It is no longer a three-dimensional word grounded in fact. Was it ever? We are living in a material world but that is not our only reality. We daydream, we imagine. Everything that ever was began as an idea in someone's mind. The non-material world is prodigious and profound.

You don't have to be religious, or artistic, or creative, or a scientist, to understand that the world and what it contains is more than a 3D experience. To understand that truth, all we have to do is log on. Increasingly, our days are spent staring at screens, communicating with people we shall never meet. Young people who have grown up online consider that arena to be more significant to them than life in the 'real' world. In China, there is a growing group who call themselves two-dimensionals, because work life, social life, love life, shopping, information, happen at a remove from physical interaction with others. This will become more apparent and more bizarre when metaverses offer an alternative reality.

Let me ask you this. If you enjoy a friendship with someone you have never met, would you know if they were dead? What if communication continued seamlessly? What if you went on meeting in the metaverse, just as always?

Already, there are apps that can recreate your dead loved one sufficiently to be able to send you texts and emails, even voice calls. And if you both entered the metaverse in your avatar form, there is no reason why the 'dead' avatar can't continue. This strange development was the push for the stories I wrote in DEVICES. Truly, technology is going to affect our relationship with death. In theory, no one needs to die. In theory, anyone can be resurrected. We can be our own haunting.

Humans are terrified of death. Will technological developments allow us to avoid its psychological consequences? Or will it give us a new way to go mad? By which I mean to detach from the world of the senses into the metaverse?

And does it matter? If *Homo sapiens* is in a transition period, as I believe we are, then biology isn't going to be the next big deal. We are already doing everything we can to escape our biological existence – most people barely make use of the bodies they have, and many would be glad to be freed from bodies that are sites of disappointment and disgust.

Perhaps we are moving steadily towards the non-material life and world that religious folks have told us is the ultimate truth. This time around, we won't have to die to get there – we join the metaverse.

There are plenty of horror stories about evil spirits impersonating the newly dead. I wonder if spirits of all kinds will infiltrate the metaverse? I am being playful here, but how would we know if a being in the metaverse has a biological self or not?

Why wouldn't ghosts hack the metaverse? Surely it will feel like a more user-friendly, at-home space to them. The metaverse exists, but at the same time, it occupies no physical space. Ghosts exist (maybe), but they have no physical being. Tangible reality is getting old-fashioned.

Once the hard boundary between the 'real' world and other worlds comes down – and that's what the metaverse intends – being alive matters less. Once the physical body becomes optional – where does that leave ghosts?

A ghost is the spirit of a dead person. An avatar is a digital twin of a living person. Neither is 'real'.

A haunted metaverse. Why not?

In a sense, the Plato sense, materialism is about the hard copy. It is impressive. But it is still a copy.

In other words, we are living in Toytown, and we mistake the substance for the shadow. The substance isn't what we can touch and feel – and we know we are not actually touching or feeling anything – that's an illusion. Substance may not be material at all.

Shakespeare put it this way: 'What is your substance, whereof are you made / That millions of strange shadows upon you tend?' (Sonnet 53)

I don't want to get into Shakespeare's Neoplatonism here – which is what those lines swirl around – but I do want to get into the fact that computing power and AI have left multi-millions of us wondering what is real – in the old-fashioned sense of the word. This will only get faster and stranger as we enter the metaverse; a virtual world with digital twins in our world – or the other way round, if you prefer.

'What is your substance, whereof are you made?'

This could be addressed to a human. Or a transhuman. Or a post-human. Or an avatar. Or a ghost.

Acknowledgements

Thanks to everyone who has worked on this book: my editors, Michal Shavit at PRH UK and Elisabeth Schmitz at Grove Press NYC. So many folks – designers, typesetters, proofreaders, and my amazing copy-editing team led by Rowena Skelton-Wallace. Thank you, Laura Evans, for wrangling the endless manuscript changes.

Thanks to my agent Caroline Michel and her colleagues at PFD. It takes so much effort to get a book into the world.

And thanks to Substack with whom I first began to explore some of these stories and themes as their writer in residence in November 2021.